The Moonstone Governess

Moonstone Landing Series
Book 4

by

Meara Platt

ARE YOU SIGNED UP FOR DRAGONBLADE'S BLOG?

You'll get the latest news and information on exclusive giveaways, exclusive excerpts, coming releases, sales, free books, cover reveals and more.

Check out our complete list of authors, too!

No spam, no junk. That's a promise!

Sign Up Here

www.dragonbladepublishing.com

Dearest Reader;

Thank you for your support of a small press. At Dragonblade Publishing, we strive to bring you the highest quality Historical Romance from some of the best authors in the business. Without your support, there is no 'us', so we sincerely hope you adore these stories and find some new favorite authors along the way.

Happy Reading!

CEO, Dragonblade Publishing

Garden of Dragons
Garden of Destiny
Garden of Angels

The Farthingale Series
If You Wished For Me (Novella)

The Lyon's Den Series
Kiss of the Lyon
The Lyon's Surprise
Lyon in the Rough

Pirates of Britannia Series
Pearls of Fire

De Wolfe Pack: The Series
Nobody's Angel
Kiss an Angel
Bhrodi's Angel

Also from Meara Platt
Aislin
All I Want for Christmas

Chapter One

Moonstone Landing
Cornwall, England
July 1823

BRENNA ANGEL PAUSED in her early morning walk along the
heights of Moonstone Landing to stare at the stranger she
had seen at this very spot for three days in a row now. He sat
upon an exquisite black steed, sweeping his gaze across the
meadow of red poppies that swayed in the gentle breeze and
ended at the edge of the nearby cliffs. From his vantage point, he
could also see the quiet village in the distance and the expanse of
crystal-blue waters of their cove shimmering in the morning light
beyond. "There is no finer view. Don't you think, sir?"

At first, the man appeared surprised by her presence and that
she had spoken to him. But then he arched an eyebrow and
dismounted to approach her. He was quite handsome and bigger
than she'd realized, for her head barely reached his shoulders now
that he stood beside her. His shoulders were nicely broad, too.

"I was going to pass the same remark to you. Do you walk
here every morning, Miss Angel? Or am I wrong in presuming
you are the elusive Brenna Angel?"

"I do enjoy a walk most days. Not in rain or snow, however.
Who are you, if I may be so bold as to ask? And what makes you

say I have been elusive?"

He laughed. "Other than the fact you have avoided me this entire week? Not to mention ignoring Mr. Priam, who happens to be Moonstone Landing's finest land agent, or so he terms himself."

"He is a persistent fellow, I will allow," she replied with good nature, supposing it was time to take the measure of this handsome lord everyone in the village had been talking about. He was likely Viscount Claymore, and it was time to discuss what he wanted from her.

"So can I be persistent, Miss Angel." His voice was cultured, but there was a determined edge to it. Although he was dressed casually, there was no mistaking his clothes were of the finest cut. Savile Row, no doubt. The white lawn of his shirt was as crisp and white as a wintery snowfall. His riding breeches were a buttery color, and the material appeared as soft as the fur of a newborn fawn.

His eyes were as blue as the sea stretched out in glistening splendor before them. Since he wore no hat, Brenna had a full view of his dark blond hair, which appeared clean and freshly washed as the sun beamed down on it and the wind gently rustled through those lovely strands of burnished gold.

Yes, this viscount, Lord Claymore—if this was indeed him— was quite good looking, which put her more on her guard. He was a man used to getting his own way by charm and seduction. She did not wish to be another of his conquests, albeit merely of the business kind.

"I suppose you are one of the posh London set presently ensconced in my cousin's hotel, the Kestrel Inn," Brenna said, keeping her voice bland, although her stomach was now twisting in a knot. "Are you the viscount or merely his lackey?"

"Are you always so blunt?" He arched his eyebrow again, but this time cast her an engaging smile along with it. "I expect you know exactly who I am. Do I look like any man's lackey? Your cousin, Thaddius Angel, is an excellent proprietor, and also an unmitigated gossip. Did he tell you about me? Or was it your uncle who tattled?"

"Which uncle? I have seven currently residing in Moonstone Landing, to be precise. But it was none of them. My family knows how to be discreet."

"Are you suggesting they do not gossip?" He laughed heartily. "Give me some credit, Miss Angel. I cannot walk down the high street without encountering an Angel curious about my business, nor can I sneeze without it being reported throughout the village within a minute of its occurrence."

She emitted a lilting laugh in response. "Perhaps you are right. But in this instance, it was Mrs. Halsey, the owner of the local tea shop, who warned me about you, my lord."

"Warned you? What have I done lately to earn my bad reputation?"

"Lately? It seems you are constantly rubbing people the wrong way."

He frowned. "Other than an unfortunate mishap with my phaeton, which was not my fault at all, what have I done to rankle anyone?"

"I think it is more what you have *not* done. By this I mean ingratiate yourself into our village life. You've been coming here for several years now, and yet you and your elegant friends continue to hold yourself apart from everyone. Are you surprised the ill feeling has amassed over the course of your visits?"

"I see you are well informed, but Mrs. Halsey's information is a little out of date. I no longer go by the title of viscount." He gave a sweeping bow. "Daire Claymore, formerly Viscount Claymore and now Duke of Claymore."

"Oh, I am sorry," she said with sincere sympathy.

"Sorry? What for?"

"Your gain obviously means the former duke has passed on. I thought he might be someone dear to you."

She saw a shadow cross over his eyes as he said with unsuppressed bitterness, "He was not."

"Ah, I see."

"No, I don't suppose you do."

She had angered him, although she was not certain why a polite expression of sympathy for the former duke should rile him. Who understood these London lords? She expected him to turn on his well-heeled boots and stride back to his horse now that he had taken offense.

Instead, he sighed and muttered, "Forgive my surliness. I have only a few weeks before my infant nephew and meddlesome mother arrive, and I have yet to find a suitable house in which to deposit them."

Brenna wondered at that remark, as well.

One deposited bottles. One *settled* loved ones.

"Your mother might enjoy the Kestrel Inn for the lively company of its guests. But your nephew might not be as comfortable there, especially if he likes to run around or squawk loudly, as infants often do. There are many fine homes in the area, although I suppose very few of them are for sale or to let. Are you familiar with the Duke of Malvern? He and his family are settled at St. Austell Grange."

He nodded. "We have met."

"But you are not friends? I suppose you have also met the Marquess of Burness at Westgate Hall and Viscount Brennan, who resides at Moonstone Cottage? By your expression, I gather they are also acquaintances but not friends. Their wives are the Killigrew sisters, and you will not meet nicer, more welcoming ladies."

"I do know them all, as you have probably heard. Is there a point you are trying to make?"

"I am just trying to determine what sort of house might appeal to someone like you."

"Someone like me?" That eyebrow of his shot up again, and he crossed his arms over his chest as he stared down at her. "Is it not obvious which house I want? Yours, Miss Angel."

If he thought to intimidate her, he had failed. "What is so

special about mine that you must suddenly have it? Not a single home has met with your approval, despite three years of searching."

"How do you know how long I have been searching? I do not believe I mentioned it."

She blushed, for not only had Mrs. Halsey gossiped about him, but so had Thaddius, numerous other members of her family, Mr. Priam—the local land agent—and practically everyone else in the village. Indeed, she had yet to hold a conversation with anyone since returning home that did not include him in it.

"One hears things here and there. You do not look happy that your family is about to join you. Why is that, Your Grace? Are you irritated they will impose on your indolent style of living? Children and parents are a blessing, I should think. I wish… Well, never mind. You would not care to hear about those dear to me."

"On the contrary, Miss Angel. I am most eager to hear of your situation, since you are obviously leaping in with both feet to pass judgment on mine. I believe you charmingly called me indolent?"

She glanced up at him, knowing she ought to feel contrite about insulting him. But she did not. This man needed to be kept at a distance lest she unwittingly fall prey to his charms, which were considerable. That insult should have done it.

Curiously, he did not walk away in a privileged huff or dismiss her in anger. What did that signify? Not attraction, for why should a duke care a whit about her? Her cousin, Thaddius the innkeeper, thought the duke was quite an intelligent man.

He did have intelligent eyes that seemed to miss nothing. She found him interesting. A bit frightening for the aura of power that circled him much like the swirl of the sea breeze off the cove waters.

But she was still not sorry she had spoken out of turn.

Why was he suddenly so keen to acquire her home?

Who was he really?

Yes, she knew he had been a viscount and probably held additional titles, including his recent elevation to the title of duke. But what did anyone really know about *him*? Despite his coming here every summer for the past three years, there was not a single person in the village who could call him a friend, not even those who were his peers. This was entirely his own doing, because everyone in Moonstone Landing was friendly, especially the Killigrew sisters and the noblemen they had married. They were all now happily settled in their fine homes on the heights overlooking the village.

Brenna's was a fine home, too. Nothing as grand as the others, but still quite beautiful, and hers possessed the finest view in all of Moonstone Landing—especially at this time of year, when those red poppies swept through the fields down to the sea.

They captivated him, too. She could tell by the way he had been looking out across them with an unguarded expression of longing.

What was he longing for?

Or was he pining for a person? Someone he cherished? Or had lost years ago?

Brenna let out a breath, ready to make a goodwill gesture and tell him a little about herself, even though she doubted he cared. He would quickly dismiss her as deadly dull by his *haut-monde* standards. After all, she was a person of no importance.

It did not matter that her cousin, Cara Angel, had fallen in love and married the Duke of Strathmore. The *ton* was still reeling from that scandal—not that Cara or her duke cared, for theirs was a love match.

She hoped for a love match, too.

However, she knew better than to look above herself. This handsome duke would not consider her fit for anything other than serving as his mistress.

The lout.

Well, he had not propositioned her.

However, she could not overlook the smolder in his eyes as

he regarded her, studying her with enough intensity to peel away her layers of clothing and see into her soul.

"Your Grace, you have not seen me around here before because I am a teacher at a prestigious girls' school in Oxford. The Rainard Academy. Have you heard of it?" When he did not bother to answer, she sighed softly and continued. "I came home this summer to settle affairs. You see, my mother passed away five years ago, and my father last year. I am their only surviving child."

"You had brothers and sisters?"

She nodded. "One brother and one sister, both older. But they did not survive into adulthood."

"I'm sorry. I see you clearly loved them."

She nodded again. "I did. Very much. This was partly the reason I needed to get away from here. Walls suddenly seemed to close in all around me. Do you understand this feeling?"

His expression softened, for the first time showing a little warmth. "I surely do."

"I thought you would." She absently brushed back a wayward curl as the wind, already warm for this hour of the morning, blew it loose. "When I was offered the position at the Rainard Academy, I jumped at the opportunity. I returned only this week with the thought of selling the house and settling permanently in Oxford. But now that I am here..." She shook her head and held out her hands in a gesture of supplication. "I cannot part with the property. In truth, I could no more part with it than I could part with my heart. I am sorry, Your Grace. It is not for sale."

"I see." His arms remained folded over his chest as he gazed toward the village and its sweep of homes down to the sea. "There is something about Moonstone Landing that draws me here, too. I have been searching for a house around here for years, as everyone in town seems to know. My land agent, Mr. Priam, must be pulling his hair out in frustration. He is convinced I am impossible to please. Perhaps he is right. I did not know what I was looking for, only that I would recognize it when I saw it."

"And after three years of searching, you have suddenly decided my home is for you? What changed from one year to the next? Surely you always knew of this house." She regarded him with a deeper curiosity, sensing the unhappiness behind his genial smile. "If it is of any consolation to you, Mr. Priam is ready to throttle me, too. I know he is salivating to sell Stoningham Manor. But I cannot bring myself to sign the papers. I am sorry, but you shall have to continue your search elsewhere. However, may I pass an observation?"

His gaze raked over her once again, those eyes of his as sharp as cut crystals, so blue and icy. He regarded her with marked impatience. However, instead of refusing her, he cast her a wry smile and said, "Go ahead. You seem to enjoy inserting that little nose of yours into my business."

She ignored his comment. "There are many fine homes in the area. I think it is not a house you are looking for so much as peace for your ravaged soul."

He stiffened, and his expression immediately darkened. "That is quite some observation, Miss Angel. Perhaps you ought to keep those thoughts to yourself in the future."

It was her turn to arch an eyebrow. "Perhaps you ought not be so prickly."

"*Perhaps* you ought to stop meddling in other people's affairs and tend to your own. Let me delay you no longer. Did you not mention you have someplace else you need to be?"

She had never said any such thing.

His arms remained taut as they lay crossed over his massive chest. Obviously, his jacket required no padding at the shoulders, for his muscles were real and meant to intimidate.

Was he dismissing her? The gall of him.

She tipped her chin up in defiance, a gesture he would certainly regard as meaningless, but it made her feel better. "Perhaps you ought to apologize to me, because this is my land you are standing on, and need I point out you are trespassing? I have every right to be here. You do not."

His arms now fell to his sides as he stared at her, no doubt attempting to determine whether she was in jest. "Are you telling me *all* of this is yours? This poppy field? This hillside and its view of the sea? As well as your house?"

"Yes. I thought Mr. Priam would have told you."

"Perhaps he did. The man is an idiot and never stops babbling." He glanced at the large stone manor in the distance behind him. "That settles it. I want Stoningham Manor. I want all of this."

She inhaled lightly. "Have you not been listening to me? It is not for sale. Besides, the manor is run-down and will not suit your family anyway."

"It is not all that run-down. I have been inside. It requires little more than a fresh coat of paint and a thorough dusting."

"And repairs to the stone. Cracked windows that require new panes. Chimneys in need of cleaning. When did you see it last?"

He shrugged. "Last year. Mr. Priam showed me around shortly after your father passed. You must have returned to Oxford by then, for I certainly would have remembered meeting you. He thought your manor would be perfect for me. But he said the same of the other twenty properties he showed me, so I did not make too much of it."

"Why, that sneaky fellow. He must have wheedled the keys from Thaddius. Why are you here now? Obviously, you found my home lacking last year."

"I never said that."

"You did not have to. Had you truly loved it, you would have made me an offer for it on the spot. Well, it was not for sale back then, and Mr. Priam should not have shown it to you. In any event, I am not going to sell a house that was once filled with so much love to the likes of..."

She clamped her mouth shut.

"To the likes of me?" he filled in for her.

She met his gaze. "My apologies. My comment was beyond

the pale."

"Indeed, it was. May I give you some advice, since you are so eager to pile a full plate of opinions on me? When selling goods, whether a bottle of wine, a gown, such as the pretty green one you have on, a horse and carriage, or a house—whatever the merchandise, do not get caught up in sentimentality. Go for the top price you can get and be ruthless about it. Sentiment will not put food on your table or provide a roof over your head. Fight for everything you can get, because no one will admire you for taking less because of sentiment."

"I did not realize that wound of yours was so raw. You hide your turmoil quite well behind a façade of casual indifference. It threw me for a moment. Is this why you choose to associate with those particular friends lodged with you at the inn?"

"What has Thaddius told you about them? That they are aimless and shallow?"

"Your words, Your Grace. My cousin would not say anything so unkind. I gather they are all about maintaining façades. So they will never look beyond the one you have so carefully crafted, and you like that just fine. All pretense. No questions asked. And no hearts at risk."

"I had no idea you were such a gifted oracle," he said with open sarcasm. "Do you also read palms? Tea leaves? Look into crystal balls?"

"Only at fairs and carnivals." She knew she was being terribly rude and intrusive. But there was something about this man that rattled her, perhaps the emptiness she perceived in his soul.

No, not emptiness. He had too much feeling, albeit suppressed. She had it all wrong. It was not that he was empty, but too full of bad feelings he could not shed.

"I must apologize again to you," Brenna said. "If I spoke out of turn—"

"Which you did."

"—it is only because I am going through a bit of turmoil myself and recognized the same in you. I am trying to figure out where I ought to be. Here, with family? Or Oxford, where I enjoy my work? All I am saying is that I thought our situations were similar, and I sought to commiserate. But I was wrong. Your concerns stem from a much darker place."

"They do, Miss Angel. I warn you, do not poke that coiled snake."

"I assure you, I mean to keep my distance. I am quite aware it is not the snake who will be hurt in the encounter."

"Once again, I commend you on your powers of observation," he said. "And yet you are still giving me that gentle look of concern. I see you are not quite ready to stop asking questions. What do you expect me to do, Miss Angel? Confide in you? Upon five minutes' acquaintance? Here's an idea—how about we confine our topics to the weather, this marvelous scenery, and Mrs. Halsey's teacakes?"

She nodded, surprised he had not simply stormed off, declaring her to be the most irritating young lady he had ever met. But he hadn't, no doubt because he was determined to have her property and would stick to her like a bee to honey until he got his way.

He was still studying her, a little too closely for comfort.

What was he thinking?

He had an ability to mask his feelings, so she could not tell what was going through his mind. However, she knew that she must be irritating him, because she was denying him something he had decided, on a whim, that he wanted.

Well, he was provoking her, too.

"So it shall be, Your Grace. I shall dazzle you with my knowledge of the weather. Isn't it a fine day? A warm sun and cool sea breeze. Nothing better for one's lungs or general constitution. How is your constitution, by the way? Do you suffer from lumbago? Gout? An embarrassing flux in your bowels?"

His lips had been twitching, and he now burst out with a deep, rich chuckle.

"Dull enough for you, Your Grace?"

"Miss Angel, I sense you are too lively ever to be dull. But your topic of conversation… Yes, it is worthy of putting me to sleep." A smile escaped his lips, one she found surprisingly charming.

This scared her, for she did not wish to like him, or begin to trust him.

"Excellent," she said, continuing their pointless conversation. "As for our local scenery, do you ride out on different paths each morning or always take the same one? They somehow always lead you back to this spot, I've noticed. Have you found something here that stirs your soul? Or evokes a memory? Is it a sad one? Or a happy one you somehow hope to reclaim? It is those red poppies, isn't it?" she said quite gently. "I am so sorry. What happened?"

"By heaven, you do not mince words, do you?"

"I apologize if I am too blunt. What am I to do about you when you keep riding over here? And do not dare suggest I sell my property to you."

He sighed. "Even your questions about the weather and scenic views are barbed and loaded with meaning, Miss Angel. Can you not try harder to keep your comments to the inane and frivolous?"

"I am not certain I can," she said with utmost sincerity, because he was a puzzle for her, and she did not wish to lie to him about her determination to figure him out. "Would you care to accompany me back to the village? I think I shall end my walk with one of Mrs. Halsey's teacakes, now that you have mentioned them."

She noticed his horse was lathered. He must have taken the magnificent beast for a hard ride, which only proved her point that he was in a dark place and unable to find a solution to whatever was plaguing him. "You ought to take it easier on your horse. No matter how hard you ride him, you will not outrun the devils chasing you."

"Blessed saints, you have a mouth on you." He said no more

as he gathered the reins, but his horse snorted in annoyance, since he was contentedly munching on some nearby gorse and did not wish to be disturbed. "Come, Scipio. There'll be sweet grass for you at the stable, old boy."

Scipio nodded as though in understanding.

Brenna stroked the horse's nose. "He's a warhorse, one you've obviously named after a much-admired Roman general. Were you cavalry?"

"What makes you think I was ever in the army? A man of my rank and privilege could have bought his way out."

"But you did not. Do not bother to deny it, for it is obvious." She began to walk alongside the duke as he led Scipio back to the village. The horse required very little coaxing from his master.

Well, his master was quite a handsome fellow and could be very persuasive. Of this, Brenna had no doubt.

He had gorgeous eyes, the beckoning bedroom sort, capable of reducing a woman to tingles and flutters with a mere glance. Not that she was responding to him in this way...

Well, she was ignoring the excited shivers running up her arms and the butterflies fluttering in her belly.

As for the duke, she did not know what else he wanted from her, or what he was thinking, or what to make of him at all.

She made the mistake of posing the question to him.

He arched that eyebrow of his, a sign of his amusement as he cast her another of his wry smiles. "Are you sure you wish to know the thoughts whirling in my head?"

"Yes, I do."

"Very well, my snoopy miss," he said, with a little heat to his voice and a heightened smolder in his eyes. He took her hand—neither his nor hers were gloved—to draw her closer. She thought his hands would be soft as hers, but they weren't. They were big and rough, and so was his voice as he said, "What I was thinking... Since you do not wish to give me your house..."

"Which I don't."

"Perhaps you might be persuaded to give me...you."

"Me?" Her mouth dropped open as she gaped at him.

Had she heard him right?

Would she be clapped in irons if she hit him? Perhaps not, since her uncle was the local constable.

She hauled her arm back, fully intending to slap him, since the entire village, including the Duke of Malvern, Marquess of Burness, and Viscount Brennan, would come to her defense against this loathsome man if he were so low as to press charges.

How dare he insult her with that revolting proposition!

He easily blocked her hand, then drew her open palm to his lips and gave it a soft kiss. "I warned you not to tangle with the coiled snake."

She had to own that he was right.

Why had she passed that comment about his demons? She could see by the turmoil in his eyes that she had ripped the bandage off a wound that had yet to heal. She ought to learn to keep her mouth shut.

What was he going to do next?

His eyes had a feral look to them…hot and raw.

"Brenna," he said with a wrenching ache that seemed to emerge from the depths of his damaged soul. "Brenna," he repeated with a throatier ache, lowering his head to hers and kissing her full on the mouth with scorching heat.

Chapter Two

D AIRE DREW HIS lips off Brenna's mouth, needing a moment to make his head stop spinning. He had expected to dazzle her with the soft crush of his lips on hers, melt her, and render her helpless to his prowess, but—what the blazes? He'd never tasted sweeter lips or felt a lovelier body pressed to his.

She pushed away, furious with him.

"Go ahead, slap me. I won't stop you this time, since even I will admit I deserve it." He held out his hands, allowing himself to be a target. "However, if you wish me to be honest about it, I am not sorry I kissed you."

"I am not going to slap you and risk another kiss, for you are just perverse enough to do something like that," she replied. "Since we are being honest with each other... I did not like your kiss in the least."

He saw the heat in her eyes and knew for a fact that quite the opposite was true. She had adored it. Women always did, especially *ton* women who understood the rules of engagement, which Brenna did not. One did not pry into the hearts of men like him without risk of getting kissed...or burned...or both.

"You are an oaf," she shot back when he grinned at her.

"And you are lying to yourself if you believe my kiss did not melt your bones." He raked a hand through his hair, and his grin slipped. "If you insist on insulting me, then you ought to be more precise about it. I am a snake, not an oaf."

"No, your anguish is the coiled snake. You are… I don't know what you are yet, other than arrogant and impossibly forward." Having said that, the snoopy bundle of froth who called herself Brenna tore down the hillside toward Moonstone Landing.

He sighed, knowing he needed to go after her and make things right, because what he had done had been unspeakably offensive, even for him.

She had asked what he wanted, and he had shown her because that plush ruby mouth of hers was irresistible.

Perhaps he had responded with too much honesty.

But she had not remained indifferent, for he saw the innocent heat of passion in her eyes.

Where was the harm in a simple kiss?

Well, perhaps no harm for someone with experience.

Brenna was surprisingly inexperienced, as it turned out. How was he to know? Of course, this was something he should have picked up on. Had any man kissed her before this? She was such a sharp little thing, he just assumed she would be sharp about everything.

His mistake.

Lush, bow-shaped lips, emerald eyes as bright as starlight, and a wild mop of hair, a glorious mix of chestnut brown and darkest red, made for a beautiful woman, but not one who necessarily wished to leap into his bed. Or kiss him.

Even if she had liked their kiss more than she would ever admit.

Daire mounted Scipio and spurred him forward to catch up with Brenna, who was now running as fast as her legs would carry her toward the village. "You will fall and break your neck hurtling down the hillside if you do not slow down," he said, cutting her off so that she was forced to stop or risk running headlong into his beast.

She was breathing hard, her lovely bosom heaving, as she struggled to restore her composure. Her eyes shimmered and her rosebud lips were lightly parted, which made him want to kiss her again. He did not reach out for her, however. That would only earn him another attempted slap, not to mention lose him any chance of acquiring her house.

"Truce, Miss Angel." He dismounted and offered his arm to escort her back into town. "You were never in any danger from me."

"Why did you kiss me in that…that…?"

"Scorching way?" Did she seriously need to ask? Had no one ever mentioned how pretty she was? He ached to kiss her every time she pursed her lips, something she had a habit of doing whenever she was thinking or fretting. "Here's a hint—it had nothing to do with your wit or wisdom."

She frowned at him. "You are quite the boor."

"I never claimed to be anything else. You are the one who sought to delve into my soul. What did you think to find? Pretty butterflies and buttercups? Or were you thinking to uncover something heroic about me? I assure you, I have not sipped a drop of elixir capable of making me brave or valorous."

"Are you suggesting you were never heroic in any respect? Yet you fought in the war when you could have bought your way out."

"Who says I didn't buy out my commission?"

"Your horse."

"I was not aware my horse could talk."

She rolled her eyes.

"Fine, fighting Napoleon does not make me a hero. It was a long time ago, and I was young and foolish."

She refused to accept his offered arm, so he dropped it to his side.

To his surprise, she proceeded to walk beside him. "You are a mass of contradictions, Your Grace. What do you have inside of you?"

"Other than bitterness and bile?"

She looked up at him as they walked along, with Scipio now

ambling contentedly behind them. "I am sorry you are so haunted. Have you always been like this, or did the war do this to you?"

"What does it matter? Do you think you are just the woman to save me? Others have tried and failed."

"Heavens, no. I am not interested in saving you. You are part gentleman, part tragic poet, and part coiled snake, as you warned. I have learned my lesson and know better than to tangle with you."

He reached out and brushed a windblown curl off her cheek. "Smart girl. Do you live alone at Stoningham Manor?"

"No one lives there at the moment. I am staying in the village, at my cousin Cara's cottage. Stoningham Manor is too big for me to manage on my own, which is why it makes sense for me to sell it. But to do so feels as though I am giving up my parents. My siblings, too. Indeed, my entire existence. I suppose you will chide me again for my sentiment."

"I have no need. You are chiding yourself."

"Not really. I value sentiment. It does have a value, no matter what you say."

"There's where you are wrong. You are going to hold on to the manor house and pour your savings into its upkeep, even though all that work and expense will never be sufficient to properly restore it. Then where will you be? Struggling because you spent the funds to preserve a memory, and winding up with a house reduced in value because the funds were never going to be enough, and it still needs fixing."

She again pursed her lips.

Ah, those exquisite lips. He wanted to kiss her again.

But even he understood he had done enough damage for one morning.

Besides, now that he realized how innocent she was, he could never take advantage. She looked quite youthful, like the breath of spring. But she had to be approaching her mid-twenties, since he knew she had taught at the Rainard Academy for several years.

Gossip flowed both ways here in Moonstone Landing. She had heard an earful about him, but he'd also heard quite a bit about her. She was beloved and admired, regarded highly for her knowledge, which obviously did not extend to men.

He was not going to make that mistake again.

In truth, he felt quite some remorse for taking advantage and kissing her. Well, he did not really regret kissing her. But he was too much of a gentleman, despite what she thought, and would not act again without her permission.

Blasted shreds of decency and honor. They were such useless things.

"You mentioned you had siblings, Miss Angel."

She nodded. "Yes, a beloved brother and a sister who always looked out for me. But a fever took them before they reached adulthood. I don't know why the fever did not take me, too."

"You might have been the littlest, but you must have had the hardiest spirit."

She shrugged.

"Miss Angel, if you are reluctant to sell me your property, perhaps we shall come to another arrangement. Would you consider letting the house to me for the remainder of the year? A six-month term? Or a full year? This will give you an income while you decide what you want to do."

She pursed her lips yet again.

Really, this girl needed serious kissing.

He grunted. What was wrong with him?

"It is a comfortable home," she said. "My father was a man of importance in the area. But you are a duke. I doubt it will be nearly fine enough for you."

"Mr. Priam would be issuing you a severe lecture right now," he said with a mock frown. "Is this not a perfect solution for you? At least a temporary one to get you through the year? Why are you trying to talk me out of tossing piles of money at you?"

She cast him a pained expression. "You are right. I am being foolish. Toss away. I'll fetch a basket to catch as many banknotes as you wish to throw at me."

"You are being sarcastic. But you should not be so quick to dismiss me, little dove. I'll need to tour the place again to make certain it is suitable for the entourage about to descend on me. Mother. Nephew. Governess. Maidservants. Butler. Cook. Groom."

"Will you reside there, too?"

"Perhaps. I haven't decided yet. The Kestrel Inn is quite comfortable."

"Especially with your lady friends ensconced there."

He arched an eyebrow. "Thaddius talks too much."

"What you do with your lady friends is none of my business, so long as you do not think to turn my home into a bawdy house."

"With my mother in residence? I can assure you, it will be as free of sin as any fine church. So, do we have a deal?"

They were almost into town now, and he knew they ought to part ways so as not to be seen returning together. For a young woman to be caught alone with a man such as himself would cause damage to her reputation if they were in London. But he wasn't quite certain how these locals would respond, especially since she was related to most of them.

"A deal? No… Maybe. Well, let me give it some thought. Set out your offer and convey it to Mr. Priam. He can bring it to me."

"Why not discuss it with me directly?"

The girl had lovely and delicate features, even as she frowned at him. "Because you think you can manipulate me with kisses. Let me assure you, I did not appreciate your forwardness. Sweeping me into your arms to kiss me will not soften me toward you in the least. It will firmly put me off. So let us keep this strictly professional. We shall deal through Mr. Priam or not at all."

He sighed and put up his hands. "Very well. I surrender to your terms. I'll ask Mr. Priam to take me to Stoningham Manor this afternoon, if that is all right with you. Care to come with us?

You needn't speak to me directly. But there will be some adjustments needed to the house, and it would be so much easier if we could come to terms on all of it today. Any work done will be solely at my cost, and if any of it is not to your liking, I shall deposit additional funds in escrow to cover the expense of restoration once the lease term has ended and we have gone back to London. As for the lease, I shall offer you double whatever the other homes in the area are being let for."

"And you chide me on my bad negotiation skills?" she said with a shake of her head. "Good heavens."

She considered his offer, one she had to know was ridiculously generous and ought to be grabbed before he came to his senses.

Not that he would, for this was mere pocket change for him.

She sighed. "Yes, I would like to be there when you look over the house."

"Good. I'll arrange it with Mr. Priam."

He waited for her to walk back into town before he mounted Scipio and made his way back to the inn. The hour was early, and Mr. Priam would not be in his office yet.

Daire was in no hurry now that he had swayed Brenna. All that was left to do was set the terms down in writing, and Mr. Priam would put his clerks to it immediately in order to secure his own fee.

There was no other pressing business to occupy Daire's day, so he took his time making certain Scipio was properly fed and curried by the inn's ostler, the chatty Mr. Matchett.

"I'll take good care of him, Your Grace. Never you worry. I hear you were looking over Miss Angel's property on the heights. Lovely girl, she is. Cleverest of us all, but we always knew she was a bright little thing and would make good someday. She could read and write better than me by the time she was a wee sprite of six. But for all her book learning, her Uncle Joseph's worried about her."

"Joseph?"

"Aye, m'lord," Mr. Matchett said. "Joseph Angel. He owns the Three Lions Tavern. Runs it with his son, William. He's a strapping lad and very protective of his cousins. Looked out for Cara, he surely did. And now he's looking out for Brenna. They are close as siblings, but that comes as no surprise, since the three of them, along with their cousin Felicity, were caught up in the squall that killed Captain Arundel, and would have killed them all had the captain not come to their rescue. Such wee ones they were at the time, and their ship about to go down. Don't think our village would ever have recovered had they drowned."

It took Daire another few minutes to disengage himself from the ostler, but the man had given him much to think about. Brenna had almost drowned as a little girl? How had this affected her, having to face death at a young age?

He did not know why it roused his protective instincts.

Gad, he wanted to take her in his arms and just hold her forever. Not that she required this from him, for she was a scrappy little thing, having survived a near drowning and the scourge of an illness that had claimed the lives of her older siblings. She was clearly a strong woman and not afraid to make her way in the world. Perhaps the ordeals she had faced had given her the strength to stand on her own.

The innkeeper, Thaddius Angel, greeted him as he strode in. "Did you have a pleasant ride this morning, Your Grace? Lovely day for it."

Daire nodded. "Yes, quite an enlightening ride."

The fellow arched an eyebrow. "Enlightening? Ah, then you finally encountered my cousin, Brenna."

For pity's sake, did everyone have to know his business?

Daire glanced at the notice posted on an easel by the entryway. "I see there is an assembly ball to be held at the inn this evening."

Thaddius looked at him askance, knowing he was mentioning it only to change the topic, since the notice had been prominently displayed there all week, and one would have to be blind as a mole not to have seen it before this moment. "Yes, Your Grace. Will you and your party attend? Brenna will be there."

Daire merely nodded and walked into the empty dining room. The hour was early for most of the inn's patrons, but he preferred the solitude, since he needed to think about Brenna. She would be at tonight's dance, he mused, taking a seat at one of the tables in a back corner of the room to discourage any of the inn's guests approaching him, should they happen to walk in.

Tomorrow there was to be a tea hosted by the Duke of Malvern and his wife at their grand estate, St. Austell Grange. He wondered whether Brenna would attend that affair, too.

No matter.

He would see the girl again this afternoon, and this pleased him immensely, although he did not know why it should when she had done nothing but meddle and poke her finger into his deep wounds.

He ordered a cup of coffee, finished it quickly, and then decided to take a walk down to the harbor. He needed to think about his summer plans and did not wish to be interrupted by his wastrel friends. Why had he brought them along when they no longer amused him? Well, it was his own fault for inviting them.

Brenna had been surprisingly quick to catch on to why he kept them about. They were toadies who did not ask questions or require him to open up his heart. The ladies among them, although still unmarried, were unapologetic in their promiscuity. They did not hesitate to join him in bed whenever it suited him. Nor did they particularly care which of them he took to his bed, or if both accompanied him.

But he hadn't touched either of them since arriving in Moonstone Landing several weeks ago. They were amoral creatures, both of them now betrothed to older noblemen who were in frail health and ridiculously wealthy. Those were irresistible qualities, apparently. They were willing to offer nights of sex during their marriage in return for scads of money upon the demise of their well-satisfied husbands.

Daire shuddered to think what kind of salons Lady Gemma and Lady Sarah would host once they were merry widows. Nor did their brother, Lord Hollinsgworth, ever show any concern for their virtue or shocking lack of it.

Ah, families.

But who was he to pass judgment on any of them when his own family was so shameful? Brutal, cruel, and completely lacking in scruples. The only one among them who stood a chance of getting into heaven was the woman he referred to as his mother. Duchess Juliana was actually his stepmother, and had married his father only a month before that bastard died. To Daire's surprise, she had taken her role as mother quite seriously, raising him and his older brother as though they were her own. She never beat them or gave up on them, despite the trouble they caused.

Unfortunately, she had come into their lives too late to save his older brother from turning into the heartless monster that their father, and grandfather before him, had been.

As for Daire himself, the outcome was yet to be decided. Had his stepmother intervened in time to save him? He simply did not know.

"Ah, Brenna," he muttered. "Perhaps you are right to want nothing to do with me."

He strode down the high street, passing the monument to Captain Brioc Taran Arundel. Daire had passed by this statue dozens of times over the years, but never stopped in front of it until this morning. The man's sacrifice now had meaning for him, for without his valor, Brenna would not be here today. The sea captain was the village hero for rescuing all the schoolchildren from that sinking schooner during the squall, as Mr. Matchett had said.

Daire shook his head.

Why did this incident now leave *him* in such turmoil?

Perhaps it was something he would talk to Brenna about later. These tragedies changed people forever, their rescuers and especially the survivors. Had he not been so changed by war? He had led his men into some fairly bloody battles.

Daire tried to dismiss thoughts of war or Brenna as he reached the dockside and looked out over the harbor that was dotted with sailing vessels. They were mostly fishing boats, but there was also a naval frigate easing into one of the slips in order to discharge its wounded soldiers. Fort Arundel, the ancient stone fortress beside the harbor, was an army outpost commanded by Viscount Fionn Brennan, and attached to it was a newly built military hospital also under his command.

Most of the naval vessels arriving at this port sailed in for the purpose of depositing their wounded.

Daire knew he ought to do something about helping out, perhaps… Well, he would talk to Viscount Brennan about it later. He turned away to walk through the nearby fish market, which was bustling at this hour. While the men were off in their fishing vessels catching their daily haul, their wives were skinning and gutting the fresh catch as it was brought in.

The ground was strewn with blood, and the air held the scent of rotting fish.

He sighed and walked back up the hill to the inn, annoyed with himself for allowing the memories of war to seep into his thoughts. Suddenly, everything he saw and every breath he inhaled reminded him of the slaughter on the bloody battlefields. Blood on all sides, young men dying needlessly, and for what?

How detestable his life had been even before he headed off to war, and how empty it was ever since his return to England once the war was over. Napoleon had been defeated years ago, and Daire's father had died years before that, so why was he still battling demons?

And why did he suddenly think Brenna could be what he needed to heal his heart?

She thought him low and repulsive for kissing her.

But, dear heaven, he thought he would suffocate if he did not kiss her again.

However, he would not attempt it unless she was willing. She already thought he was an arrogant rogue and did not like him. Well, she did not *want* to like him, which was not quite the same thing. If he had any sense, he would keep his arrangement with Brenna completely professional and keep to the *ton* ladies for his amorous affairs.

Yes, it would be so much easier to keep to those easy women who tossed themselves at him and offered him whatever he wished, without need for him to expend any effort or make any promises to get them into his bed.

But Brenna… He would have to work hard to claim her. It was his fault they had started off badly. In his own defense, it was not every day he brazenly kissed a woman he had just met. In fact, he had never done it before.

She assumed he wanted her as a bedmate.

But she was wrong. It was very possible he wanted her as someone more permanent.

However, not merely as his mistress. First of all, he did not believe in keeping a mistress, and never had, since they were a responsibility and could be as demanding as a wife. Nor did he like the thought of keeping a pretty bird trapped in a gilded cage. It was still a cage, and the pretty bird was not free, no matter how many expensive trinkets her *keeper* provided.

Second of all, Brenna was completely innocent and would not know the first thing about enticing a man in bed.

Though that innocence was enticing in itself. She was an angel, a glorious, beautiful, celestial being. And this was her family name, too. Angel. He had done some low things in his life, but never had he befouled an angel.

Perhaps she could become someone dear to him over time—he simply did not know.

She certainly remained in his thoughts, and he had never felt so invigorated after meeting someone. It made no sense, for she was nothing more than a prim, overly sentimental schoolteacher on the verge of becoming a spinster.

But gad, what a stunning spinster she was.

He liked her, despite her insolent attitude...which probably made him like her more.

Why was he thinking so much about her? It must be boredom, or a momentary madness on his part.

What else could it be?

Chapter Three

DAIRE DECIDED THESE surprising feelings he had for Brenna were indeed a momentary madness, for who but a madman contemplated marriage within minutes of meeting a person? Not that he was seriously contemplating it, certainly not with this girl, who was nothing like the biddable ladies he usually came across.

Nor would Brenna be in any way suitable, since he was a duke and she had not an ounce of noble blood. It did not matter that his body was still thrumming and his heart had not stopped racing from their earlier kiss.

She had said what he needed was salvation, not a home.

What if she turned out to be his salvation?

Blast, he was doing it again. Why could he not stop thinking of this girl?

Not that his thoughts were at all serious about her.

However, if they did turn serious, then what did he care what anyone thought about who he chose for a wife? Only his opinion mattered. If the Duke of Strathmore could marry an Angel, why couldn't he?

"Botheration," he muttered, chiding himself for allowing these far-fetched musings to invade his thoughts and completely swallow them up. His mind had been on nothing and no one but her since meeting her this morning.

Since kissing her this morning.

Bollocks.

He was being an idiot, and Brenna would be the first one to call him out on it.

Nor would Brenna ever believe or trust him if he chose to pursue something beyond the leasing of her house. How could she when he did not trust himself? He was still that coiled snake, and too dangerous for an innocent like her to handle.

He pushed thoughts of her out of his mind, yet again.

His friends were now awake and seated in wait for him at one of the grander tables in the inn's dining room when he returned. They caught his attention as he tried to stride past them, so he could not ignore their gestures to come over.

They looked like a muster of peacocks, all of them overly dressed for this casual village, and impatient for him to relieve their *ennui*.

"Really, Claymore," Lord Hollingsworth said, seated idolently in the chair beside the one Daire now took. "How long must we rusticate here? Why don't we all head to Bath for the summer?"

Daire glanced at the others. "Is this what you all wish to do?"

Hollingsworth's sisters, Lady Sarah and Lady Gemma, had bored looks on their faces. So had their cousin, Lord Danson, who adored bright popinjay colors and thought he struck quite a dashing pose in them. All he did was blind everyone with his colorful silks. He looked quite out of place and ridiculous.

The others were similarly out of place with their bejeweled attire and pale complexions.

"I intend to settle my mother and nephew here," Daire said with finality. "Leave if you wish, but I am staying."

His edict did not please them, but they quickly assured him they would stay on. It was not out of friendship, because these were not true friends but merely hangers-on. He was footing the bills, and these Hollingsworths were more than happy to go along with his plans, since they did not like to pay for anything themselves. Their own funds were spent on glittering trinkets. Hollingsworth, Danson, and the ladies routinely went through the generous allowance given them every month by their uncle, the Marquess of Haverlock, every last farthing frivolously applied to their own selfish purposes and nothing set aside for future needs.

Perhaps he would ship them off to Bath. They would only be in the way while he supervised repairs to Stoningham Manor. There was little time, and all had to be in order before his mother and nephew arrived. Besides, his mother did not care for his friends.

In truth, neither did he.

Well, Hollingsworth could be all right sometimes. The man wasn't a complete dullard. But Daire had little patience for any of them right now. He could easily afford to ship them off to his townhouse in Bath. Of course, it was located in one of the most elegant crescents, because his family only acquired the finest. Yes, he would send them off once he and Brenna had firmed their terms.

"I'm afraid you will have to entertain yourselves today," Daire said. "I will see you this evening at the assembly ball."

They responded like lost children, whining and questioning why he would leave them on their own in this boring backwater. "What is so important that will occupy your time? Why can we not join you?" Lady Sarah asked, casting him a pretty pout.

"It is a business matter, and you will only delay me." He slapped his hands to his thighs and rose.

"But you will be back in time for the assembly ball?" Lady Gemma asked. "Who are we to dance with if you are not there?"

He nodded. "I shall be back well before then, and you shall have your dance."

He returned to his suite of rooms and ordered up a bath. Once washed and properly groomed, he walked over to Mr. Priam's land office, which was on the high street along with most of the village shops and businesses.

The man's eyes lit up when Daire strode in and told him he wanted to see Stoningham Manor again for the purpose of letting it. "Merely to let, my lord? I thought you wished to purchase."

"But Miss Angel does not have a mind to sell, so I am authorizing you to offer her leasing terms. But I must tour the house again before I sign my name to anything. Tell her I wish to see it this afternoon, Mr. Priam. Make certain she is present on the tour. I do not intend to waste time haggling."

"Yes, my lord. I shall arrange it at once. Miss Angel happens to be at the tea shop. I saw her there not ten minutes ago. If you will be so kind as to wait right here, I shall—"

"I'll go with you," Daire said, not caring that it was probably a bad idea, since Brenna had insisted on having him deal exclusively through Mr. Priam. But since when did Daire take orders from anyone?

Good thing he was put in charge of his cavalry regiments during the war, for he truly was not good at taking orders, and rarely bent to the will of others.

The little man cleared his throat. "It might be best if I—"

"No, Mr. Priam. We shall go over there together."

Brenna was just finishing her tea when they arrived at Mrs. Halsey's popular establishment. The aroma of cakes, pies, and bread baking in the ovens struck Daire as he strode in, and was enough to make his mouth water.

However, the most tempting morsel for him was Brenna.

Gad, she was pretty…in an impudent way. Big eyes, a pursed and pouty mouth that was as sweet as cherries, and unruly hair that blazed more red than brown in the sunshine.

She maintained an even countenance as he and Mr. Priam approached her table. "Do sit down, gentlemen."

They took chairs on either side of her, but these wrought-iron chairs were ornately designed and meant for a dainty woman's frame, not for big men such as Daire. He sat quietly as Mr. Priam began to do the talking for him.

"Miss Angel," the man said, his beady eyes shining as he silently counted his profits, "His Grace, the Duke of Claymore, is seriously interested in your property. I have told him how exquisite it is, and he is eager to make you an offer on it. Now, I know you have mentioned it is not for sale. But he is a generous man, willing to offer generous terms. And we all know you are hard-pressed to maintain—"

"That is enough, Mr. Priam," Daire said. "Miss Angel will not respond to your tactics. My offer, which I made clear to you, is merely to let the house from her for the remainder of the year. I know she is not yet ready to sell, and do not appreciate your coercing her."

"Thank you, Your Grace," she said, staring at him with marked surprise and a hint of appreciation.

He could be nice when he wanted to be.

"Miss Angel," he said, trying not to smile at her continued expression of surprise, "will you be amenable to meeting us at Stoningham Manor this afternoon? I would like you to walk me through the property, after which we can discuss leasing terms that will suit us both."

She nodded. "Very well. Two o'clock this afternoon at the house."

He smiled. "Until then, Miss Angel."

Daire rose and walked to the tea shop door, sparing a greeting for Mrs. Halsey, who was quite the gossip but also baked the best pies he had ever tasted. "Have a good day, Mrs. Halsey."

"And you, Your Grace. Will you and your party be stopping by later for tea and cakes?"

"Yes, as always. It is the high point of our day." Which was not far from the truth, since little went on in this quiet village to amuse his friends. As for Daire, he enjoyed the quieter life and had never been much enamored of the typical London entertainments. After all, how many dinner parties, balls, musicales, and theater outings could one attend with the same people? How could one speak of the same trivial things, and listen to their infuriatingly petty complaints?

He had long ago lost any feeling of excitement in bedding the same bored ladies, most of whom were married and unhappy with their lives. Not a one would have traded their wealth and titles for a true love match, but that did not stop them from bemoaning their plight.

He looked back, sparing a glance at Brenna, who was chatting with Mr. Priam.

She was the romantic, impossibly idealistic sort who would insist on a love match.

Perhaps this is why she fascinated him—this refreshingly innocent hope she had of finding love. And yet she was also sensible, quite independent, capable enough to teach at an elegant girls' school in Oxford, and not afraid to live on her own.

In her own way, Brenna was formidable.

He had yet to cross the street to return to the inn when another of the tea shop's patrons hurried out after him. "Good morning, Lady Dowling," he greeted her.

"Good morning, Your Grace." She flashed him a seductive smile that did not impress him in the least. Many considered Lady Dowling to be the most beautiful woman in Moonstone Landing, and he had to own she was quite nice looking. But the lovely widow was also an opportunist and not above breaking up a romantic couple if it served her purpose. He had seen her in action trying to break up Viscount Brennan and Lady Chloe Killigrew—fortunately, a failed attempt on her part.

She smiled at him quite prettily. "A lovely day, isn't it?"

Daire sighed, for he did not like the woman very much. Not that he had a conscience to speak of, but he knew love was something important and rare. He did not like to think it could be so easily destroyed by this temptress. "Yes, quite a pleasant day."

She took his arm as they walked toward the inn, although he had no idea if this was her destination. "Will you be attending the assembly ball this evening?" she asked with a charming lilt to her voice.

He nodded.

"Excellent. I shall see you then. I was thinking of taking a room at the inn for myself."

What was she suggesting?

"For tonight, Lady Dowling? Why? You live close by, and any of a dozen gentlemen would not hesitate to see you safely home."

"Are you offering? I do so appreciate it."

"Of course." He cursed silently, for being seen in her company would not endear him to Brenna. She would never believe his actions were innocent. Not that his affairs were any business of hers, but the girl already thought he ran a brothel in his room. He did not want her mistaking a simple offer to walk Lady Dowling home as something more and refuse to lease her property to him.

Not that he intended to stay the night, which was obviously what Lady Dowling was offering. Now, if Brenna were to invite him, his answer would be quite different. But she would never do such a thing.

He left Lady Dowling in the dining room with the others of his party, who had not budged and were once again complaining they had nothing to do. "Really, Claymore," Lord Danson drawled, "must you leave us when you see we are so miserable?"

"Alas, I must." Daire retired to his suite to attend to the packet of business delivered yesterday by his man of affairs.

There was not much to do, for Daire's detestable brother had not lived long enough to inflict much damage to the dukedom their grandfather had ruthlessly built up to be one of the most profitable estates in England. Daire's brutal father had died shortly after his grandfather, to everyone's relief, and Morgan, his reckless bastard of a brother, had inherited next.

The only good that could be said of Morgan was that he left the business matters to Daire, for the most part, while he wreaked havoc in his tenure as duke, running up gambling debts and siring a slew of illegitimate offspring, all but one of whom had died.

The boy, Matthew, was as wild as wolves.

Perhaps it was a mistake for Daire to bring his mother and

Matthew here. Well, he had made the decision, and hoped it would not prove to be a bad one. The boy's mother had died, too. Daire was the only one left to look after him.

He finished the most pressing matters and delivered his mail to Thaddius. "See that it is put on the next mail coach to London."

"At once, Your Grace," Thaddius said with an amiable smile.

Since the hour was nearing two o'clock, Daire strode up the high street to the land agent's office. Mr. Priam had his curricle hitched and was waiting for him to climb in before he flicked the reins and they headed to Brenna's manor. "What about Miss Angel?" Daire asked.

"Oh, I am certain she is there already. She likes to walk. It gives her time to think, she claims. In my opinion, she thinks an awful lot but does not seem to resolve anything."

"Mr. Priam, that is unfair. You know she is the sentimental sort, and it must be quite hard for her to part with this beautiful property, even if it is only for a few months."

The man eyed Daire curiously. "You seem to know an awful lot about her, Your Grace."

"I make it my business to know whom I am dealing with."

"Ah, then you've heard she is also contemplating an offer of marriage."

Daire's heart leaped into his throat. "I've heard some conflicting accounts."

This was an outright lie, for no one had mentioned Brenna having a beau until this very moment. Why would this be kept from him when the entire village must have known of it? Not a blessed soul could control their mouths about anything, so why fail to bring up the fact she had a beau?

The fellow could not be much of a man if he had not even kissed her. Or if he had, it had been a botched affair, for Daire would wager his dukedom that Brenna had not been kissed in a romantic way before this morning.

"What do you know about him, Mr. Priam?"

And how was it possible a girl as beautiful as her had never been properly kissed? Perhaps those seven uncles had scared the lads off. But those uncles had not been with her in Oxford.

"Well, Your Grace, it is not my place to say." Mr. Priam looked straight ahead and flicked the reins again to hurry his old bay up the small hill toward the house.

"But say it anyway, Mr. Priam. It is pertinent information. Not that I care about the gentleman, but Miss Angel's feelings for him will certainly affect her decisions regarding Stoningham Manor. Who is he?"

"I hear he is an Oxford professor. Quite respected in his field."

"And what might that field be?"

"Oh, that I do not know. I'm sure Miss Angel will tell you if you to ask her."

Daire doubted she would open up to him and discuss something this personal. But he would do his best to draw her out in casual conversation. Why was she determined to hold on to this house if her beau truly meant to marry her? A full professorship at Oxford University had to be much coveted, and this fellow of hers was not likely to give it up to reside in some out-of-the-way village in Cornwall, such as Moonstone Landing.

If this man was indeed serious, did Brenna feel the same about him?

The possibility made Daire's stomach churn.

Brenna was already at the house, standing in wait on the front steps as they rattled up the overgrown drive in the jouncing curricle. Daire did not take his gaze off her the entire time, soaking in the uncommon beauty of her face and that sweet body of hers. She would hit him again if she suspected what he was thinking.

But how could he not ache over her? This girl sparkled. The air fairly crackled around her because she had so much vitality. That she should settle for a staid Oxford professor who did not know how to kiss her properly would be a gross injustice.

"Blast," he said quietly, raking a hand through his hair.

"Your Grace, did you say something?" Mr. Priam glanced at him as they drew up in front of the house.

"No, merely thinking aloud." Why should Daire care whom she chose to marry? He'd only met the girl this morning.

It was mad to care, but he did, and his stomach was churning again.

Botheration.

What was it about Brenna Angel he found so fascinating?

Chapter Four

BRENNA TRIED TO maintain a calm façade as she showed the Duke of Claymore through her home. She had brought along a small writing journal and a graphite to jot down details that would go into the lease. "Three broken windows."

"I'll have those repaired," the duke said, examining them closer.

"Should they not be my responsibility?" She was not comfortable with his taking over every aspect of her home's restoration, although it was quite silly on her part. If the man wanted to storm through her house like a big, commanding bull and insist on taking on all the expenses, why should she care?

He cast her a look. "Miss Angel, it shall be my cost, and that's an end to it."

"But—"

"Mine," he said with an arch of his eyebrow, daring her to challenge him.

"Very well," she grumbled, her lips twitching at the corners in a smile, because they were both being stupidly stubborn. She was the more foolish because he was wealthy and this cost was nothing to him, whereas it was a significant expense to her. "Thank you, Your Grace."

Mr. Priam merely watched them in confusion.

"My Uncle Simon is a builder and can handle this list of repairs for you as well as the painting," she offered, finally giving in, since this was the sensible thing to do. "Do you wish to see his references?"

Daire chuckled. "No. You Angels are a close-knit family. I doubt he would do anything other than his best work on your home for fear your constable uncle would lock him up."

"He won't mind being locked up by Uncle Malcolm, but he will howl and put an ancient curse on us if Uncle Joseph—he owns the Three Lions Tavern—ever barred him from enjoying a pint there again," Brenna said with a light laugh. "That threat would be far more effective. But I merely jest. My family is honest and hardworking. Uncle Simon will always do his best, even if it is for you, a stranger none of us trust yet."

Daire chuckled. "You have such a flattering way with words, Miss Angel."

She held up her journal. "Shall we decide on the colors for these rooms to be painted? Does your mother have a particular favorite?"

He shrugged. "I have no idea. What do you suggest?"

She shook her head. "You cannot leave the choice to me."

"Why not? What do I know about home decorations? Choose your colors, and if my mother does not like them, I shall have the rooms repainted at my expense."

"For pity's sake, you toss your coin around with such little care."

He shook his head. "On the contrary—I am well aware of everything I spend, and all of it is carefully considered."

She sighed. "It does not feel as though you have given careful consideration to this undertaking at all. Don't you think you are behaving rashly?"

"How is wanting a beautiful house made fit for my family in any way rash? Besides, as I've told you, it is something I can easily afford."

The rest of their tour went much the same way, with his being annoyingly agreeable to her suggestions and insisting on footing all of the bills.

"The garden will require upgrading as well," she said, wondering whether he had reached his limit of patience yet.

He merely nodded. "Who maintains the Kestrel Inn's gardens? They are quite excellently done."

"That is my cousin, Felicity Angel."

"A woman?"

She tipped her chin up. "What is so wrong with a woman taking charge?"

He grinned. "Nothing. But you are delightful when indignant, and I take perverse pleasure in riling you just to see that little chin of yours shoot to the moon. I do not care who does the work, so long as it is done well and completed on time. Engage your cousin for me, and need I say it?"

She frowned. "Say what?"

His voice was rich and resounding as he said, "I shall be responsible for the cost."

"Very well," she said, unable to hold back another lilt of laughter. "I shall make certain Mr. Priam includes it on the list of your responsibilities under our lease. You really don't mind that a woman will be in charge of your garden?"

"Not in the least. When it comes to engaging workers, my only requirements are that the person I hire is competent to do the job, reasonable in price, and reliable. In truth, I find women generally to be more reliable than men. They are always better organized and able to handle more than one task at a time."

"That is surprisingly forward thinking of you."

He shrugged. "I am not a complete ogre, Miss Angel."

There was something in the sincerity of his smile that softened her heart. "In this, you are not an ogre at all. You will berate me again, but it must be said… You are far too generous."

Mr. Priam groaned.

The duke laughed. "Have no fear, Mr. Priam. I am not going to lower my offer, no matter how badly Miss Angel negotiates on her behalf."

"Very good, Your Grace. Because this is the finest home, and—"

"I know its value, Mr. Priam," he said, cutting the land agent off before once more turning to her. "Walk outside with me, Miss Angel. Let's discuss the gardening work that will be required."

He stopped Mr. Priam with a stern glance when he sought to follow them out.

Brenna shook her head and *tsked* at him once they were alone outdoors. "You are giving that poor man heart spasms."

"On the contrary," Daire replied, "you are the one who is giving him the spasms with your constant mention of my generosity. Do you think he gives a fig that I am overpaying? Why should he care how much I spend on this house? He is probably thinking up reasons to raise the price even higher in order to increase his fee. One does not succeed in his business by growing a conscience. You, on the other hand, my little dove, need to toughen that soft heart of yours, or some unscrupulous bounder might come along and hurt it."

"Are you speaking of yourself?"

"Am I the only man in your life?" he asked.

"You are not in my life at all. Do not think a single kiss is enough to make you anyone special to me." But the way he was looking at her, as though he could read her mind, made her blush. It was bad enough that the handsome oaf had kissed her and she'd liked it.

More than liked it, for she had melted in his embrace.

Had she the slightest amount of brazenness in her, she would have thrown her arms around his neck and held him in a wrestler's lock while he probed and plundered her mouth. Had she been less of a coward, she would have urged him to kiss her again.

And again.

Dear heaven, even the delicious scent of him was etched into her soul. Musk and male heat, and the slightest hint of leather.

Her first kiss had been more splendid than she ever dreamed

possible. Did he know it was the first time she had ever been kissed?

Now she had to worry about what Albert would think.

Oh dear.

Had the duke heard rumors about her and Albert Swanson, her Oxford professor beau? She hoped not, for she did not want this man knowing anything about her private life.

Albert had asked her to marry him and was growing impatient for an answer. His latest letter had arrived only yesterday, demanding a response that she was not yet ready to provide. Perhaps he would give up on her and simply resolve the matter by withdrawing his offer and finding someone else.

Easy enough. Decision made for her.

She was startled out of her thoughts when she felt a light caress to her cheek.

"Brenna, I know you think I am an oaf and a bit of a bounder," the duke said, his voice smooth as melted chocolate and achingly gentle. "I know I also warned you about this darker side of me… That coiled snake. But I give you my word of honor, I would not hurt you for the world."

She shook her head.

No, she dared not believe he could be sincere. He was just very good at faking it.

"Your Grace, we ought to concentrate on the landscaping."

"Call me Daire. I cannot abide this formality between us. You are not my lesser."

She groaned inwardly. Why was he being so cozy with her?

She could not even fault him for it. He had been generous and polite to her the entire afternoon. "You are a duke. Why do you claim we are equals? Is this a trick?"

He cast her a wry smile. "No, little dove. I am in earnest. Call me Daire whenever we are able to converse privately. I doubt it will be too often, since you are afraid of me."

Her chin shot upward. "I am not afraid of you."

"Oh, Brenna," he said, emitting a chuckle, "you are. And do

not tip your pretty chin to the moon again and pretend indignation. Let us be honest with each other, shall we? You like me and are not happy about it. This is what scares you."

"That is utter rot." She stared at him. "And what of you?"

"Is it not obvious I like you? Yes, enough to want to be a gentleman around you. Ignore what happened this morning. I would like us to be friends."

She gave a most unladylike snort.

He grinned. "Perhaps in time you will come to see I am not such a bad fellow."

"Even with that dark snake inside of you?"

"It is mostly intent on destroying me and not anyone else. Now, let us get back to business. Will you ask your cousin to come by here and take a look at the grounds? Have her write up a proposal for me with an estimate of the costs. Do you think she can do this by tomorrow?"

Brenna nodded. "Easily."

"Good. Same for your Uncle Simon—have him prepare an estimate for repairs and painting. I'd like to get started as soon as possible. I suppose they'll need funds to purchase supplies. Let me know what they will require to start. I'll make arrangements with the bank manager today and have him deposit the funds in your account."

Her gaze shot to his. "Mine? Why?"

"This is your house, and no one will look after this renovation work better than you."

"But I don't understand. You speak as though you are leaving the entire matter to me."

"Not entirely, for I must insist on all final approvals. But I do not expect to be here day in and day out while the work goes on. You, however, will be."

"How do you know this is what I will do?"

Her question appeared to amuse him, for his lips twitched at the corners in the hint of a smile. "Because this is your beloved home, and you have quite a bit of a controlling streak in you."

"That is absurd! If anyone is a controlling oaf, it is you."

He laughed. "Now you are just being defensive. To be controlling and frugal is in your nature, so do not bother to deny it. I am not suggesting it is a bad thing. In fact, I rather like these qualities in you. You are going to know exactly what is going on, have opinions at every step, and be far more tight-fisted in spending my coin than I would ever be."

She cast him an indignant frown. "I am not controlling… Merely dutiful, responsible, and cautious. Nor am I miserly, but I do think before I toss my money around, unlike you. And I shall certainly be careful with yours, since you will likely hold me to account for all I expend."

"Which is precisely the reason why I trust you, Brenna. I mean it as a compliment, for I never trust anyone." He glanced around. "We've gone over just about everything necessary. Have I overlooked anything?"

She shook her head. "No, not a single thing. Not so much as a nail has been overlooked."

"Good. If you think of anything else, just let me know. I'll keep out of the way as much as possible, since I am certain anyone who works on this house will respond better to you than to me."

"All right," Brenna replied. "I'll bring Felicity and Uncle Simon around tomorrow morning before the tea party. I'll leave word for you regarding the time so you may join us if you wish. It will have to be early in the morning, because the Duke and Duchess of Malvern have invited the entire village to their estate, so we will all be going up to the grange tomorrow just after midday. Their tea is an annual affair and not to be missed. I suppose they have extended an invitation to you and your friends, as well."

"They have. Seems I will be seeing quite a bit of you these next few days. I understand you will also be at the assembly ball tonight. Is that so?"

She nodded.

"Save me a dance."

She laughed.

"I'm serious, Brenna."

"Very well. But only one, otherwise everyone will talk. And you must promise to dance with other village ladies as well. I cannot be the only one to claim your attention."

He nodded. "I shall dance with others. But ours must be a waltz. If I am to share only one dance with you, I ought to make the most of it." He tossed her a grin and pressed on before she could comment. "And now I need your guidance on another matter entirely. Since you are a teacher, you are just the one to advise me. My nephew is six years old and a bit wild."

"Six?"

"Yes. What is so odd about this?"

"You described him as an infant, so I assumed he was no more than two or three years old. Well, I suppose you do not have much experience around children. Never mind—do go on." The duke obviously regarded every child under the age of fourteen as some toddling creature to be avoided at all costs.

"The boy needs some distractions. What would you suggest I have in readiness for his room?"

"Books, for certain. I can help you select some suitable reading material for his governess to read to him. A large slate board and chalk. Tin soldiers and marbles, as well. I think he will enjoy playing with those. Children also enjoy spillikins. A ball for him to kick or toss around. I have a few cousins with children of similar age. Would you be averse to having them play together?"

"Matthew will like that. He isn't suited to London and the confines of my townhouse, even though it is quite large by any standard. He feels lonely rattling around the halls with no one to speak to but his grandmother."

Brenna frowned. "What about his governess?"

"He has not liked a single one of them yet. They march in like commanding generals but rarely last the month before dashing out like frightened rabbits."

"Perhaps this is their mistake, to come at him with brute force instead of gentle understanding."

The duke shrugged. "In truth, I do not know. I require each governess, as part of her duties, to take him to the park whenever possible, for he's a handful and never seems to tire. I thought being outdoors and having the chance to meet other children might do him some good. So far, my idea has not worked out very well. He comes home sullen. The governesses complain. They make it quite clear he isn't an easy lad."

Brenna nodded. "Does he come in with his shirt tucked in or out?"

"What does it matter? I did not take notice."

This man, as well-meaning as he was, certainly knew nothing about children. Had he never been a child himself? "Boys at that age need to expend themselves, run around, get messy. Simply have fun. If he returns as neat as he left home, then one can assume the governess did nothing but restrict his fun."

He appeared to give her comment serious consideration. "I never gave it a thought, to my shame, I suppose."

"I think it is more to the shame of these governesses who hold themselves out as experts in dealing with children. Give it thought now, Your Grace. I think it is important for the boy. I will own that girls at this age are often easier to manage. I'll ask my uncle to fix the swing in the garden. Matthew will like that, too. He might enjoy long walks in nature, because everything fascinates children at that age. The shape of the grass, a fallen leaf, frogs and insects. Did you notice the stream running behind the house?"

"Yes, one can hear the sound of softly rushing water whenever the wind shifts directions."

She nodded again. "The stream forms a little pool in the glade not far from here. It is an excellent place to swim. Your nephew will enjoy that, too. Does he swim?"

"No," he said with some dismay.

Brenna did not want the duke to think she was criticizing

him, since he obviously cared for the boy and wanted to do what was right. "Then you can teach him. It is an excellent way for the two of you to build a rapport."

"What makes you think I can swim?" He cast her a sardonic grin.

A trill of laughter escaped her lips, but it soon died down and she gentled her voice. "Your Grace, you accused me of having a controlling nature, but I pale in comparison to you. That coiled snake haunts you, and you spend much of your time running from it. You fear it will strangle you and drown you. Swimming is one of the first things you must have sought to master, I expect. I think you have the prowess to swim across the sea to France if this is what it takes to escape your snake."

He groaned. "Bloody blazes, Brenna. Where do you think up such nonsense?"

But she knew it wasn't nonsense. "Can you swim?"

"Yes," he said, letting out a long, deflated breath.

They walked back into the house and began to close it up before returning to Moonstone Landing, each of them silent and lost in their thoughts as they went about the task. Mr. Priam was eager to get back, and made no secret of it, drawing out his watch fob and continually checking on the time. "I must return to my office if I'm to have my clerks prepare the lease in time to be signed tomorrow."

They all climbed into his curricle, the three of them squashed together, as these rigs were only designed to comfortably accommodate two persons. Brenna found herself practically on the duke's lap. There was nowhere else to be while trying to keep out of the way of Mr. Priam's elbow as he struggled with the reins.

"Sorry," she muttered, falling against the duke.

"Quite all right, Miss Angel."

"Sorry," she muttered again, accidentally poking him in the ribs with her elbow as she fell into him again. She emitted a soft cry when it happened a third time, and he suddenly drew her onto his lap. "Your Grace!"

"Do not turn prim and feign outrage. It is the only sensible solution, unless you wish to walk back to Moonstone Landing. You look tired, Miss Angel, and the sun is beating down on us relentlessly."

"You could walk."

"And leave the seat to you?" He tossed her that irritating look of detached amusement he must have perfected over the years, lifting one eyebrow as though obviously bored. His eyes shimmered with insolence and insufferable mirth. "Yes, I could. But I am not going to do it."

"Fine, if you don't care, then I won't either." It was not much of a threat, and she could see he was doing his best not to laugh at her. She was doing her best not to melt against his body, resisting when he wrapped his arms around her to hold her steady as the curricle rumbled and rattled its way down the steep roadway.

"Rest against me, Miss Angel," he said a short while later. "You will only hurt yourself if you insist on teetering on the edge of my lap. You'll tumble off the curricle if you are not careful."

"I'll be fine," she snapped. "You needn't hold on to me."

"You are not fine. How can you be when you are unbalanced and holding your back as stiff as a board?" He grinned. "Of course, I refer to your being merely physically unbalanced, although your decision to remain as uncomfortably situated as you are is not very sensible."

Would he simply not drop the subject? Were they not already giving Mr. Priam fodder for gossip? "I am not stiff or unbalanced."

"Miss Angel, you will crack if you are any stiffer."

She knew he was right, but she would rather swallow worms than ever admit it to him. "As for unbalanced, I—" Her protest was cut short when the curricle hit a rut and she almost went flying off it.

"Miss Angel!" the duke and Mr. Priam cried out in alarm at the same time.

Fortunately, the duke caught her and drew her back firmly

against his chest. "Enough," he said with raspy heat, and wrapped his muscled arms around her. "Lean on me and do not utter another word."

Her heart was still pounding from her almost tumble, so she obeyed and rested her head against his shoulder. "Do not make anything of this, Your Grace."

"Of what? Your being sensible?"

The lout. Why did he always have to be so smug?

Ignoring him proved impossible. Try as she might, she could not overlook his insanely appealing musk scent, the hard contours of his body, or her tingles as she remained enfolded in his sinfully strong arms.

The curricle hit another rut that would have sent her flying into the poppy field if not for his secure embrace. "Mr. Priam, are you purposely aiming for every bump in the road?"

"No, Miss Angel. I am doing my best."

She wanted to say something more, but her lips were too close to the duke's jaw. He had only to tip his head in the slightest for her mouth to graze his skin. Did he know it? Yes, of course he did.

"Comfortable yet, Miss Angel?" he asked, arrogantly tightening his arms around her as the curricle jounced over several more rough patches.

She prayed they would get into town fast and her ordeal would finally end, for his hands, despite their light touch, were burning into her skin.

Was this how it felt to be touched by a man who knew his way around a woman's body?

She hated to think she was as easily conquered as all his other women. She certainly was not one of *those* women.

Her face was in flames by the time Mr. Priam drew his horse to a halt beside the Kestrel Inn's stable. In her haste to get down, she tripped over the duke's feet, and was about to take a dive onto her head when he caught her yet again and drew her back hard against him. "Blast it, Brenna," he whispered, his lips against her ear. "Stop running from me."

"I am not—" She made the mistake of tipping her chin up in defiance as she turned her head to face him.

Their lips touched.

Mr. Priam gasped.

She struggled to right herself, something not easy to do while flames wildly leaped through her veins.

Dear heaven.

First an unforgettable kiss this morning, and now this?

She had never been in such close contact with any man before, much less one with a hard, muscled body like his.

"Have a care, Miss Angel," the duke said with a husky chuckle.

"You too, Your Grace." Oh, that made absolutely no sense, and now he had to be silently reveling in his smug victory.

A bead of moisture somehow transferred from his neck to her lips, because he was still holding her too close and she was still facing him, though their lips were no longer touching.

She scowled at him.

"I am always careful, Miss Angel. Stop pretending you do not like me."

She began to sputter in outrage. "Like you? Are you always so full of yourself? The horse suddenly shifted forward and I lost my balance. Were you truly a gentleman, you would have refused a ride in the curricle and walked."

Mr. Priam was looking on with beady-eyed interest.

The duke must have noticed. "Mr. Priam, as you can see, Miss Angel is out of sorts, and I will admit to having behaved perhaps a bit boorishly toward her. But if you breathe a word of anything between Miss Angel and myself, I shall personally see to destroying your business."

"Your Grace!" the poor man said, his eyes wide in alarm. "I am the soul of discretion!"

The duke's eyes were a soft blue, but his gaze turned lethal as he coldly said, "Good."

Mr. Priam bade her a hasty farewell and ran off as though the devil were chasing his tail.

At first the duke said nothing, merely hopped down and then placed his hands on her waist to assist her off the curricle. "Do not be angry with me, Brenna."

"That is Miss Angel to you. I did not give you leave to address me so informally." How could she not be furious? "You are an arrogant, heartless rake. How could you scare Mr. Priam like that? You must apologize to him at once."

"And have him gossip all over town that I had you on my lap? Or that my lips touched yours? I don't think so. Before you know it, that accidental touch of our lips will become a heated, tongues-swallowed, passionate kiss, and who knows where they'll say my hand roamed?"

"Tongues swallowed?" What was he talking about? "Why would we swallow our tongues?"

"We… It's not… Dear heaven, you are innocent." He stared at her incredulously for a long moment, and then his expression turned achingly soft. "My point is that the damage would be to you, little dove. Something you might realize if you ever stopped glowering at me long enough to think things through. Dukes are impervious to gossip. We are beloved no matter how naughtily we behave. But you? I would be forced to marry you if your reputation were tarnished."

She shook her head. "I would never force you to do such a thing. How can you think I would ever impose on you in that manner? Nor would I want to marry someone like you. I think I have been clear on wanting a love match. Why did you not simply walk back to town? Or ride up separately on Scipio?"

"Enough, Brenna. I had matters to discuss with Mr. Priam on the way up, and riding with him made most sense. Nor did I expect you to be walking back and forth on your own. Where was your horse? Or your curricle?"

"I don't have either."

He sighed. "So you walk everywhere? You must have been

fatigued."

"I was," she grumbled.

"I know I behaved like a lout," he said, his manner gentler. "But in my own defense…it was because of you."

She folded her arms over her chest. "So we are back to putting the blame on me?"

"I am not blaming you. All I am saying is that you are different from the other ladies of my acquaintance, and I was not ready to part ways with you. I am truly sorry if I caused you any misery. Now, let us put an end to this squabble. I have apologized." He raked a hand through his hair. "It is quite a concession on my part, for I never apologize to anyone."

She nodded, for she had done her bit to blow the incident out of proportion. "I apologize for my part in it, too. I am no priggish miss and could have just kept my mouth shut. This might have caused scandal in London, but would have earned me no more than an afternoon of teasing from the village ladies, and perhaps a lecture from my uncles to borrow one of their carts if I need to meet you at the manor house again."

Her apology obviously surprised him. His eyes widened slightly and his gaze turned thoughtful as he regarded her. "Indeed, you are different from the ladies of my acquaintance."

"Why? Because I admitted I might have also been in the wrong?"

He nodded.

"I will own up to my mistakes. As for you, is it not obvious you are keeping company with the wrong sort of ladies?"

"Yes, so I have been telling myself for quite some time now." He cast her a boyishly appealing smile, one she had no idea he was capable of giving after seeing the ruthless way in which he had dealt with Mr. Priam.

Poor Mr. Priam. Hopefully the commission he would make on the duke's lease would go a long way toward mollifying him.

Mr. Matchett, the ostler, hurried toward them. "Your Grace, forgive me. I did not realize Mr. Priam had left you with the task of handing me his curricle."

The Kestrel Inn stable served not only the inn but the local business owners, and sometimes housed the army horses as well.

Brenna grabbed her journal off the curricle's seat, bade the ostler and the duke a good day, then hurried off to find Uncle Simon and Felicity to make arrangements for tomorrow. After the scene between her and the duke, it was a wonder he had not changed his mind about leasing her manor. Apparently, the thought of canceling had not crossed his mind.

She decided to leave well enough alone. Yes, she was still irritated by their completely avoidable curricle incident. She had gotten an apology from him, which was quite something because, as he'd stated, he clearly was not the sort who ever apologized for his misdeeds. That he had offered her one was quite a concession on his part.

She had yet to cross the high street when the duke caught up to her. "Your Grace? What now?" she asked.

"Daire," he said, falling into stride with her. "Call me Daire. I'll let you go in a moment, but can you tell me where I might find those items you mentioned for Matthew?"

She stopped walking to stare at him askance. "Do you plan on choosing them yourself?"

"Yes, I do. What is so difficult about it? You forget I was a little boy once."

She did not think he had ever been a little boy—not in the sense of having a youthful upbringing that was in the least enriching or innocent. "I'm sure you were more of a terror than young Matthew."

He nodded. "I was not the best-behaved lad."

"If you can wait until tomorrow, we could stop by Mr. Bedwell's mercantile before you leave for the tea party. I'll be done going over the Stoningham Manor items to be repaired with my uncle and cousin by late morning. Shall I stop at the inn to fetch you once I am back? Or do you have other plans?"

"No other plans. In fact, I'd like to go up to the house with you in the morning, since it might be simpler to make swift changes if your uncle finds something else that must be done."

"All right, that's an even better plan," Brenna replied. "We'll pick you up in my uncle's wagon. Felicity and I can ride in the back while you sit up front with my uncle. It is not nearly as fine as your posh carriage."

"Nor as cramped as Mr. Priam's curricle, I imagine. Too bad. We were quite cozy, weren't we?"

She frowned at him. "Do not ever bring that up again, not even in jest."

"Wagon is fine. I don't mind riding with the rabble," he teased, then held up his hands in mock surrender.

She gave up and sighed.

He was naturally charming, but so full of himself. And yet not anything like his elite friends. He thought highly of workers, for he had not thought twice before accepting Uncle Simon or Felicity for the work proposed. He judged people on their merits.

"Once we are done and return to the village," she continued, "it will only take us a few minutes in Mr. Bedwell's shop to select some games and books for Matthew. I'll give serious thought to what he might like. Mr. Bedwell can send to Plymouth or Exeter for whatever he does not have."

The duke was agreeable to all her suggestions.

"We'll be seeing a lot of each other over the next few days, Brenna. I really wish you would call me Daire."

"No, Your Grace," she said softly. "It is better that we maintain a professional rapport."

He sighed. "Very well, but we can remain professional while still dealing with each other cordially. Why are you so reluctant? Are you concerned your beau might disapprove?"

She stopped walking and turned to look up at him. "Who told you about Albert?"

"Your distinguished college professor who has never properly kissed you? Everyone in Moonstone Landing gossips, Brenna. Half the time they don't realize they are doing it because it is so innate to them. Why do you think I had to come down so hard on Mr. Priam? I took no pleasure in doing so, but I could not risk harm to your reputation. Especially since you are completely innocent. But since we are on the subject of your Albert, why don't you tell me about him? Isn't it better that I hear the facts from you than wild rumors from unreliable sources?"

She shook her head vehemently. "Oh, no. I will not have you undermining him."

"Why do you think I would do such a thing?" the duke asked.

"It is none of your business whether he has ever kissed me."

He tucked a finger under her chin and raised her gaze to his. "That is not the question I asked you, little dove. Why are you mentioning kisses?"

Her cheeks heated. "I will not discuss Albert with you."

He released her and folded his arms across his chest. "What are you afraid of, Brenna?"

"Well, *Daire*… I'll tell you." She mimicked his stance and frowned at him, but her mention of his name obviously pleased him, even though she had uttered it sarcastically. His eyes lit up and his smile was one of genuine delight. She found it irritating, and frowned harder. "You are going to ridicule him because he is earnest and serious and does not know how to seduce women as you do."

"I am not going to ridicule him."

"Then what are you going to do to him?"

"Nothing." He lowered his hands to his sides. "I do not give two figs about him. It is you I am concerned about. How can you consider marrying a man you do not love? How can he possibly love you, either? Men in love cannot keep their hands off the women they desire. What is wrong with him that he remains a gentleman around you?"

She lowered her hands and balled them into fists. "He respects me."

"You know, that is the lamest excuse either of us has ever heard. Brenna, your eyes are an emerald blaze of fire."

"So what? I am angry with you. Yet again, I might add."

"Which proves my point. You have too much passion bubbling inside of you ever to be happy with a cold fish like Albert."

"He isn't cold!"

"He just doesn't care to touch you, is that it?"

She gasped. "This is why I am not having this conversation with you. He is a decent man and holds himself to high standards."

"Why does he want you, Brenna? It took me three seconds to decide I wanted to get my hands all over your body, which I promise I will not do without your permission. So do not start huffing in indignation again. It is an important question, and one you ought to be asking yourself before you give him an answer."

She turned on her heels and hurried toward the Three Lions Tavern, where she hoped to find Uncle Simon enjoying a pint.

"He's still up at the Duke of Malvern's residence, helping him and Duchess Hen prepare their grounds for tomorrow's tea," said her cousin, William, while drying off some freshly washed mugs.

"What about Felicity?"

"Oh, she's up there at St. Austell Grange, too. You and I are just about the only Angels not there at the moment. Even Mum and Da took the wagon up to deliver kegs of ale."

Brenna turned back to the duke, who had followed her into the tavern. "I ought to have realized they would be busy. I'll seek out Felicity and Uncle Simon as soon as they return."

He nodded and escorted her out of the tavern. "What if we head to Mr. Bedwell's mercantile now?"

She shook her head. "Would you mind terribly if we saved it for tomorrow? I would like to give your nephew a little more thought and come up with a proper list of items."

"You do love your lists," he said, his voice soft and teasing.

"It helps me organize my thoughts. I'll bid you good day for now. I must return to Cara's cottage. There's correspondence I need to get out."

"Ah, yes. Albert must be impatient for your response."

"Gad, you are irritating." She walked on toward her cousin's cottage, where she was living for the duration of her stay.

The duke strode beside her, completely ignoring the fact she had not invited him along.

Honestly, this man needed a good comeuppance.

"I will not invite you in." She came to a halt in front of the charming cottage that was nestled on one of the quaint streets just above the beach. Her cousin Cara's former home was a simple place, but its view overlooking the cove was quite stunning.

"I have no intention of going in. I merely walked you to your door." He glanced at the beach and then turned to study the house. "Cara is the one who caught herself the Duke of Strathmore, isn't she?"

Brenna looked up at him and huffed. "She did not *catch* him as though he were a trout. Cara and the duke fell in love."

"Unlike you and Albert. What exactly do the two of you see in each other?"

In truth, she did not know.

Mutual respect? Friendship? Shared intellectual pursuits? It was hard to say. Those reasons had seemed enough until the duke came along and kissed her with enough heat to turn her insides liquid. What had seemed a simple plan—visit Moonstone Landing, stay a few weeks to sell Stoningham Manor, and then return to Oxford and Albert's waiting arms—was not so simple anymore.

But Albert would never take her in his arms, certainly not if anyone else was looking. Would he be more amorous if they were alone?

She simply did not know, because they had never been alone. He had never even *tried* to get her alone.

Would he ever kiss her as the duke had? Or make her body melt?

"You cannot marry him, Brenna. Is this what you will tell him?"

She refused to answer. "Good day, Your Grace."

She opened the door to the cottage and walked in, quickly slamming the door in his face. Only then did she groan and lean against it.

She heard his rich chuckle on the other side of the door. "I'll see you this evening, Miss Angel. Do not forget to save a waltz for me."

She wanted to fling open the door and tell him she would never dance with him, but who was she hurting other than herself?

He was infuriating.

But he was also the handsomest man in Moonstone Landing, and a duke, no less. Why give up the chance to share a waltz with him?

She could school her features, appear to appreciate his offer of a dance, and keep a polite but unaffected smile on her face while he twirled her about the floor.

He was to be her tenant. Should she not maintain a cordial relation with him?

However, there was one small problem. A tiny one that she ought to be able to overcome...

Ought to be able, but how did one prevent one's traitorous body from turning molten in response to this gorgeous duke's touch?

Chapter Five

THE KESTREL INN was quite lively as Daire walked down the hall with his entourage toward the large dining room, now devoid of tables so that it might serve as a ballroom for the evening. The orchestra was tuning up in a far corner beside some potted ferns, and the inn itself was packed with villagers standing in the doorways and spilling out of all the main rooms that had been set up for the entertainment of the attendees.

The library now served as a cards room, and one of the smaller, private dining rooms had long tables lined against the walls, upon which had been placed trays of sweets, glasses of champagne, bowls of orgeat and ratafia punch, and kegs of ale.

The villagers had donned their finest clothes for the festivities. Of course, Hollingsworth, Danson, and the ladies wasted no time in passing their condescending remarks.

"Have they never heard of silk?" Lady Sarah remarked as she eyed several of the local ladies whose gowns were of muslin, to which they had attached lace collars in an attempt to transform their attire to suitable evening wear.

"Oh, and those horrid scraps of lace. Not to mention every one of them is wearing cheap jewelry," Lady Gemma said with a sneer. "They would be laughed out of Almack's if they dared appear in those appalling garments."

"Now, I say. She's not bad," Danson interjected with a leer

toward Brenna, who was chatting with several locals Daire presumed to be her cousins, since they bore a slight resemblance to her. She looked breathtaking in a cream silk gown she must have acquired in Oxford, because it was fashionably elegant. She wore no jewelry other than tiny diamond earrings.

"She's worth bedding," Hollingsworth drawled.

Daire shot him a quelling glance. "Touch her and you shall never see your hand again."

His friends stared at him in surprise.

"Fine, Claymore. If you want her that badly, she's yours," Hollingsworth said. "Looks like a virgin, anyway. Too much effort required."

Daire sighed.

Yes, he was dispatching them to Bath right after tomorrow's tea at St. Austell Grange.

He left his group and made his way to Brenna, who was obviously debating whether to smile at him or scowl. Fortunately, she decided to smile as he greeted her. "Your Grace, may I present my uncle, Mr. Simon Angel, and my cousin, Miss Felicity Angel. We were just making our plans for tomorrow."

He nodded to acknowledge them as they bowed to him. "Then I am just in time to be included."

They agreed to pick him up at the inn at seven o'clock in the morning. That settled, Brenna's uncle and cousin moved on to chat with others, leaving him alone with her. He eyed the delicious girl but said nothing.

She pursed her lips in that kissable way he quite adored.

"What are you thinking, Brenna?"

"If you must know, I am trying not to snap at you. Why are you looking at me that way?"

"How am I looking at you?" The music began to play, and guests began to hurry onto the dance floor. Daire ignored everyone, for only Brenna existed for him in this moment. The dance was a country reel he vaguely recognized. He ignored that, too.

Only a waltz would do for him and Brenna.

"You are gloating," she said.

Daire shook his head. "I am not at all. Why should I gloat? Did you decide to refuse your Albert?"

A blush stained her cheeks. "No, I haven't replied to him at all."

"And you think I will consider this a victory?"

She nodded.

"Brenna, what I think should not matter to you. It is you who must bed the man, not I."

The little blush now spread across her face and neck. "Why do I even bother to talk to you? Our conversations always manage to turn highly inappropriate."

"Because we speak of intimate desires."

"See, you are doing it again."

"Perhaps, but what do you expect me to say when this matter of marital intimacy is on topic? This is something that troubles you deeply. In theory, your Albert seems perfect for you. Respectable. Intelligent. Able to give you a comfortable life. But it will be a dull life, a safe one with absolutely no excitement above the frenzy of finding him a suitable cravat to wear to the annual university luncheon. That life, my fiery little dove, will crush your soul."

She tipped her chin up in defiance. "It will not."

He shrugged. "Lie to me all you want, Brenna. But you cannot lie to yourself. You do not want him to be respectable in the bedchamber, and this is what worries you. You want him naughty and thirsting for you, but he has shown no inclination to do so. Alarms ought to be ringing in your head."

She gulped down the orgeat in her glass. "Oh, that is vile," she said with a moue of distaste, and handed her glass to a passing servant Daire recognized as her cousin William. The lad was obviously a hard worker, for he was always at his father's tavern, the Three Lions, serving, cleaning up, fetching barrels, running errands—and now he was busy handing out drinks and clearing them away here at the inn's assembly ball.

Daire was always looking for good workers, but he tucked the thought aside for now, since Brenna was foremost on his mind.

"How about some champagne?" he suggested, as Brenna was obviously trying to get the taste of orgeat out of her mouth.

She shook her head, causing her lively mass of curls to bob. "No, I dare not."

"Why not?"

"I will fall atop you when we waltz if I have any. I do not hold my spirits well."

"Good to know," he said, tossing her a wicked smile.

She frowned at him.

He sighed. "Stop reprimanding me. I've told you, I am never going to take advantage of you. I merely spoke in jest."

"You kissed me and had me sitting on your lap," she said in a chiding whisper. "Is this your idea of behaving?"

"Yes, actually. If I were seriously misbehaving, you would know it."

The country reel ended and the orchestra struck up a waltz.

Daire held out his arm to her. "Our dance."

She hesitated, and for a moment he thought she might refuse him. But in the next, she nodded and placed her hand gently on his arm. Warmth flooded through him, but it was far more than a sexual urge that heated his blood. He had been attracted to women before, and had even considered courting some—but those efforts had been halfhearted, and not once had his heart truly been at risk.

He was not certain why he was responding so strongly to Brenna, but he was going to pursue it, no matter the consequences. If they were caught in a compromising position—which, Lord help him, he hoped would happen, because he agonizingly ached to explore this girl's body—he would not be averse to marrying her. Yes, he would leap into the parson's trap and tie the knot, no matter the scandal created, since he did not care what anyone thought.

He wanted her, apparently wanted her beyond reason, since he was ready to do the right thing if he ruined her.

Take that, Albert.

Brenna is mine.

She blushed as he placed his hand to the small of her back and drew her closer. Music filled the air, and dancers began to twirl in time to the melodic strains. "You're a graceful thing," he said, surprised by how easily they moved together, as though their bodies had always been one.

How would they move together in bed?

He shoved the dangerous thought aside. Brenna was not, nor should she ever be, a sport for him.

"We held several dances at the Rainard Academy. It was an important part of a young lady's training."

Yes, of course. These girls from elite families were expected to become consorts to dukes, earls, and even princes. "Were you their dance instructor?"

She laughed. "Heavens, no. I taught mathematics and literature. Dancing, fan fluttering, the intricacies of pouring tea, and general deportment were left to others."

He grinned. "I'm not surprised they chose you to feed their young brains with the more substantial topics."

"Families pay a lot of money to properly shape their daughters. We could not have them come out complete dunces. Many girls were quite clever and took to the academic subjects. I am proud of my small contribution."

"Never think it is small. I am sure you inspired these girls to be more than they imagined possible."

"Thank you," she said with genuine appreciation. "Albert never once acknowledged my contributions."

Because her beau was an elitist arse who thought women had no place outside the home. Would Albert require Brenna to give up her position at the school once they married?

He asked her.

She cast him a pained look. "We never discussed it."

"Why not?"

"I…I…don't know. It never seemed the right time."

"Brenna, I am arrogant, impatient, and difficult in many ways, as I seem to be constantly proving. But even I know this cannot be good. If you and he are truly a love match, then you should have no qualms about confiding your hopes and dreams to your husband-to-be. Nor should you hold back from disagreeing with him if you feel he is wrong about something. You certainly do not hold back with me."

"But you are—"

He kept his gaze on her as they slowly spun around the room. "What am I, little dove?"

She sighed. "You are easy to berate. Oh, you deserve it. But you take it rather well, considering who you are."

"Thank you—I think. I'll take it as a compliment."

"I meant it as such. I also find it easy to talk to you. You are surprisingly open-minded."

"Well, well. The little dove is starting to like me," he gently teased. "But does this not make my point? I have not met Albert, but I think you are never yourself around him."

He expected a vehement denial from her lips, but she simply turned silent.

It was as though her entire body turned inward, curling up in a protective shell.

"Forgive me," he said as they continued to twirl with exceptional ease around the dance floor. "Tonight is meant to be enjoyed, and I am burdening you with my concerns."

She looked up at him. "I appreciate what you are saying. For someone who has avoided love quite deftly all these years, you seem to understand it quite well."

"It is not love I am avoiding. In truth, I may be more desperate to find it than anyone else here. What I seek to avoid is being caught in the parson's trap with someone who is completely unsuitable for me, as all these young ladies pushed at me by their scheming mothers have been so far."

"I have never had a beau other than Albert. I am never myself around him and his friends. They engage in esoteric debates among themselves and shut me out if ever I attempt to offer an opinion. Sometimes, they are more insufferable than your elite friends."

Daire laughed. "Dear heaven, that bad?"

She cast him the softest smile. "Yes."

The waltz came to an end, and Daire felt considerable regret, for he was not yet ready to leave Brenna's side. But to remain with her any longer would only embarrass her and stir up gossip. He returned her to her Uncle Malcolm, who was the village constable and much respected by the local citizenry.

After greeting her uncle, he turned to Brenna and bowed over her hand. "A pleasure, Miss Angel."

He spent the rest of the evening sharing a lively reel with Mrs. Halsey, and another with her daughter, then a steadier quadrille with Lady Dowling, and waltzes with Lady Gemma and Lady Sarah. But his eyes were on Brenna all the while. This inability to get her out of his thoughts disconcerted him.

He had told Brenna to stop worrying and simply enjoy the evening. He decided to take his own advice.

This made for a rather cheerful evening, until Lady Dowling approached him while he once again happened to be speaking to Brenna and her Uncle Malcolm. "Your Grace, you promised to escort me home," she said in a suggestive purr.

His smile faded.

She placed her arm in his with a bit too much familiarity, leaning into him so that her breast grazed his arm. "I am quite fatigued and look forward to jumping into bed."

Bloody blazes.

He looked around for Hollingsworth or Danson, hoping to fob her off on one of them, but they were nowhere to be seen. "Very well." He turned reluctantly to Brenna and her uncle. "I shall return shortly to continue our conversation."

How much more obvious could he be in assuring Brenna he was not going to spend the night with the merry widow?

"Do not concern yourself," Brenna said, her voice sounding brittle. "I must leave soon as well."

He sighed. "Stay, Miss Angel. I will not be gone long."

But it was a lost cause.

Brenna was convinced he had planned an assignation with Lady Dowling and was now merely trying not to look like the bounder she knew he was.

"Good night, then." He gave a curt nod. "I will see you in the morning."

He walked the widow back to her house, making certain nothing was amiss before he turned to leave. Although this was a quiet village, it was starting to attract the usual assortment of unsavory characters who followed the idle rich. A widow alone was an easy target. As irritated as he was with the woman for purposely stirring up trouble between him and Brenna, he was not going to ignore her safety.

"Do stay," she purred, this time rubbing her full body up against him like a cat in heat.

"No." He unwound her arm from his. "To be clear, Lady Dowling, do not play your games with me, for I do not take kindly to being manipulated. You asked to be walked home, and you are now home. Good night."

He strode out, hoping to make his way back to the inn before Brenna left.

But he was too late. She was nowhere to be found among the crowd.

"Blast," he muttered, grabbing a drink for himself and stalking off to the inn's garden to calm himself down.

To his surprise, he saw Brenna seated alone on one of the garden benches, staring up at the milky stars and a moon that was big and silver against a clear, dark sky. "You're here," he said, not bothering to mask his surprise. "I thought you had gone home."

She turned to him in shock, her features beautifully illuminated by the flame of a nearby torch, and cast him a hesitant smile. "And I thought… Well, you know what I must have been thinking."

"Which is exactly the impression Lady Dowling hoped to give you, but all I ever intended to do was walk her home. Not that I offered, but she trapped me earlier with the request, and there was no way for me to politely decline. Even though you think quite little of me, I am a gentleman most of the time."

She gave a light snort.

"I am, Brenna. If I weren't, I would be kissing every delectable inch of you right now."

"Oh." She cleared her throat. "I had better go inside."

"Yes, I suppose it is wisest, considering my reputation. Are we all right, little dove?" He took her hand and gently held her back when she started to walk away. "By the way, you look beautiful tonight. I ought to have mentioned it earlier."

"Thank you." The amber glow of firelight from the torch mingled with her own soft blush, stirring the fire within him. "Yes, we are fine. I really must go before anyone sees us together."

"And reports it to Albert?" He groaned. "Never mind. Forget I said that. I'll see you in the morning."

He released her hand, and she flitted away like a butterfly in cream silk.

He remained outdoors a while longer, listening to the strains of a lively reel while sipping his champagne and breathing in the scent of roses and the salt of the sea.

This place.

He wanted to settle here.

He wanted to get to know Brenna better and perhaps make her a permanent part of his life. But that thought came out of nowhere. One did not think of permanence upon one day's acquaintance with an opinionated young woman. Besides, she was nowhere near ready to trust him. Nor was he quite ready to be trusted. He was the first to admit he was not by nature a nice man.

He still had much to work through before he would ever consider himself reliable when it came to women.

Could he ever be faithful to one woman for all of his life?

He thought he could with someone like Brenna.

Dear heaven.

All this talk of permanence. He certainly was surprising himself.

The more immediate problem was to make certain Brenna remained here long enough to get to know him and develop an unshakeable faith in him.

He had not thought to ask before, but now it was important for him to know when she planned to return to Oxford. She valued her teaching position at the elite girls' school and did not seem ready to give it up, even if she held on to Stoningham Manor.

And what of this Albert character who was eager to marry her? This troubled him most of all. What was Albert's true motive?

It could not be love, because the man had never properly kissed Brenna, who was irresistibly kissable. Any beau in his right mind would have had his lips on hers at every possible opportunity.

Nor could Albert's motive involve Brenna's wealth, because she had little to speak of beyond this charming manor house that was too far from Oxford to be of any use to him. If Brenna ever sold it, the proceeds would allow her to live out the rest of her days in modest comfort if she chose not work again.

Perhaps this was enough of a lure for her Oxford professor. A wife to mend his stockings, embroider initials on his handkerchiefs, and bear him children. In addition, he would gain control of the tidy sum from her sale of Stoningham Manor, to be used for his purposes.

Daire shook his head.

Something did not feel right about this beau of hers.

He was still thinking of Brenna by the time he retired to his suite. In truth, he left the assembly ball well before it ended because nothing more interested him. As he undressed, he could hear the orchestra playing a waltz. A smile escaped his lips, for he caught Brenna's subtle lavender scent upon his jacket.

Her warm skin.

That delightful body of hers.

Their waltz was something he would not soon forget.

He removed his jacket, waistcoat, and cravat before sitting at the edge of his bed to remove his boots. He had not bothered with more fashionable footwear, since the villagers did not have the funds for such luxuries as dancing slippers, and he refused to look like an elite toad among them. He left the trappings of wealth and rank to Hollingsworth and Danson.

Next, he shrugged out of his shirt and took a moment to wash his hands and face before pouring himself a glass of port wine, then dousing the lamplight to leave him in the dark. He settled into the elegant *chaise longue* in his sitting room to think about Brenna once again.

She was afraid of her feelings for him, and he could not blame her. Whatever was simmering between them was going to erupt eventually, and could end badly if he did not handle it properly.

He had meant it when he promised never to hurt her.

Still, what if she fell in love with him? It could happen even if he made no attempt to seduce her.

He had never been in love.

He wondered what it would feel like to fall in love with Brenna.

But he quickly shook out of the thought, because it was a terrible idea for so many reasons. What did he know about love, anyway?

Nobody had ever shown him love beyond a motherly affection from his stepmother. How desperate her family must have been to force a marriage between her and his odious brute of a father. Well, she hadn't long to suffer, since he had died within a month of their marriage.

He used to wonder whether she had poisoned him and gotten away with it, but the woman he now referred to as his mother was genuinely kind and compassionate. If anyone had done away with his father, it was likely Daire's odious older brother, Morgan.

He sighed and took a sip of the sweet port.

As had become his custom, he had ordered the windows left open to allow in the night air. Despite what others thought, he never found this cooler air to be harmful. In fact, it was quite a relief, since thoughts of Brenna now had him in a fiery roil.

Gad, he adored Brenna's hot body.

He had been completely in the wrong when refusing to give up his seat in Mr. Priam's curricle. He would have done it for anyone else, for the walk back to the village was mostly downhill and easily accomplished in spite of the heat.

But the chance to have Brenna up against him… Well, it was not well done of him. He really had to do better whenever he was with her.

She seemed to have come to terms with their curricle incident, and he was not going to raise it again.

Blessed saints.

She did look beautiful when angry, though. Her eyes genuinely sparkled, and he could only hope one day they would sparkle for him in passion.

It was not such a stretch, for even though she hid behind a prim façade, the girl was incandescent. It only required the expert touch of a man—namely him—to set her body on fire.

But he needed to keep her in Moonstone Landing long enough for them to get to know each other. He did not mean getting familiar in the physical sense, although that possibility was never to be ruled out.

He meant it in an abiding friendship, mates of the soul way. Hearts united. Troths plighted.

He now had her house, albeit merely a leasehold. She had

now agreed to the repairs he wanted. What he needed was something more.

He would sleep on it, and perhaps the answer would come to him. He wasn't certain how she had gotten in his blood and become this important to him in the span of a day.

Did he hope to win Brenna's heart? Marry her and make her his duchess? He could not imagine anyone more qualified for that role.

He shed his trousers and fell naked atop his sheets, falling asleep to the strains of a violin and the scent of a light, salty breeze off the water.

THE SUN FILTERED into Daire's elegant suite shortly after dawn, and the bright light momentarily blinded him as he awoke. He rolled out of bed with a grunt, shoved into his riding clothes, and managed a quick ride through the countryside on Scipio, both of them working up a lather before returning to the village.

Once back at the inn, Daire shaved, washed, and dressed at his leisure, since he still had a little time before Brenna was scheduled to fetch him.

He ordered breakfast brought to his suite, since he had received a mail packet late last night that he had yet to go through. He wanted to get the most important items addressed before hopping onto the wagon with Brenna and her family in what promised to be a glorious morning.

Of course, he could have met them at the manor house, riding up on Scipio after giving the beast a run. But these Angels intrigued him. He had never seen such a close-knit, genial family. They all seemed happy, as though infected with a curious disease that left them chirping and smiling throughout the day.

He did not ever recall a happy moment with his family, unless he included watching those bitter, cruel, ruthless men die—

grandfather, father, and even his brother. It worried him that they shared a bloodline. He did not want to be anything like them.

Yet he had inherited the ruthless Claymore streak, becoming quite adept at always getting what he wanted. However, it was through coaxing, outsmarting, and sometimes manipulation, never cruelty. In this, he had decided early on never to use his power to destroy others.

Besting others was acceptable. Crushing them was not... Unless they thought to crush him first.

He settled in the tufted leather chair behind the small desk he had ordered placed in a corner of his bedchamber, and began to sort through the mail pouch. There were not very many documents in it, and reading through each did not take very long. These business affairs proved simple enough to resolve. An approval required to commence repairs on the grist mill. Two investment opportunities that he declined. A third that he approved.

At the bottom of the pouch was a letter from his stepmother, Juliana, the widowed Duchess of Claymore and the one he referred to as his mother because she had been the only one to ever care for him. He quickly opened her missive and read the unsurprising news. The latest governess had walked out on them, and she no longer knew what to do with the incorrigible Matthew. "Well, I know what must be done," Daire grumbled.

He quickly penned a reply, urging her to come to Moonstone Landing with her entourage and the little devil's spawn as soon as possible. Of course, he referred to his nephew by his given name, although the child truly was a concern and seemed bent on a path of evil.

Do not bother to engage another governess, he wrote. *Let our housemaids take turns serving as nannies for the lad on your journey here. I shall take responsibility for hiring a governess and tutors, as necessary.*

Clearly, one governess was not enough. The boy needed a full regiment watching over him.

Upon finishing, he strode downstairs and handed off his letters to Thaddius. No sooner had he given them over to the innkeeper than Brenna hurried in, her cheeks rosy and her smile forced. Her eyes revealed she was troubled. "What is wrong, Miss Angel?" he asked.

"Nothing, Your Grace."

He sighed and ran a finger lightly across her brow. "Try again. Worry is written all over your forehead. Something happened, and you are overset by it. Is it something I did?"

She pursed her lips. "Will you tell me the truth if I ask you?"

He did not know what she was talking about, but he nodded. "Of course." Was this about Lady Dowling and last night? Daire thought the matter had been resolved.

She withdrew a folded parchment from her bosom.

He knew better than to stare. Or grin.

"Did you cause this?" She handed him the letter, which turned out to be from the headmistress of her elite girls' school, expressing sadness that Brenna would not be returning to them at the start of the term and wishing her well in her future endeavors.

He frowned. "How could you think I had a hand in this? When would I have had the time to send a letter off to your school informing them you were not returning? It would take three days' riding in good weather on a horse as fast as Scipio. Not to mention the time it would take for a response to arrive."

She put her hand over his. "I'm sorry. I *am* overset and lashed out at you unfairly. I know you are not to blame for this…misunderstanding. I think I must return to Oxford as soon as possible to straighten it out."

"Don't, Brenna. At least not before you hear me out."

"Hear you out?"

"Yes. I also received a letter and now have a proposition for you." He reached into the breast pocket of his jacket and withdrew the letter his mother had written. "As she reports, we've lost yet another governess. That's the fourth in as many months."

She looked up at him, her eyes gentle. "Oh my."

Daire nodded. "Matthew is a troubled boy, but so was I at his age. I do not think he is a hopeless cause. In fact, I believe the right governess will do him a world of good. But we won't find her in London. I think London is part of the problem. He and my mother will arrive here within a fortnight. Would you consider taking on the duties of governess? More than that…tutor, mentor, confidante. The lad desperately needs someone like you. Name your wages. Make up a list of supplies. I'll make certain you have everything you need."

"Your Grace, I—"

"Is it not fitting you should remain at Stoningham Manor with them? It is your home, after all. Choose whichever bedchamber you desire. You'll not be relegated to the nursery. Take the largest room, if you wish. I'll have your Uncle Simon freshen it up to your specifications."

"Your Grace, stop! It is impossible."

"Why, Brenna?" Thaddius had been listening in all the while. "Were you not just remarking to the family how much you wished to stay? And His Grace has just offered you terms that are more than generous."

"Yes, but…this is different."

"How?" Thaddius asked.

Daire listened quietly, knowing he had said whatever needed to be said. For him to now press Brenna would only put her off. But he saw that she was listening to Thaddius.

She scowled at Daire.

He sighed. "What do you not like about my offer?"

"All of it," she grumbled. "Who are you? My fairy godmother?"

He and Thaddius chuckled.

"Brenna, you do realize how foolishly you are behaving, do you not?" Thaddius said, his manner gentle but stern. "You cannot possibly be angry because His Grace is giving you everything you hoped for. Stop protesting. You only sound ridiculous and ungrateful."

She turned to study Daire once more. "Be honest with me. Why are you being so generous? First with repairs to the manor, and now with the position you are offering me?"

"Stop viewing it as generosity but as the price I know I must pay to get what I want," he replied. "Believe me, you will more than earn your keep with Matthew. I am the one getting the bargain here."

"Assuming I accept your offer."

He nodded. "Do not be so hasty to reject it. There is a good chance you might not be able to get your teaching post back if the headmistress has immediately moved to fill it. More important, we both know who must have advised the headmistress that you were not returning."

She folded her arms across her chest and frowned at him again. "Who?"

"Must I say it? Are you not thinking the same thing?" He sighed. "Very well—I shall tell you what you already know. It was your underhanded sneak of a beau. I thought I was ruthless, but he puts me to shame. I would never do such a thing to the woman I loved."

Tears formed in her eyes.

Daire groaned. "We'll work it out, Brenna. If you still want your position at Oxford, I'll use my clout to help get it back for you. But I hope you will seriously consider my offer. It is sensible and more than fair... Even if it is coming from me."

She stood quietly while he withdrew his handkerchief and cupped her chin to dab at the tears now streaming down her cheeks. "I cannot believe Albert would do this to me."

"I know, little dove." He should not have called her that in front of Thaddius, but the innkeeper was the most discreet of all the Angels in Moonstone Landing, so hopefully news of the endearment Daire had just called her would not spread throughout the village like wildfire. "What he did to you was harsh, even for my jaded sensibilities."

"I am better now. Thank you."

"Are you certain?" Pain still filled her eyes, and she was going to cry again if he did not do something to ease her distress.

But she hurried out of the inn before he could utter another word.

Daire stared at her as she climbed back into her Uncle Simon's wagon.

"Your Grace," Thaddius said, his expression one of concern. "Do you really believe Professor Swanson was the culprit?"

"Who else would have reason?" Daire said. "He's offered to marry her. She has been putting him off. How better to cut her off at the knees and give her no option but to accept him?"

"It is a dastardly scheme, Your Grace. But I suppose if he loves her, he would be desperate to win her consent, even if it is by unsavory means."

"Thaddius, I do not see how he loves her. Your cousin is as pure as a newborn lamb. He has never even kissed her."

The young innkeeper's eyebrows shot up. "He hasn't? How do you know?"

"Do not take out your shotgun. I respect Brenna and would never use her badly." Which Daire had upon their first meeting and his giving her that scorching kiss. But was he not reforming? Had he not promised to do her no harm? "However, I am an experienced hound and understand such things. It is obvious Brenna has never been kissed, and this has me even more concerned."

"What do you mean?"

"Any man with functioning eyeballs can see how beautiful she is. And yet this man has not even *tried* to kiss her. So, why is he determined to marry her?"

Thaddius stared at him blankly for a long moment. "Well, he's a respectable professor and must hold to a certain standard of comportment."

Daire dismissed the remark. "He's a man, Thaddius. Yet not a kiss. Not a touch. I doubt they have exchanged tender words.

Well, you and I are not going to resolve anything by standing here. I'll try to talk to her while we are up at the manor house."

He strode out and climbed onto the front seat beside Brenna's uncle, stretching his long legs before him as the wagon rocked and rattled up the hill. As they approached the house, Daire glanced back to take in the scenic view, the field of red poppies and the glittering sea beyond it.

Daire noticed Brenna studying him and cast her an affectionate smile. He ached for this innocent girl and did not like to see her so unhappy.

She was now trying to deal with the loss of a job she loved and the betrayal of the man who claimed to want to marry her. Most of all—and it did strike Daire as quite amusing that he should be the valiant knight in this situation—she resented the fact that Daire was being so nice to her and offering her a generous solution.

He understood the true reason for her distress. She wanted him to be vile and reprehensible because she was afraid of falling in love with him.

He was not afraid of falling in love with her. In truth, he expected she would be good for him.

One problem at a time, he warned himself. He had known Brenna for all of a day.

That she felt completely right for him was irrelevant, and would remain irrelevant until sufficient time had passed for him to make a meaningful decision. He needed to see how she got along with Matthew and his mother. He sensed she would be wonderful and they would love her.

Well, his mother would. Matthew might chew her up and spit her out, as he had done with all his prior governesses.

When they arrived at Stoningham Manor, Daire remained in the background while Brenna went through the house from top to bottom with her uncle, and then did the same with her cousin with respect to the garden.

Brenna and Felicity chattered easily while they strolled along the flowerbeds. Daire suspected they were speaking of him as well as what to do with the flowerbeds.

No matter.

Brenna was not likely to reveal that he had kissed her.

He smiled when she brought out her journal and jotted down details of whatever Felicity was telling her. When they finished, she walked over to him and handed him her journal. "It is still a bit sloppy, but you will find a comprehensive list of the work to be done in the house and in the garden. Beside each item is an estimate of the cost."

Daire skimmed through the pages. A few entries were left blank, to be filled in later as her uncle and cousin checked on the price of supplies that were yet to be confirmed, but those were minor omissions. "You'll make an excellent estate manager," he remarked when he finished his perusal. "You are extremely thorough and well organized."

"I try to be," she said evenly, but he noticed the sparkle in her eyes and knew his compliment had pleased her.

They returned to the wagon, but he merely helped the ladies up and did not climb in himself. "I'll walk back to town."

To his surprise, Brenna scampered down. "So will I. Do you mind if I walk back with you?"

He smiled at her. "Not at all. We have plenty to discuss, I think."

Although he motioned to her journal, reviewing details about the house was not at all the discussion he had in mind.

She did not look at him again until they had walked out of earshot of Felicity and her uncle. "Your Grace, are you going to lecture me about Albert?"

He arched an eyebrow. "Do you want me to?"

Chapter Six

"I DO NOT lecture," Daire said, tossing her an affable smile. "I give sage counsel."

She smiled at him and nodded. "Shockingly, I agree. Everything you have said about my nonexistent love life has made sense."

He held out his arms and glanced skyward, taking in the bluest sky he'd seen in an age. But everything was vivid and beautiful here. The brilliant red of the poppies. The dark red clay of the towering cliffs. The azure shimmer of the sea. The vibrant blue of the sky. "Do you hear that, Lord? Brenna admits I am sensible."

She laughed. "Just this one time. You are far from perfect. I would not gloat if I were you."

He dropped his hands to his sides and shook his head. "Oh, no. I am taking that compliment and will never let you forget it, especially since it is the last one I may ever receive from you."

"Am I that difficult?"

"No, little dove. You are a delight, but you are still afraid of me."

"How so? I am walking alongside you, and we are alone."

He pointed in the distance. "In plain sight of your cousin Felicity. Your uncle has purposely slowed his wagon to be certain we are always in view."

"I suppose they do not fully trust you yet."

He nodded. "Nor should they, for they do not really know me."

"None of us do," she said, her brow furrowed in thought.

"My fault, I know. I have done nothing to ingratiate myself, as you took pains to point out when we first met."

"Well, we can work on that over the summer, since I…" She sighed. "Since I am going to accept your offer. I will do my best to take care of your nephew. But are you serious about my residing at the manor house? And having my choice of living quarters?"

"Yes." He had expected more of a battle in convincing her to take on the role of governess. But she had a compassionate nature and was already thinking of all the things Matthew needed, starting with a strong dose of kindness that she could provide.

He wanted to reach out and caress her cheek, assure her that she had made the right choice, but she would turn skittish if he touched her. In any event, he had won this battle, and nothing more needed to be done thanks to Albert's high-handed and callous undermining of her teaching position.

"Brenna, I will make it clear to everyone that you are to be treated as one of the family…*my* family, with all the privileges that affords. You shall dine with us, take tea with us, and have a lady's maid to assist you."

"But my care of Matthew ought to come first."

"I know you will put all of your heart into helping him out. I don't want you to be merely a caretaker, but a tutor for him in academic studies and a mentor in building his character. It is a lot to ask of you. My mother and I will help in any way we can. Consider us all in this endeavor together. I do not want you taking meals in your room or walking about the place as though you are a mere notch above a servant."

They walked slowly down the hill as they spoke, and while there should have been nothing particularly special about this moment, Daire could not help but feel more at peace than he had ever been in his life.

He knew it was because of Brenna. There was something quite steady and calming about her—perhaps magical.

"What do you think I ought to do about Albert?" she asked, cutting into his thoughts.

He was surprised but flattered she wanted his advice, because he had very strong opinions about that scoundrel. "Reject his offer of marriage."

She pursed her lips. "What if we are unfairly blaming him and he is innocent?"

"Seriously, Brenna? He isn't. But go ahead and write to your headmistress for confirmation. Write to Albert, as well. See what he says."

"I will. It is only fair to hear him out before I pass judgment, don't you think?"

"Little dove, you ought to refuse him even if he is completely innocent and it was all a terrible misunderstanding."

Her eyes widened, those big, bright eyes so lovely as they shimmered like emeralds while staring up at him.

Indeed, she was magical.

"Why are you so adamant about this?" she asked. "Simply because he has yet to kiss me?"

"Yes."

"But we were rarely alone. It would not have been proper."

"Brenna, part of your charm is that you have no idea how pretty you are. But I see it, and Albert must have seen it, too. He should have been hungry for you and wanting to devour you. What would it have taken to gather you in his arms or give you a scorching kiss? No more than a few seconds. If his heart does not go into spasms every time he looks at you, then something is very wrong."

She was still studying him with her big gemstone eyes. "I think you are describing your own wolfish ways. Hunger? Devour? You are describing a predatory animal. But I suppose this is what you are. Albert is nothing like you."

"He would be if he cared for you."

She stiffened at the remark. "He does care for me. Sabotaging my teaching position was wrong, but he did it—assuming he is guilty—to force my hand because he loves me and wants me to marry him."

Daire decided to end the conversation, because he did not wish to rile Brenna and undo his victory. But for pity's sake, how could she not want to take a hunting rifle to that puffed-up, professorial arse and shoot him in the gut? "Truce, little dove. What do you plan to wear to the Duke of Malvern's tea party?"

She laughed. "Goodness, you must be desperate to change the topic of conversation if you are asking me about my clothes. Do you really care what I intend to wear?"

"Would you believe me if I said yes?"

"No, Your Grace. That is too much of a stretch."

They were nearing the village and would soon part ways. The field of poppies was just behind them, and Daire could hear the light whoosh of their petals swaying in the wind. He glanced at Brenna as they walked along in silence. True, he did not care about her clothes other than in the way she filled them out— which she did spectacularly well, no matter what she wore.

This morning she was clad in a pale green muslin gown with the barest of lace trim at the modest collar and sleeve cuffs. The sun shone down on her hair, setting the red tones ablaze amid her dark locks. Her lips were a lush pink and gracefully shaped, and her eyes shone like dark emeralds. All these colors about her ought to have clashed, but each enhanced her beautiful features instead.

Or was it just him falling under her ensorcelling spell?

She would laugh heartily if he dared to call her an enchant- ress.

For one mad moment, he contemplated what his life might be like if he were married to her. But the fleeting moment of madness passed, the spell somehow broken when the mail coach thundered by on its way to the inn and jolted him out of his musings. He knew it was on its way to the Kestrel Inn because the inn served not only as the village's hotel but the local post office as well. Thaddius, who seemed to be quite the enterprising businessman, was its postmaster.

"Your Grace, I—"

"Bollocks, Brenna. Call me Daire. I've given you permission to do so whenever we are alone."

"I know, but it does not sit well with me."

"Only because you want to keep me at arm's length from you. I've already given you my oath to behave around you."

"Which is something any gentleman ought to do, so do not make it out to be a sacrifice or reason for reward. It is only polite behavior."

He grunted.

"Obviously, I trust your word, or I would not have agreed to move back to Stoningham Manor and work with your nephew. I hardly think I am pushing you away."

"This is you being friendly?"

"Let's just say cautiously friendly. You know I cannot let down my guard around you. And our definitions of friendship are not quite the same. Your notion of a lady friend is one who is a bit too…willing to surrender herself to your amorous advances."

"The women approach me. I do not approach them."

"What is the difference? You do not turn them away from your bed."

"Why should I turn them away?" he asked. "I am not betrothed or married. You are frowning in disapproval, little dove. If it is any consolation, they use me as much as I use them. Nor do they care about me beyond the pretty trinkets I might give them. Do you think I would ever dare open my heart to any of them? Or trust them?"

She looked at him but said nothing.

"To them, I am nothing beyond my title, first as Viscount Claymore and now as Duke of Claymore. Just a title and deep pockets."

"Is this why you keep yourself aloof? To maintain your protective barriers?"

"Yes." He raked a hand through his hair. "Although I have lowered them for you. Is it not obvious?"

She regarded him with some surprise. "Why me?"

"Because your friendship, if ever freely given to me, would be genuine and something worth treasuring."

"Half the time you want to throttle me."

"Is that not part of friendship, being confident enough to express your opinion and knowing it will be valued even if we happen not to agree? You are impudent and do not hesitate to challenge me."

She arched a delicate eyebrow. "Is that an insult or a compliment?"

He grinned. "A compliment. In truth, one of the highest I can give."

"Then I feel quite worthy." She dipped into a quick but graceful curtsy.

"I like that you care nothing for my status and always expect better of me. You do not pander to my whims or say what you think I want to hear."

"Dear heaven, that is true. I shall never do that."

"From the moment we met, you poked and prodded to find the man I am inside." He pounded lightly on his heart. "You may yet decide you do not like me, but that decision will be made upon knowing who I really am."

"I am honored." She cast him a wry smile. "Well, *Daire*, now that we are on our way to becoming good friends, do you wish to stop in at Mr. Bedwell's mercantile and look over the supplies needed for Matthew? It should not take us long. I think we will have to order most of what we need from Exeter or Plymouth. Some items might have to be ordered from as far away as London."

"Sure, I have time." Since they were now walking into town and surrounded by passersby, her uncle had hurried his wagon along and was no longer in sight. Daire was in no hurry to part from Brenna and was glad she had suggested browsing in the mercantile. "You haven't asked me, Brenna."

She looked up at him. "Asked you what?"

"We have yet to discuss your governess wages."

"Oh, that." She told him what she earned while at the girls' school.

He emitted a groan and then laughed. "You are a terrible negotiator, little dove. Why would you volunteer this information to me? I might have offered you more."

"I only want what's fair. Will you match it?"

He sighed. "I'll double it. Settled."

Her jaw dropped open. "Daire, you are mad."

No, he was euphoric.

She was now calling him Daire and not averse to considering him a friend. She had no idea how much this pleased him, and it had nothing to do with how pretty she was or how much he desired her in his bed, which he did with a molten and unbearable ache.

But he would lose her if he acted upon his urges now. She needed to trust him.

Yes, this had everything to do with gaining her trust, just as she was gaining his.

This was something completely new to him, trusting a woman. But Brenna was a gem. A Moonstone gem.

Honest, earnest, compassionate. Truly someone special.

He ought to triple her wages.

She would berate him and smack him across the back of his head if he considered anything so insane.

But who could put a price on a woman like this?

Chapter Seven

DAIRE ESCORTED BRENNA into the mercantile.

It took them no more than thirty minutes to select reading material and toys for his nephew, because Brenna had a very good idea of what a young boy needed and approached the task with skilled efficiency. Daire purchased the books, games, and toys that were readily available and asked for them to be delivered to his suite at the inn.

"Right away, Your Grace," Mr. Bedwell said, obviously pleased. The man's smile broadened when Brenna then handed him an additional list of supplies the entire length of a page and instructed him to purchase the items from wherever he could find them. "I'll do my best, Brenna."

"Thank you, Mr. Bedwell. And do negotiate the best price possible for us."

"Of course."

As for their current purchases, Daire was certain the mercantile prices were hiked for him because he was a wealthy peer, but they were not so very much out of line. He placed a hand lightly over Brenna's to quiet her when she started to haggle with the shopkeeper. "We are done, Miss Angel. No need to come to my defense."

She rolled her eyes the moment they were out on the street and beyond the shopkeeper's hearing. "Honestly, everyone will fleece you if you do not stop treating your coin purse as though it is bottomless and there is an endless supply."

He grinned at her. "But there *is* an endless supply."

Her mouth rounded in an *O* as that sharp brain of hers took in his words. "Seriously? Are you suggesting you can buy this village ten times over?"

He nodded. "Probably closer to twenty. Little dove, stop fretting for me. I am contributing to the economy of Moonstone Landing, am I not? This is good for everyone."

It was especially good for him because it was time for him to ingratiate himself with the villagers. But he also liked that Brenna was trying to be frugal on his behalf. Not that he wanted her to do it, but everyone turned beady-eyed and conniving once they realized how wealthy he was.

Not Brenna, however. There was no greed in this girl. She did not want his money.

Of course, she did not want *him*, either. He hoped her feelings would change in time.

Though perhaps he should not desire this. If there was one thing Daire did not wish for, it was complication.

"How are you getting to St. Austell Grange?" Daire asked as he walked Brenna back to her cousin Cara's cottage. Another thing he did not like was that she was living alone. It did not matter that half the cottages on this quiet beachfront street were occupied by members of her family. What was to stop Albert from sneaking in one night and having his way with her? Or abducting her?

Well, that was probably not going to happen. The man was a professor, not a pirate.

"I'll ride up with one of my uncles," she said with a casual wave of her hand.

"You are welcome to ride in my carriage," Daire offered.

She laughed and shook her head. "Oh, dear me. No. Your friends are too glittery for me. I shall look like a lump of coal and have to endure their sneers the entire way there."

"I won't be sneering."

She arched a delicate eyebrow. "Daire, surely you realize that you are more dangerous to me than all of your friends combined."

She had called him Daire again.

Yes, he was dangerous to her.

Despite all commonsense efforts to resist this girl, it was inevitable she would end up in his bed, because he could not seem to get enough of her. He was not the sort to settle for less than claiming all of her.

And it was just as inevitable that if he bedded her, he would feel honor-bound to marry her, because she deserved better than to be used by him for a single night or to be taken on as his mistress.

Besides, once he got a taste of her, he did not think anything less than forever with Brenna would satisfy him.

Daire sighed. He walked her to her door and waited for her to disappear inside before he strode back to the inn to prepare for the tea party. He ordered a bath brought in, then marched to his suite of rooms, noting the elegant furnishings in the small sitting room that served as his private parlor, the blue silk settees and matching silk curtains. The decorative pillows were embroidered in tones of blue and yellow, and the carpet was clearly of finest quality, perhaps Aubusson or a fine imitation. The tables were of finely polished mahogany.

He strode into his bedchamber, an equally elegant room decorated in those same shades of blue and yellow, and stripped out of his clothes. He put on a robe of black silk, loosely fastened the belt at his waist, and then poured himself a port while waiting for the inn's staff to bring in the tub and buckets of water.

He had no sooner poured his drink than he heard a knock at the door. "That was fast."

Setting aside his glass, he crossed the room and paused with his hand on the knob. Thaddius was an excellent innkeeper and must have anticipated his needs.

To his surprise, Lady Gemma was at his door when he opened it, her eyes gleaming with a predatory hunger when she saw he was undressed. "I see I've come at the perfect time," she said, her voice low and breathy.

Her nimble fingers undid the tie of his belt and teased aside the robe before he could stop her. In the next moment, she had her hands on his bare chest and was sliding them lower. He grabbed her wrists to stop her. "No, Gemma."

She frowned. "Why not?"

"I've ordered a bath, and the inn's staff will be along at any moment."

"So what? That never stopped you before. I'll wash your back for you," she continued in that breathy purr that he found quite annoying at the moment. "I don't mind being your serving maid."

"For pity's sake." She was about to cup his privates, but he caught her hand once more, trying to be gentle with her despite his impatience. He turned her toward the door. "Out, Gemma."

But she resisted and turned back to face him. "It's that girl, isn't it? You haven't touched me or Sarah since we arrived here. Are you saving yourself for her? What is so special about that prim little nobody?"

"This has nothing to do with her. Can you not see I have responsibilities that are occupying my time?"

She rubbed against him. "What occupies your time is that virgin. Can she do this for you?"

"Dear heaven," he muttered, stopping her as she attempted to kneel before him and take him into her mouth, giving not a care that his door was open and anyone passing by could see in.

He picked her up and set her in the hallway, then shut the door and retied the belt of his robe while chiding himself for ever bringing these toady friends along with him when he had long since tired of them. He would speak to Hollingsworth, Danson, and the ladies while in the carriage on the way to St. Austell Grange. It was time for them to leave. They would not mind too much, since he planned to ship them off to Bath and would settle them in his fine townhouse on the fanciest crescent. Gemma and Sarah were beautiful women who would easily find some other clots to indulge their sexual appetites.

No wonder Brenna was determined to keep her distance from him. How decadent and depraved must he appear to her?

Would she ever believe he had not lain with a woman since arriving in Moonstone Landing? One would think he had reformed his wastrel ways in anticipation of meeting her. Perhaps he had unconsciously done so.

When the tub arrived, he washed, dressed, and then strode past the inn's registration desk as the noon hour approached, more determined than ever to be rid of these hangers-on and actually attempt to behave like a gentleman where Brenna was concerned.

His carriage awaited him and his toadies in the front court-yard.

They all climbed in.

Daire cleared his throat as it rolled away from the inn. "I've mentioned this before, but it is now time for all of you to go to Bath. You've begged to go practically every day since we arrived in Moonstone Landing."

Gemma's eyes widened. "Finally! It is about time you came to your senses and quit this place."

"No, Gemma. Not me. I am talking about the four of you."

He went on to offer them use of his townhouse. Danson and Hollingsworth were delighted with his proposition. "And we may remain there for the entire summer?" Danson inquired.

Daire nodded.

Lady Sarah frowned. "Do you have it properly staffed?"

"Yes—not a full staff, mind you. But it should be sufficient for your purposes." He provided more details as his carriage wended its way past the familiar poppy field and Stoningham Manor.

"Then it looks like Bath it is," Hollingsworth said. "One wea-ries of the ignorant milkmaids found around here, although a few are quite robust and a delightful handful." He cupped his hands and mimicked grasping lush, bouncing breasts.

Lady Gemma was still pouting. "You make it sound enticing, but what you are really doing is pushing us away."

Danson nudged her lightly. "I am sure you will find plenty of young bucks to satisfy you, my dear. Just remember to be discreet about it. After all, you are betrothed now to that old goat, Viscount Handly. He's just stupid enough to believe he has bought your fidelity. He's already settled a generous sum on you with the promise of more to come."

Her brother, Hollingsworth, nodded. "Try to show some restraint, Gemma. Do not ruin it for yourself."

"Claymore is to blame," Lady Sarah interjected. "She is angry that he has suddenly become a monk around us." She turned to frown at Daire. "You have not been any fun at all lately. And now you are sending us away. It is because of that little virgin."

"She is a pretty thing," Danson said. "There's something quite invigorating about claiming a virgin—isn't that so, Claymore?"

"I wouldn't know," Daire replied. "I do not make it a practice to seduce innocent young ladies."

Gemma sneered. "You'll tire of her and her priggish ways soon."

He was never going to tire of Brenna. She was the sort of girl a man never forgot.

"This is not about her. My mother and nephew will be here soon, and I mean to devote my time to them this summer."

Danson laughed. "Claymore, you look so earnest. But you cannot fool us. First of all, your mother is no more than your stepmother. No blood relation at all. And your nephew is a by-blow. Why are you bothering with them at all? Unless you are doing this to look like a hero in your virgin's eyes?"

"Danson, you are an idiot." Daire silently cursed his own stupidity in attaching himself to this sad lot.

His fault, of course.

He turned away to stare out the window as his elegant carriage rolled past Westgate Hall and then Moonstone Cottage. "I hear that place is haunted," Lady Sarah said. "By a very handsome ghost."

"Isn't this where that other pretty young thing lives?" Hollingsworth remarked. "You liked her once, didn't you, Claymore? But she had eyes only for Major Brennan at the time."

"Chloe Killigrew," Daire replied.

"Yes, that's the one. I must say, she's a far better choice than your virgin. Chloe is the daughter of an earl, while this Brenna Angel is merely a tradesman's daughter. You're not thinking of courting her, are you?"

"Me? I am not courting anyone. Nor do I intend to." First of all, he had no idea how to actually court a woman. He doubted he would ever have the patience to whisper sweet nothings in some giggling goose's ear, or bring her flowers, or recite sonnets to her beauty.

Nor would he ever patiently wait his turn among a queue of suitors.

No, if he wanted something, he simply charged in like a bull and took it. That approach would never work with Brenna, however.

"You can afford to be brash and set your own rules," Hollingsworth said with a note of wistfulness. "I always admired this about you. Ruthless, that's what you are when you want something. I hope to be like you someday, but I have to wait around for my uncle to die first. I am convinced he will live forever just to thwart me."

They turned up the drive to St. Austell Grange, a magnificent country house overlooking the sea. Daire could not wait to get out of his carriage and away from these friends. This afternoon tea was not going to be easy for him, because he would be seeing Lady Chloe Killigrew for the first time since her marriage. She was Lady Brennan now, having wed Fionn Brennan, a mere major at the time but now a viscount.

Not that Daire minded seeing her again, for they had parted

on good terms.

Her husband was not too fond of him because Daire had thought to propose to Chloe. Being eminently sensible, Chloe had cut him off fast back then. She did not love him, and Daire had not been in love with her. But he liked her, and she would have made him a good wife.

It was never going to happen. He would not have made her a good husband, and she knew it. The danger signs were obvious to Chloe, because even while thinking to court her, Daire had been dallying with Gemma and Sarah in their casual nighttime romps.

Looking back on it now, he knew it was not well done of him.

Some bad habits were hard to break, especially when there were so many easy women around, those who took no effort to lure into his bed and could be appeased with trinkets. He chose these conquests because they did not give a fig about him.

Chloe was not such a woman. Nor was Brenna.

Things were different for him now. Some might say he had finally grown into a responsible man.

As for him, he had never thought of himself as a thoughtless bounder. But he had closed himself off to everyone. It was the only way he knew how to maintain a shred of dignity after all those years of abuse from his father. The old bastard claimed to be beating strength into him. Ironically, Daire was only beaten when he attempted to stand up for himself. He was never quite sure why his father was doing it, only that the old man took too much pleasure in it.

The war and the senseless brutality of every fierce battle had only closed him off further.

What was he now but an unhappy man who could no longer bear to carry the festering burden of a damaged heart? He was desperate for it to heal.

Perhaps this was why he enjoyed Brenna's company as much as he did. Brenna, with her refreshing innocence and opinionated ways, was better than any healing balm. He particularly liked her unwavering belief in love.

Perhaps she could convince him such a thing existed and was possible for him.

He had already acknowledged the need to change his ways. Elegant courtesans, expensive brandy, and nights at the gaming table were not providing any satisfaction. He was already on the path to redemption, or whatever one called it.

He had abstained from touching a woman in over a fortnight. Nor did he have any desire to be with anyone other than Brenna… At least for now.

Bollocks.

Was this what he had to look forward to? A summer of celibacy?

And yet he would not hesitate to turn into a monk if this was what it took to heal.

He set aside the thought as he approached the reception line. Viscount Brennan was looking on, and pinned him with a glower.

The man was obviously not happy to see Daire.

He recognized that apish look, that *Chloe is mine, so keep your hands off her* glower. The viscount had nothing to worry about. Daire's attention was completely on Brenna, never mind that he'd known her for little more than two days now.

Daire wondered whether he would be as jealous of Albert if that pompous rat ever dared come to Moonstone Landing in search of Brenna.

The answer was yes. Daire would go at him like a wild ape and rip that man apart.

Ah, men were such possessive creatures.

He sighed and shook his head in dismay. He was not even courting Brenna. Courtship implied patience, politeness, and care for another's feelings. This was never in his nature.

Once again, he shook out of his thoughts. They were mostly inappropriate anyway. He cleared his head as his turn on the receiving line came up.

Although this was the Duke and Duchess of Malvern's tea

party, both of the duchess's sisters and their husbands stood beside her to greet their guests. Daire, heeding Brenna's words, strove to be more engaging—even to Viscount Brennan, who was still eyeing him warily.

The Duke of Malvern was far more jovial in his greeting. "Claymore, I heard you were back," the big, gruff bear of a man said, giving his hand a hearty shake.

His duchess, Henley, who was as gentle and amiable as could be, greeted Daire with warmth and a merry lilt to her voice. "Brenna says you are bringing your mother and nephew to Moonstone Landing for the summer. That is wonderful. Do send word once they arrive, and we will have you over for supper. A quiet party, nothing as hectic as today's affair."

"Thank you, we'll be delighted to join you." He moved on to greet Lady Phoebe and her marquess husband. "Burness," Daire said with a nod, uncertain how the marquess and his outspoken wife would receive him. "Lady Burness, a pleasure."

Daire had acquired a reputation as a rake, but his reputation was nowhere near as reprehensible as the one earned by this marquess before he had met and married Lady Phoebe. For this reason, the love that burned in Burness's eyes for his wife surprised Daire. If anything, it seemed the marquess was falling more deeply in love with his wife with each passing year.

Daire wondered if he could ever fall in love so completely, or think in terms of years instead of mere days or months when it came to being a faithful husband.

He glanced at the Duke of Malvern and saw that same doting expression in the man's face whenever he looked upon Duchess Henley.

These men were committed to their wives, all in with their heart and soul. They were not likely ever to break their wedding vows. Daire hoped Chloe was as fortunate with her husband.

"Brennan," he said, offering his hand to the viscount, who did not look particularly pleased to shake it.

"Claymore," he replied, his tone still icy.

Lady Chloe showed no such reserve. "I am so glad you found your way back to us. And I hear your mother and nephew are to join you. Hen and Cain are going to grab you first, but we look forward to having you with us, too. Don't we, my love?"

The viscount's expression softened when Chloe reached up and kissed his cheek. Yes, this viscount was completely besotted with his wife.

Daire was glad for Chloe. She deserved the best.

He chuckled at the viscount's chagrin. "That is very kind of you, Lady Brennan. I haven't done much to endear myself to any of you, but I hope all this will change as my family and I settle in."

"Settle in?" Her husband frowned. "I thought you were only here for the summer."

"I hope to be here much longer, but that will depend on how my nephew and mother adapt to Moonstone Landing. As I am sure you've heard, I have let Stoningham Manor until the end of the year, but I hope to work out a longer arrangement."

Chloe smiled. "We knew of it before the ink was dry on your lease. Fionn was not very happy about it," she said, giving her husband a playful poke in the ribs, "but I think moving here will be very good for you."

Daire nodded. "I hope so. I need to devote more time to my nephew, be a better man for him, and London is simply too distracting."

The marquess overheard his statement. "Good for you, Claymore. My little nieces saved my sanity when I lost my arm." He glanced at the empty sleeve hiding his missing limb. "I knew I had to do better for them. Then I met Phoebe and knew she would never have me unless I shaped up, not only for them but for myself."

Daire nodded. "I have a bit of fixing up I need to do for my-self. Not all of it can be blamed on the ravages of war." He turned to Chloe's husband, who was still regarding him with a strong dose of skepticism. "You were never in any danger of losing Chloe to me. You were the only one she ever loved."

Brennan's manner softened. "I know. I still cannot figure out what she sees in me."

Chloe gasped. "Fionn! How can you say such a thing? To work your way up from nothing…less than nothing, the way you did? You have more strength of heart than anyone I know. There is no finer man than you."

Chloe's husband turned to Daire with a lopsided grin. "I hope you find someone just as outspoken who feels this way about you…so long as it is not my wife."

Daire laughed. "It will not be Chloe, so put your sword away and stop scowling at me as though you intend to gut me."

"Have you found someone?" Chloe asked, her eyes alight.

"I don't know. That's my problem, isn't it? I would not know a good thing if it struck me in the face."

"Well, you won't be able to think clearly while you keep those friends of yours around," she remarked, frowning as Hollingsworth, Danson, and the ladies approached.

"I'm shipping them off to Bath tomorrow."

She cast him a brilliant smile. "You are? Then you have found someone, haven't you?"

He moved on without answering, leaving Chloe and her sisters to greet his *ton* friends. He took a few minutes to wander about the nicely landscaped grounds of St. Austell Grange, for this is where all the tables had been set up.

Additional long tables, their linens blowing in the soft breeze, had been placed on the terrace and were laden with tea sandwiches and fancy cakes, no doubt supplied by Mrs. Halsey. He recognized several specialties from her tea shop. There was also heartier fare set out on other long tables for those who came with large appetites.

Smaller, round tables dotted the lawn and formal gardens, and chairs were set around them for those who wished to sit. Several footmen walked among the throng offering champagne, and others carried out teapots to serve tea.

It seemed as though everyone from the village was here, and

Daire's first thought was that a thief could tear through the town and steal whatever he wished, for there was no one left to protect the homes and businesses.

Malcolm Angel, the village constable, must have noticed his expression. "Your Grace, is something troubling you?"

"Good afternoon, constable. I was merely wondering, who is left in town? Everyone seems to be here."

"Most of the businesses closed shortly before noon, since no one was going to shop now that the tea party has started. Let me assure you, the town is well guarded. My men are working in shifts so that everyone has a chance to attend at some point in the day. Those who are here now will leave early to allow those on duty to come up. Major Brennan does the same with his soldiers, including those on staff at the hospital. Everyone takes turns so no one misses out on this grand affair, but our quiet village remains fully protected."

There was a harpist set up beside a rose bower.

"That's my daughter, Verity," the constable said, beaming with fatherly pride.

"She's talented." Daire meant it, for he had been to enough *ton* musicales and listened to plenty of sweet young things torture their instruments in the hope of gaining his admiration and attention, when all they managed to do was torture his ears.

"Thank you, Your Grace. When she finishes, the orchestra will take over and start playing their tunes. The villagers enjoy her harp music, but what they really want to do is dance. The guests will get a bit rowdy once the teapots are put away. But it is all in good fun."

Daire continued to wander the grounds.

The house, which was quite grand in size, was open to those who wished to sit indoors. Not that guests were permitted to roam wherever they wished. Footmen stood guard to make certain those wandering in remained confined to the parlor. But they did not stop him from exploring the rooms beyond, no doubt because he was a duke.

No one interfered with a duke.

Daire took a quick look around the main rooms, curious as to the decorations and wall colors Duchess Henley had chosen. Not that he particularly cared, but he wanted to be prepared if Brenna insisted on his making decisions about Stoningham Manor.

He ambled through the parlor, the dining room, the entry hall, and finally strolled into the library. He thought he would be alone, but was surprised to find Brenna with her trusty journal in hand, too busy jotting down notes to notice him.

He laughed and leaned a shoulder against the doorjamb. "I might have known you would be snooping. How did you get around the duke's watchdogs? They were not letting anyone past the parlor."

"They let you through, didn't they?" She smiled at him. "One of the footmen is a cousin of mine."

Daire emitted a hearty chuckle. "Of course."

"I suppose you got through because of your noble rank. No one is going to stop a duke from doing whatever he pleases." She held up her journal. "I thought to prepare myself for the Stoningham Manor renovations. Your mother will expect a certain level of elegance, and I do not want to make any garish mistakes."

"You won't. You have naturally elegant tastes." He left the door wide open and kept his distance, for he did not want any scandal arising should someone walk in on them. "Have you seen enough? Care to take a turn in the garden with me and tell me about your findings?"

She glanced upward. "In truth, I would love to see the bedchambers. But I think that is too much of a trespass."

The library was near the grand staircase. The butler and footmen who were usually around had all been drawn to the parlor or outside, and had their hands full with the entire village on their lawn. "Come on, little dove," Daire said. "I'll stand guard while you scamper upstairs."

Her eyes widened. "What if I am caught?"

"I will shoulder the blame. Go on. You know you want to snoop. I'll whistle a warning if the duke or duchess come upstairs."

"All right." She cast him an adorable, conspiratorial grin. "You are a terrible influence, you know."

"Yes, yes. Morally corrupt and all that. Get on upstairs before the party is over."

She scurried up the steps, her derriere wiggling delightfully as she raced up. He waited at the foot of the staircase for her return. This girl really needed a little dose of wicked in her. Gad, she was so refreshingly innocent. Had she *ever* misbehaved?

She hurried downstairs a few minutes later, a guilty blush on her cheeks. If Daire had to place wagers, he would bet it would take Brenna no more than a day to tearfully confess her so-called crime to Duchess Henley.

"What did you find, you naughty girl?" he teased.

She opened her journal and began to check off the colors of each bedchamber. "Peach. Yellow. Cream. Ivory. Pale mint green. Lilac, although I was not enamored of that color on the walls. It is much prettier on the drapes and bed curtains alone."

"Too much if slathered on the walls?" He folded his arms across his chest. "Consider lilac banished."

"The mint-green and floral curtains looked beautiful. I think your mother might like that for her bedchamber," she said, still blushing over the fact she had trespassed on the privacy of their host and hostess. One would think she had just stolen the Crown Jewels.

She was so sweet and good hearted.

"Done," he said, suppressing the urge to wrap her up in his arms and kiss her. "Where will we find those fabrics?"

She pursed her lips. "Not in Moonstone Landing. You'll probably have to go to Exeter for those."

"Me? You are the one who ought to choose them."

"Oh." Her eyes were big and bright again. "You would trust me with the task? But I cannot go alone."

"We'll go together." He raised his hands when she took a deep breath and was about to excoriate him for suggesting such an improper thing. "Surely you must have a relative who can serve as chaperone. But we won't go until your uncle starts on the repairs and painting first. Same for your cousin's work on the garden. We'll get them underway before we rush off, all right?"

She gave a wary nod.

"However, before we plan our wild tryst in Exeter," he teased, unable to resist riling her, since she was quite irresistible when flustered, "I suggest you simply ask Duchess Henley if she happens to have discarded fabrics. I'm sure she ordered books full of samples."

"Wild tryst, indeed," she grumbled, tossing him a disapproving look, which was not convincing at all because she could not suppress the gleam of curiosity in her eyes. "But your idea about the samples is an excellent one. Will you ask her?"

He arched an eyebrow. "Why me?"

"Because you are a... Um, and..."

"What were you going to say, Brenna? That I am a duke and you are a nobody, so why would she ever accommodate you?"

She nodded, then shook her head, then simply sighed. "She isn't haughty like that, but this house is the height of elegance. She might consider me a usurper and resent that I am attempting to make my home as fine as hers."

"Do you hear yourself, little dove? A usurper? Because you like her taste in draperies?"

"Well, I would certainly not copy her exact designs. I have no intention of turning Stoningham Manor into a miniature of St. Austell Grange. I am only hoping to get ideas about what makes a home elegant." She cast him a wincing smile. "Am I being ridiculous?"

"Yes." He took her arm and placed it in his. "We'll talk to her together, if you cannot summon the courage to talk to her on your own. But we cannot bother her now. She's too busy entertaining her guests."

He led her outdoors and guided her toward the gazebo, which overlooked a beach tucked away in the cove. The wind was blowing lightly off the water, causing Brenna's gown to swirl in becoming waves around her body. "You look pretty, Brenna."

"Thank you, Your Grace…Daire."

By the scuffs on the wood floor of the gazebo, Daire knew a small table and chairs were usually placed here. But they had been taken away, no doubt set on the lawn as one of the tea tables. He was glad, for it kept others away. There was no place to sit in here, and it allowed him time alone with Brenna.

She looked lovely in a simple gown of ivory that had delicate pink roses with green stems and leaves embroidered on it. A silk band in the same leafy-green hue circled her body just under her breasts, drawing attention to those full mounds.

Not that he cared a whit for the gown itself, only that she looked elegant and beautiful in it. Perhaps it was the Oxford influence, because her clothes, despite being simple, were very well made and unmistakably stylish. "Brenna, tell me more about yourself."

"What do you wish to know?" She turned away from him to peer out toward the sea, which shimmered in shades of green and blue under the force of the sun.

He came to her side, standing close enough so that their shoulders almost grazed. "Whatever you wish to tell me."

"I don't know. There isn't much you would find worthy of your interest."

"What about your experiences teaching at the Rainard Academy? Or your life growing up here in Moonstone Landing? Or the things you like to do? Hopes? Dreams? Victories? Disappointments?"

"Do you really want to hear all this about me?"

He nodded. "I would not have asked otherwise."

I want to know everything about you.

He waited patiently, hoping she would begin to open herself up.

"Have you heard of our local moonstone lore, *Daire?*"

He smiled, liking the sound of his name on her lips and the impertinent stress she put on it because she did not feel comfortable yet with the familiarity. "No, little dove. Tell me."

"The moonstones glow for those who find true love. They did not glow for me when I held up Albert's letter, the one where he demanded an answer to his proposal. I read it aloud as I looked out over the water."

"And received not a single glimmer in response?"

"You are mocking me."

"No, not at all. The entire village believes in this lore, so I expect there is some truth to it. Perhaps the lore is enhanced because the sight of those moonstones shimmering across the water puts one in an amorous mood and makes a man propose to the lady he is with. Or perhaps being caught alone with an unmarried young lady late at night puts said young lady in a compromising position, and a hasty marriage is the result whether or not those moonstones shine."

"Must you be so cynical? The moonstones only shine when there is true love. This is why they are magical."

"But they did not shine for you and Albert. I would have been shocked if they had. Have I not told you he is not the man for you?"

"Yes, but the moonstones don't care about your opinion."

He chuckled. "Unless I am the one you love."

She cast him a pained look. "Don't ever say that. You know we are not suited. And do you think I would ever consider you while you travel around with your harem?"

"Brenna, I've sent them away."

"What?" She eyed him warily.

"They're leaving for Bath tomorrow."

"Because you are sending them off? Or did they decide to leave of their own accord?"

"It was all my doing, but they are eager to go. Moonstone Landing's society leaves much to be desired for them. They will be much happier in Bath…and I will be much happier with them gone."

He noted the turmoil in her eyes as she stared at him. "Why did you send them away?"

"It was time," he said quietly.

"What made you decide it was time?"

"Oh, several reasons, the most important being that my nephew needs me to be a presence in his life. If I wish to shape him into a man of good character, then I ought to set the example. Should I not?"

She nodded, and her expression softened. "I'm glad you realize it. You carry more influence than anyone else, and he will notice your deeds more than your words. What were your other reasons?"

"For a while now, this casual life has not satisfied me. I am ready for more serious attachments. Did you know I had started to court Lady Chloe before she married Viscount Brennan? It was a halfhearted attempt, I will be the first to admit. I knew she would never take me seriously while my lady friends remained with me, yet I made no effort to shed myself of those ladies. They stayed, and Chloe dismissed me, as I fully expected she would."

"So why send them away now? She is married and will never leave the husband she loves for you."

"This has nothing to do with Chloe. I never loved her and she never loved me, but she was not married at the time and had many qualities I did like. However, the most important quality was always missing. There was no spark between us. Those moonstones would not have shimmered for us. But I think…" He tucked a finger under Brenna's chin and tipped her face upward so that her gaze met his. "Must I spell it out for you, little dove?"

"Yes, because I am dense and will probably come to the wrong conclusion. Or be angry with you because you are taking advantage of the moonstone lore to make a jest of it and me."

"Brenna, I would never do anything so cruel. Especially to you. I have enjoyed our time together immensely. Yes, we only met recently. But we've been in each other's constant company, and I haven't stopped thinking about you ever since."

He saw at once this admission scared her, for she pursed her lips in that fretting way of hers. "Are you suggesting I am one of your reasons?"

"A small part of it for now, but yes. I am not going to do anything to interfere with your governess duties for my nephew, or having my mother comfortably settled here. I don't know what will happen between us. Quite possibly nothing, because I still need to change many things about my life. I've sent my *harem* away, but who is to say I will not change my mind in a month and bring them back?"

"I will never respect you if you do."

"I know, little dove. If it is any consolation, I do not expect I will ever ask them back. It would be a sign of my failure if I did."

She shook her head. "I think you are capable of commitment, since you take your duties as duke quite seriously. You also provide generously for your family, I expect. It is not commitment so much as trust that is your stumbling point. Trusting someone with your heart, that is the difficulty. Allowing yourself to be vulnerable. What happened to you? Why is your heart so ravaged?"

He gave a short, bitter laugh. "I wanted to find out more about you, and here you are trying to draw out the secrets of my soul."

"Is it not relevant? I think there is a lot to learn about you, Your Grace."

He shook his head. "Daire."

She sighed. "Yes, Daire. Any other questions you wish to ask me?"

"So you can turn the tables on me and get me talking more about my life? No, little dove. This is enough for today. But I will have lots of questions for you throughout the coming days. This is not the last conversation you and I are going to have."

"If you say so," she said with a soft laugh. "My life is not that complicated. Nor is it very deep or particularly filled with turmoil. I can tell you all of it in under five minutes."

"I'm sure it will take much longer than that. You almost drowned as a child. How did this incident affect you?" He had not meant to ask more questions now, but neither of them seemed eager to move away from the other, and he really did want to know more about her.

She thought she had little to offer, but this was not true.

She pursed her lips yet again in that kissable way as she pondered his question. "I will own that it was the most frightening experience of my life. I haven't gone in the water since that day. Cara reacted similarly. We are both deathly afraid of drowning, although she will go in now if her husband is beside her and holding tightly to her. But she will never go in alone. Nor will I. I suppose it is ridiculous, because this is a seaside village and our lives revolve around the sea."

Tears formed in her eyes, but she hastily wiped them away. "However, fear of drowning is not what guides my life. It was Captain Arundel's heroic actions that had the strongest impact on me. He sacrificed his life to save ours. He did not even hesitate to do this brave thing. This is why it is so important for me to honor him by doing something worthy with my life. This is what I have been striving for, and it has shaped me more than anything else, not some silly fear of water."

Daire took out his handkerchief and handed it to her so she could dab away her tears as they threatened to fall. "That is quite a story. It is powerful, Brenna."

"I knew in that moment I had to do something meaningful," she said, her lips trembling as she struggled to maintain her composure. "Captain Arundel had given us all a second chance. This is why I sought to become a teacher, to add value to the lives of others."

"You have, little dove. I'm sure you inspired every girl you taught."

"I hope so. I tried… But Albert has now taken this meaningful thing away from me, hasn't he?" She sniffled and turned away. "Well, I have to find out what really happened. It is not fair of me to leap to any conclusions. I need to gather all the facts."

Daire wanted to put his arms around Brenna, but thought better of it. Everyone was watching them and must have seen her dabbing at her tears. Now they would be wondering what oafish thing he had said to make her cry.

He moved to the opposite side of the gazebo while she composed herself. It was not a large enclosure, and he was still within easy reach of her. But he understood now why she was such an earnest thing, determined to do good in the world.

In truth, he was quite proud of her. He could not think of a better way to honor the man who had saved her life.

What had he ever done to honor those who had sacrificed for him? Absolutely nothing.

Brenna was teaching young ladies to think for themselves and find their strengths. He was romping in bed with sexually active debutantes, bored widows, and unhappily married wives.

No wonder he had become disgusted with himself.

Perhaps this was why he was so fascinated with Brenna.

There was a depth to her that he had not seen in other women. Certainly never in the spoiled and pouty *ton* diamonds he had seduced.

Gad, he hadn't even needed to seduce them. Women flocked to him of their own accord. He had only to choose whom he wanted for the evening…or the ten minutes in a shadowed alcove if he only had time for something quick.

He could fall in love with someone like Brenna. He did not give a fig about the scandal it would create among the *ton*.

Still, he dismissed the notion. It was too soon to make that dramatic leap. What was he thinking? Well, clearly he was not thinking carefully.

The summer season was hardly underway. They would have plenty of time to get to know each other over the coming weeks.

"Stay here, little dove. I'll fetch you a lemonade."

Brenna nodded. "Thank you."

She meant to hand him back his handkerchief, but he shook his head. "Dry your tears. I'll take it back later."

He strode off to fetch a drink for each of them, needing a little distance between them, for she seemed to be wrapping herself around his soul, and he was not ready for this.

Was there anything about this girl he did not like?

He could not think of a single thing.

Chapter Eight

RETURNING TO BRENNA took a few minutes longer than Daire expected because others approached him, and he did not wish to appear rude. This was the new Daire Claymore, ever patient and engaging. What a jest!

Would people so easily forget what an arse he was?

But being this better version of himself felt effortless when he was with Brenna.

He strode back to her side and immediately cursed himself for ever leaving her alone. Gemma and Sarah were now beside her, no doubt bent on destroying any illusions about his valor the little dove might have held.

By the looks on their scheming faces, they were spilling every dirty detail of their nighttime frolics. He did not owe Brenna any apology or explanation for his past behavior. He did not owe her an explanation or apology for present behavior, either.

He had been an amoral hound. She knew this.

Still, their attempt to demean him made his blood boil. It was done for no other reason than to maliciously retaliate for sending them away.

Their spite was utterly ridiculous, for both were betrothed to wealthy old men who were suffering maladies that would likely kill them within the year. He was a novice compared to them when it came to using people to advance their selfish purposes.

This was why he never opened himself up or dared to trust anybody. He'd paid for their stay at the Kestrel Inn, had footed all the cost for these ladies in addition to buying them sparkly trinkets, and would now pay for their time in Bath. He had been generous to them for years…and yet they did not hesitate to turn on him with a vengeance.

Was there no gratitude? No understanding? Not a shred of loyalty?

"Ladies," he said curtly, handing Brenna her lemonade. "Don't you have somewhere else to be?"

They laughed and skittered away.

He groaned. "Dare I ask?"

"No, it is better that you do not." Brenna turned to him, not looking particularly horrified. "The Marquess of Burness had a hideous reputation, one even worse than yours. Look at him now. He would die before ever hurting Lady Phoebe. The Duke of Malvern was often his partner on their debauched jaunts. He is completely reformed as well. He adores Duchess Hen."

"So, I am absolved?"

"No," she said with a gently admonishing laugh. "You have yet to prove yourself. I hope in time you will, because it appears you are sincere in the attempt. However, it is not me or your family or any of these villagers to whom you owe your proof. You owe it to yourself. The desire to change the arc of your life must come from within you. We may supply the first push, but making the important changes in your life is ultimately up to you alone."

"Do not dismiss your importance to me, Brenna."

"Do not say that. We hardly know each other. Nothing will come of us beyond a cordial friendship. Your rank and my lack of it can never be overlooked. So, let us be sensible. What I think of you cannot be all that important."

"You are wrong." Her opinion could prove to be his salvation, but she did not want to hear this. She would never believe him, because she placed more importance on the difference in their status than he did. *Everyone* placed importance on it.

He, however, did not.

She sipped her lemonade and turned to watch the dancers gathering for the first dance of the afternoon.

"Care to dance with me, little dove? The orchestra is tuning up, and I can think of nothing more enjoyable than hopping about and making a complete arse of myself as the entire village looks on."

Her eyes were mirthful and her laughter flitted on the breeze. "You are an excellent dancer, as you well know. All eyes will be on you because you are too handsome for words. But you must promise to dance with other ladies, too."

"Yes, I shall have a care for your reputation. But no one will be fooled. Their eyes may be on me, but my eyes will be on you, and everyone will know it."

"Don't say these things to me."

"Why not? Should I not be honest with you?"

"Yes, you should... But..."

"What is troubling you?" He slowed his pace as they walked toward the makeshift dance floor, which was nothing more than long planks set out across the lawn.

"Your lady friends said you returned to Lady Dowling's after last night's assembly ball."

He was not surprised they would make up these ridiculous lies. "But you saw me return. All I did was walk her home and come straight back to the inn."

"I know. They were speaking of later, after I had gone home."

"And you believe them?"

"Actually, no."

He sighed in relief. "Thank you, Brenna."

"Do not be grateful. I only find it easy to believe you because Lady Dowling has done nothing but cast me venomous looks since I arrived. She has claws, that one, and would have been looking at me with the smug confidence of a cat who had just polished off a bowl of cream if you really had spent the night with her."

"I see." He raked a hand through his hair. "Then good thing she is angry."

Brenna frowned. "I do not like to be caught up in these manipulative games."

"I know. I am sorry you are. The only way to avoid being drawn in is to have nothing to do with me, but this is the last thing I want. Hollingsworth's sisters and Lady Dowling, for all their fine clothes and jewels, for all their elegant training and titles, are nothing compared to you. You are the true pearl among them."

"Hardly."

"A natural, exquisite pearl," he continued. "People are always going to scheme because this seems to be the nature of most, especially those who want something from me. It is all the more reason why you are so important to me."

"I suppose this is why you must be cautious, always alert to those who seek to use you because you are a wealthy duke…or trap you because you are one of England's most sought-after bachelors."

"I can do little to control them. However, I promise always to be honest with you. We are building a friendship here, and friends do not lie to each other."

"Learning to trust you will take time."

He nodded. "I look forward to the challenge."

"I don't. I am very afraid of what is going to happen."

He took her hand as they joined the line of dancers. "And I am afraid of what might not."

"What do mean?" She stared at him as they moved down the line in time to the music.

He could not answer as they parted to twirl with the couple in front of them, each of them now standing with a new partner for the moment.

But was his concern not obvious?

Brenna had the capacity to believe in others, for she had been raised with love and had a supportive family willing to come to her aid when necessary. She understood how to trust and what it meant to have unquestioned faith in a loved one.

She would not be afraid to make the leap and trust him once she felt the time was right.

But he had never put his faith in anyone in his entire life… Well, one person came close, and that was Juliana, the stepmother he always referred to as his mother, another of those rare, kind souls.

Perhaps this was all it took. If he had the capacity to trust his stepmother, then he might have the capacity to trust Brenna, too.

How closely was trust connected to love?

Now, he certainly knew that caring for a mother was a far different thing from caring for a woman in a romantic, burned-into-my-soul way.

He thought about what Brenna had told him of the moonstones and how they did not shine for her and Albert. If the moonstone lore was real, was it possible they would one day shine for him and Brenna? Or was his heart too damaged to ever be capable of finding love?

This was what he feared—hurting this lovely girl. Having her fall in love with him, and then finding himself unable to love in return despite all his efforts to reform.

He glanced at Brenna, whose cheeks were pink from hopping about to the lively tune, and her smile was as soft as a summer breeze.

How could he not fall in love with this girl?

The partners twirled once again, and she fell back into his arms.

She cast him a dazzling smile.

How could she not be right for him?

Chapter Nine

B Y THE FOLLOWING day, business had returned to its normal, unhurried pace in Moonstone Landing. Daire caught the scent of pies baking in Mrs. Halsey's tea shop ovens as he strode to the stable to take Scipio out for his early-morning run. Good weather had smiled on them all week, but the threat of rain was finally upon them today.

He rode off, hoping to beat the impending storm, but felt a tug of disappointment as a heavy mist hung over the poppy field. He could hardly make out the vibrant reds of the flowers. His view of the sea was completely obscured by low, wet clouds.

The air was thick and so uncomfortably damp that his shirt stuck to his clammy skin as he rode along the now-familiar pathways.

"We're going to take it slow this morning, Scipio." The visibility was bad, and he did not want the beast to stumble over an unexpected obstacle. He decided to cut the ride short and return to the inn as droplets began to fall.

He heard the roll of thunder in the distance.

"Blast," Daire muttered, for he had not bothered to don anything other than his shirt, riding breeches, and boots. He had not given a moment's thought to bringing along an oilcloth for protection against the rain.

This was a minor nuisance compared to the delay the rain

would cause in the work needing to be done at Stoningham Manor. He knew Brenna's uncle and cousin had planned to start this morning. Simon Angel and his crew intended to work on the chimneys first. Since this could not be done while a storm raged, Daire hoped they would have sense enough to shift their attention indoors.

The garden work would be a total loss and would have to wait until the weather cleared. However, this was of less concern to him, since his mother could sit outdoors with or without a view of flowers in bloom—and besides, she rarely sat outdoors anyway.

A heavier rain began to fall as Daire gave Scipio his lead and allowed him to gallop back to the inn. They neared Moonstone Landing's familiar high street.

Mr. Matchett scurried out of the stable to grab Scipio's reins as soon as Daire rode up. "There's a deluge coming, Your Grace. I feel it in my knees."

"I heard the clap of thunder."

"Aye, storm's rolling toward us like a mighty army. Let's hope it passes fast. This could still turn into a glorious day. One must always look on the bright side."

Daire nodded.

"Won't delay yer house repairs, though," the chatty man went on. "Miss Brenna and Miss Felicity have already been up to Stoningham Manor and back. Simon and his men are at Mr. Bedwell's mercantile purchasing their supplies. But they'll wait out the rain before loading their wagons and driving them up the hill. Those wagons will just get stuck in the mud if they attempt it now. I'm sure the girls are also smart enough to work around the rain."

Daire certainly hoped so. He did not like to think of Brenna or her cousin caught in a dangerous storm. But she and Felicity were clever and understood the weather in these parts.

"I expect they know what they are doing."

"Aye, m'lord. The Angels are good workers, every last one of them. Brenna's been up since daybreak toting those big books around. She's a busy little bee."

What big books?

Not that it mattered. Daire would see Brenna later and find out what the ostler had been talking about.

Right now, he had to avoid the rain.

Daire patted Scipio, made certain he was safely returned to his stall, and then ran to the inn. But the sky opened up the moment he stepped out of the stable. It was as though mischievous goblins had been lying in wait for him to run out in the open before immediately pouring tubs of water down on him. Pour down it did, right atop his head. Despite the short distance between the stable and the inn, he was soaked to the teeth by the time he stepped inside.

Thaddius called out to him, but Daire waved him off. "Later, Thaddius. I am drenched."

He took the liberty of darting along the servants' hallways, since his boots were muddied and he was shedding water everywhere. There were a few steps up to reach his elegant suite, and he took those two at a time.

"But my lord—!"

He ignored whatever the innkeeper was trying to tell him. "Not now, Thaddius!"

His clothes weighed him down, and every inch of him was sopping wet thanks to this deluge of biblical proportions. Cursing, he burst into his suite, shut the door, and immediately began removing his clothes. He started with his shirt and unceremoniously tossed it to the floor. "Bloody rain," he muttered, raking fingers through his hair as he watched the shirt land with a squish beside the door.

Since he did not wish to track mud all over the impressively carpeted floor of his suite, he decided to take his boots off as well. He hopped about, tugging off one and slamming his back against the wall as he lost his balance and fell against it. "Bloody boots."

He thought he heard a faint female gasp, but dismissed it as coming from somewhere in the hall, since he glanced around and saw no interloper in his suite.

He began to work on his other boot, this time striking his elbow against the doorknob as he yanked the stubborn thing off. "Bloody knob."

He had just started to undo the falls of his riding breeches when he heard a feminine cry that definitely came from inside his sitting room. "What the...?"

It was then he turned toward the hearth and noticed Brenna poking her head out from behind one of the big leather chairs set beside it. She stared wide-eyed at him, her cheeks aflame and her mouth agape.

He growled low in his throat. "Bloody blazes! Who let you in here?"

Of course, he knew it had to be Thaddius, and this was what the innkeeper must have been desperately trying to convey to Daire as he tore past the registration desk.

Sighing, Daire strode toward her.

He ignored the droplets of water sliding down his neck, and took no note of them as they fell onto his chest and continued lower, into the waistband of his breeches.

If Brenna's eyes bulged any wider, they would pop out of their sockets. She followed the trail of water down his torso.

"Like what you see, little dove?"

She nodded numbly, then groaned and hastily turned to face the wall. "Oh, dear heaven! I have to get out of here."

"Why were you in here in the first place?"

Her breaths turned rapid as she began her explanation, still staring at the wall instead of at him, and chattering so fast that he could not immediately make sense of what she was saying. "I was delivering books to you," she explained, finally slowing down. "Thaddius said it would be all right if I brought them in here myself, since you were out for your morning ride and would not return for another hour. Why are you back early?"

"Need you ask?" The wind was howling and a violent rain

now pounded against the windows with enough force to make them rattle. "I did not wish to drown in the deluge."

"Yes, yes. Of course. May I go, please?"

"In this downpour? What books are you talking about? What did you bring me?"

"Fabric samples. You will never guess what happened as I was about to leave yesterday's tea party."

He turned her to face him, suppressing a laugh as Brenna made a deliciously breathy sound and closed her eyes. But not before she took in another eyeful of him without his shirt. Her cheeks caught flame again. It really was not well done of him to prolong her embarrassment, but he was not used to dealing with innocents, and he found her reaction quite refreshing and charming.

Not to mention arousing.

Heat thrummed through his veins. She was still making those breathy little noises that would have him spilling himself if she were making those sounds in bed.

Bollocks.

It was sheer folly for him to delay her departure, and yet he could not get enough of her.

"Open your eyes, Brenna."

She shook her head vehemently. "No."

"I'll step aside so you do not have to look at me. But you must open your eyes to see your way out of here." To be caught with him in his state of undress was as compromising to her as if she were caught naked in his bed. Her reputation would be in ruins, while he, being a duke and above condemnation, would be under no obligation to marry her because she was merely a tradesman's daughter. "Wait for me in the dining room. I won't be long."

"All right." She made another of those deliciously breathy noises and cracked one eye open.

Sighing, he took her by the shoulders and guided her to the door. "Wait, let me make certain there is no one in the hall.

When you leave, take the servants' passageway. The hour is early, but some guests will be awake by now, so it is very important to be as quiet as a mouse and rouse as little attention as possible."

She nodded.

And licked her rosebud lips. And made another of those deliciously breathy sounds.

"One more thing..."

She opened her eyes and looked up at him with her shimmering green orbs.

"Little dove, if I catch you alone in here again, I am going to peel the clothes off you, pin you up against the elegantly painted wall, and kiss every inch of your naked body."

Which was exactly the wrong thing to say to this innocent, because she tore out of his suite without giving him the chance to check the hallway. In the next moment, she slammed into one of the inn's maids, who happened to be twice Brenna's size and had the shoulders of an ox.

Brenna bounced off the maid, who had been rolling a tea cart to the room across from his. The cart spilled as Brenna knocked it over and tumbled over it to the floor.

Trays clanged and banged. Teacups shattered. Tea spilled all over the carpeted floor. The maid started screaming. Doors flew open and guests peered out to see what was going on, only to find Brenna sprawled on the floor and Daire—still shirtless— rushing to her side and about to lift her into his arms.

The maid began to yell at Brenna.

Daire silenced her with a quelling glance. "Summon the innkeeper. Not a word out of you," he said with arrogant authority, hoping to cut off this obviously angry woman before she revealed Brenna had run out of his room. "Get staff to clean this mess up. Now!"

He stifled a groan when Brenna's delicious body melted against his as she wrapped her arms around his neck and rested her head against his shoulder. "Daire, your skin is so warm," she whispered, her lips grazing his jaw. "So deliciously wet and warm."

Did she just lick his neck?

Fire shot through him. "And have the doctor summoned! She may be delirious."

The maid was about to toss another surly remark when Thaddius came running toward them. He took note of the situation and started to panic. But he quickly recovered and began to make up an excuse for his cousin. "Your Grace, I am so sorry you were disturbed. My apologies to everyone," he said, glancing up and down the hall to address the guests who were standing beside their open doors. "I had asked my cousin to take measurements for new hall decorations, but she must have taken a tumble off her ladder and…"

Gad, these Angels were terrible liars. There was no ladder in sight.

Daire hoped he was the only one to notice, since everyone else appeared to have been startled out of bed and looked quite groggy.

Thaddius turned to another maid who had just run up with mop and pail in hand. "Mary, run to my desk and fetch the vouchers. These guests are all to have breakfast compliments of the inn this morning."

He then turned once again to Daire. "Your Grace, I am truly sorry for the inconvenience. I hope you were not too greatly disturbed. I'll help my cousin into the dining room, and we will not interrupt you again."

Daire had no intention of letting go of Brenna, who was now nuzzling his neck in her inept but adorable way and setting off an inferno within his loins. "She's hurt, Thaddius. Let her rest in my sitting room until the doctor arrives. Send in a maid to serve as her chaperone. I'll keep the door open."

Thaddius raked a hand through his hair as he eyed the scene, which included taking in Daire's lack of a shirt. Since these Angels were very protective of each other, he expected Thaddius to be back here shortly, armed with an arsenal of questions and perhaps a shotgun. "Very generous of you, Your Grace."

Daire had claimed Brenna was hurt merely as an excuse to bring her back into his suite, but he quickly realized she was truly injured. "Thaddius, no jest. Send one of your lads for the doctor. She's bleeding."

"Dear heaven, she is. I had better go for him myself." The innkeeper tore down the hall, all the while shouting orders to his staff.

Daire, momentarily left alone with Brenna, set her down on the fashionable *chaise longue* and studied her eyes, which were slightly dazed. "Brenna, did you hit your head?"

She winced. "I think it caught on the upended edge of the cart as I fell."

"I'm so sorry, little dove. This is all my fault. I should not have said to you what I did."

"And I should not have stood there gawking at you while you shed your clothes. I have never seen water trail down anyone's body quite like that."

"Glad you liked the show," he gently teased.

She groaned. "It wasn't intentional."

"I know." He ran his thumb ever so gently along her brow. His humor faded when he spotted a cut along her hairline that needed to be cleansed. "You might need stitches. Let me check the rest of you."

Fortunately, he found nothing else of concern beyond a small scrape on the palm of her hand where she might have fallen on a broken teacup. But it had hardly pierced her skin, and there was no shard to pick out. "Do you have a handkerchief?"

She nodded and withdrew it from the sleeve of her gown. "It's clean."

"Good." He applied it to the area of her cut. "Hold it there. Lie quietly."

"What are you going to do?" she asked when he left her side.

"I need to toss on some dry clothes before the Mongol horde

arrives."

"Oh. Yes, that is wise."

He hurried into his bedchamber and closed the door firmly before anyone else walked in and saw him bare-arsed naked as he removed his breeches, quickly washed up and dried off, and donned buff breeches, a work shirt, and a polished pair of boots. He did not bother with a cravat, waistcoat, or jacket just yet, since it was more important to get back to Brenna.

The handkerchief must have fallen, for she was holding a hand to her head when he returned to her side. "Don't touch the cut, love." He saw blood ooze through her fingers when she obeyed and removed her hand. "Bollocks, don't move. I'll be right back."

He hurried back into his bedchamber, took out several clean handkerchiefs, and carried the ewer, which had been freshly filled last night, and its matching basin into his sitting room. He doused one of his handkerchiefs with water and another with brandy from the corner cabinet that Thaddius kept well stocked to his specifications.

"Dr. Hewitt will do a better job of this, but I dare not wait any longer to cleanse it. We saw these sorts of wounds all the time in battle. When treated, they healed fast. If left untreated, they festered and… Well, we need to take care of this."

He knelt beside Brenna and rinsed away the blood from the cut as carefully as he could manage without hurting her. She gasped several times, but there really was no way to wash it out properly without causing her a little pain.

Once done, he also washed the blood off her hands.

He then took the brandy-soaked handkerchief and held it close to her brow. "This will sting, love. Close your eyes and hold your breath."

She shuddered when he pressed it carefully to her cut, but she was a brave thing and did not cry out. As a precaution, he also applied the brandy to the scrape on her palm.

By this time, Thaddius and Dr. Hewitt had arrived. "Doctor,

she'll need stitches," Daire said. He quickly told the doctor what he had done.

"Excellent work, Your Grace. I see you've had experience with such wounds. In battle?"

He nodded.

It turned out Brenna did need stitches, but fortunately only three were required. Daire held her hand while the doctor sewed them to close her gash.

She had such a delicate hand, so little and soft.

He ran his thumb in gentle circles along her palm and whispered words of encouragement while the doctor worked on her. But his heart remained stuck in his throat all the while. Why was he such an arse? He knew the girl was innocent, and yet he'd uttered that stupid remark and set this latest mess in motion.

She was such a sweet thing and did not deserve any of what had happened.

"Your Grace," she said, her voice soft as she struggled with her pain, "it is still raining. May I stay until it stops?"

"Yes, Brenna. Of course. You'll stay as long as the doctor requires…even if it is for the entire month."

Dr. Hewitt nodded. "I would rather Brenna not go home tonight. She should not be alone at least for the next twelve hours."

Daire turned to Thaddius. "Leave your cousin here with one of your staff to watch her. She will not disturb me. We'll figure out arrangements later. I'll move into one of the rooms vacated by my friends, since Brenna should not be moved. Have any of them stirred yet?"

"Lord Hollingsworth has called for a valet, but the others are still abed."

"Blast," he muttered. "They won't be out of here before nightfall at this rate."

As soon as the doctor left, Thaddius began to ask Daire questions. The usually genial innkeeper now assumed the role of protective father, determined to make certain nothing amiss had happened to Brenna, or he would toss Daire out along with his indolent friends.

Brenna sat up with a wince. "No, Thaddius. He was a gentleman. I behaved like a goose. I had just finished carrying in the books when he strode in and surprised me. He had no idea I was here until I darted out and ran straight into the tea cart."

Daire knew he had not spoken to her like a gentleman, but he did not contradict Brenna's version, since there was no need to stir up more trouble. It was bad enough the rain was still pounding down and little work would be done on the house.

And now Brenna was hurt.

Thaddius began apologizing to him. "I'm so sorry, Your Grace. I did not think you would mind having Brenna bring those books into your suite, since you were eager to move ahead with the business of repairing her house. and I just assumed—"

"Thaddius, no apology necessary," Daire said, because he was not going to allow himself to accept the role of innocent bystander when he had been the instigator. "In fact, charge the cost of this tea cart mess to my account, including those breakfast vouchers you handed out. Send word to Dr. Hewitt that he is to charge me for Brenna's stitches. I ought to have mentioned it to him before he left."

Brenna frowned at him. "But—"

"And have one your maids bring up some tea and scones. Lots of them. Your cousin needs nourishment."

Thaddius left them to put in the order himself.

The tea and scones were quickly delivered by one of his staff, who then bustled off to attend to other duties. Daire and Brenna were left alone again for the moment, but the suite's door was open, and he expected someone would be sent in shortly to serve as Brenna's chaperone.

For the moment, he had her all to himself.

Daire poured Brenna a cup of tea and placed a scone on a plate beside her. "I am truly sorry," he said quietly. "What I said to you—"

It was her turn to cut him off. "I should have made my presence known the moment you walked in and began taking off your shirt. We were both stupid. All right? We seem to have a knack for being stupid together."

He cast her an affectionate smile. "Seems to be something we must work on, how to be around each other without giving each other fits. Now, what is this you wish to tell me about books?"

Her eyes lit up. "The best news. You'll never guess."

He smiled. "Tell me, little dove."

She wrapped her graceful fingers around her teacup to warm her hands. "As yesterday's tea party came to a close, I approached Duchess Henley and asked if she might spare some time within the next few days to give me some guidance regarding refurbishing Stoningham Manor to your mother's liking."

"And?"

"She grabbed my hand, and that very moment took me through every room in her house, including the bedchambers." She cast him a guilty look, revealing she had not confessed to sneaking upstairs during the party. "Then she took me into their storage room and showed me an entire bookshelf filled with books and boxes of fabric samples. She said the duke's father had engaged one of England's foremost decorators to do most of the work. Duchess Hen made a few changes after they were married, but not much. His father was a meticulous man who kept meticulous records. And do you know the best part?"

"He kept all the sample books in pristine condition?"

"Yes, that too. It turns out the fabric shop they used, Dumbley & Hayworth, is in Plymouth. We do not need to send all the way to Exeter or London for the materials. *And,*" she said with emphasis, her eyes taking on a starlit glow, "it turns out the sewing itself is all done there, too. Right on the premises. How long do you think it will take us to go to Plymouth and back by carriage, Your Grace? Their shop is on Plym Square, one of the more elegant shopping streets in town. Do you know of it? Is it possible to ride there in a day, place our orders, and return before nightfall? Felicity and I were at the manor at break of day this morning, taking precise measurements for each room and sketching out specific designs for your mother's bedchamber and those she will likely use to entertain her guests. I have a design in mind that will be perfect for her private salon."

Daire listened to Brenna as she chattered excitedly, but stopped her when he realized she only meant to decorate the rooms his family would occupy and meant to do nothing for herself. "Brenna, you are to redo the entire house. Have I not made myself clear on this?"

She nodded. "But is it not wasteful to—"

"No, it is not. My mother is a duchess. The entire house must reflect her status." He did not really believe his own words, but it was not very far from the truth. Besides, he could not bear the thought of Brenna depriving herself or appearing of lesser worth than his family.

She sighed. "All right. In fact, Felicity insisted we measure all the rooms, so we did. The details are all set down in my journal. But—"

"No, you may not pay for any of it."

"Gad, you are the most irritating duke I have ever met." But she cast him a smile that touched his deadened heart. "The fabric books are stacked in the corner." She pointed toward the hearth wall. "I was bending over them when you walked in and suddenly began tossing off your clothes. This is why you did not see me. You were quite funny, hopping about like a rabbit as you tried to remove your boots."

"Good thing you said something before I dropped my breeches."

Flames shot into her cheeks again.

He sighed. "Brenna, being curious about my body does not make you wanton."

She winced. "Well, it does not make me respectable, either."

"You are curious, that's all. Never mind about this little incident. We are past it now. Do you have more to tell me about our project?"

"Actually, is this not a perfect day for us to go through these fabric books and make our selections?"

He leaned back and propped his hands behind his head. "Oh, joy," he said dryly. "Can't wait to get started. Selecting drapery. What man can resist such fun?"

"I see your point. It is rather dull for you."

"I am exaggerating, Brenna. Why don't you sort through them and then show me your selections? I have some Claymore estate matters that require my attention. We can work side by side. Interrupt me whenever you feel it is necessary."

"All right. That sounds nice."

Yes, it was nice having her beside him as they each attended to their tasks. The doctor had wrapped a protective bandage around her head and given her some laudanum to quell the pain. She ought to have looked exhausted and disheveled, but to Daire, she looked like a beautiful, doe-eyed waif.

Daire truly felt bad about what had happened. "Feel free to treat this suite as your own, Brenna. Don't overdo it. Take a nap if you feel tired. Tug on the bellpull if you require anything to eat or drink. Take your meals in here, or if you are feeling strong enough, you can join me in the dining room. And to be clear, because you are very thick about this, all is to be charged to my account."

She pursed her lips, but did not object.

Daire spent the next hour attending to Claymore estate matters. He was just finishing up when Felicity rushed in carrying a leather satchel that turned out to hold her designs for the Stoningham Manor garden.

"Stay," he said, wanting her to serve as chaperone to replace the sourpuss maid whom Thaddius had installed as watchdog over Brenna. The maid was the same one Brenna had accidentally bumped into this morning when darting out of his suite. This woman had a perpetual frown that Daire, quite frankly, could not abide.

Brenna smiled in relief when the dour woman left. "Felicity, I'm so glad you're here."

"I had to come as soon as I heard you were hurt. What happened?"

Brenna told her the cleaned-up version, omitting Daire's stupid remark that had shot her out of here like a fireworks rocket.

"Let me see your garden designs, Felicity." Daire motioned for her to take a seat beside Brenna and make herself at home. "Would you care for tea?"

She nodded. "I'd love a cup. It is so raw out there, but the rain has slowed to a drizzle and should end soon."

She and Brenna chatted quietly while he skimmed through her drawings. "These are excellent," Daire said with some surprise. Yes, Brenna had told him that her cousin was good at her work, but this was professional quality. He had few modifications to suggest and was surprised she had put something this impressive together so quickly.

"You must have worked all night after yesterday's tea party to complete these drawings," he remarked.

Felicity nodded. "Yes, but I didn't mind. I'm looking forward to putting these ideas into effect. With your approval, of course."

Since Felicity obviously had a good eye for color and form, he suggested she assist Brenna in choosing the fabrics for Stoningham Manor's new bedding and drapes.

"I would love to help," she said, scooting her chair even closer to Brenna's and asking about her choices so far. "Oh, these are lovely."

Brenna nodded. "I thought so, too."

As the mantel clock struck the eleven o'clock hour, he excused himself and headed down the hall in search of Thaddius. It felt as though an eternity had passed since he'd run into his suite completely drenched, but it was no more than late morning now, and only a few hours had gone by. "Thaddius, have my friends started packing yet?"

"No, my lord. As far as I know, only Lord Hollingsworth is ready. The others are still dawdling abed."

"Abed? Blast," he muttered. "Send one of your maids to rouse them. If they give her trouble, she is to tell them it is at my command."

"Well, can you really blame your friends? It is not a day for travel," Thaddius remarked. "Even the morning mail coach is several hours late."

"I don't care. The storm is ending, and I want them gone."

Thaddius swallowed hard, no doubt caught off guard by his harsh tone. "Yes, Your Grace."

Daire noticed a look in the innkeeper's eyes and understood what he was thinking. Would he behave like this toward Brenna when he tired of her? He had been kindness itself to Brenna this morning, but what about tomorrow? Would he curtly toss her out on her ear, as he was now doing with the Hollingsworths and their cousin, Lord Danson, all of whom had joined him here year after year?

Daire knew he would never treat Brenna so uncivilly, for she was neither a toady nor a leech. Nor would she ever be the wanton sort to hop from bed to bed, or go out of her way to demean him as Gemma and Sarah had attempted to do at yesterday's tea party.

He would have to sink to the lowest depths to treat Brenna that way.

But he was not going to engage the innkeeper in that conversation now.

As it turned out, Hollingsworth happened to walk by on his way to the dining room. "Ah, Claymore, have you had a change of heart and decided to join us in Bath?"

Daire walked over to the lord. "No, I meant it when I said my family must come first."

"Well, we shall all be pleased if you change your mind. I'm going to have a cup of coffee, and then I'll go rouse that lazy bunch. Do not judge my sisters too harshly."

Daire arched an eyebrow. "It isn't my place. My conduct has been no better."

"We've all been rather dissolute, haven't we? I suppose their behavior is more shocking because they are women, and we have been taught those of the fairer sex are delicate creatures. Ha! That is quite a jest. I stopped lecturing my sisters years ago. They were never going to be sweet young things. But they have grown into beautiful women who know exactly what they want and how to use their wiles to get their way. In truth, it relieves my burden. They are a pair of nimble cats who will always land on their feet. If all goes according to their plans, they will be two of the richest widows in England within the next five years."

Daire cast him a wry smile. "Send word when they are packed and you are all ready to be on your way. I wish you a good journey, Hollingsworth. While you are in Bath, may you find yourself a beautiful, *young* heiress who dotes on you, provides a pot of gold for you once you marry, and will not mind if you continue your wastrel ways."

To his surprise, Hollingsworth turned wistful. "These wastrel ways grow tiresome, do they not? Did it not surprise you that Malvern, Burness, and Brennan have yet to stray? Nor does it appear they ever will."

"I noticed, but those Killigrew sisters are something quite special."

Hollingsworth nodded. "You liked the youngest one… What was her name again?"

"Chloe."

"Yes, that's her. But you did not appear put out at all when she chose Brennan over you."

"Because I did not love her."

His expression turned surprisingly sober. "I wonder what it feels like to be in love? Were you ever curious about it, Claymore?"

Daire nodded. "Sure."

"But I cannot see you ever falling in love."

They stepped out of the entryway to allow other guests to walk into the dining room and find their tables. "Why do you think I am not capable of it?" Daire asked.

"Claymore, I admire you. In fact, I wish I were you. But I haven't your intelligence or steely resolve, so I will never be you. Let's face it, you are competitive, cunning, and ruthless in getting what you want. A look springs in your eyes that chills me to the bone sometimes."

Daire frowned. "What sort of look?"

"I don't know…predatory? You train your gaze on your prey and then move in with the stealth of a jungle cat. Of course, the ladies seem to adore this masculine power and are happy to become your willing conquests."

"My prowess is much exaggerated."

"I think you are actually quite modest about your abilities. But my point is, you win over these ladies and they will do anything for you."

"And?"

"You always win. You always *need* to win," Hollingsworth replied.

"You exaggerate."

"Do I? When have you not gotten your way? When have you ever lost control of a situation and not come out on top? You give in to no one. Seems to me, the important question to ask is…will you ever find the woman whose desires are more important to you than your own?"

Daire gritted his teeth, for hadn't Hollingsworth just put his finger on exactly the problem!

Hollingsworth cast him a wry smile. "They call it sacrifice, Claymore."

"I know very well what it is," Daire said with an irritated growl. Since when had Hollingsworth become so wise? Daire supposed he wasn't the only man thinking about what he wanted out of life and sensing something important was missing.

"Well?" his friend prompted him. "Have you met anyone

whose happiness you would put ahead of your own?"

The image of Brenna with her bandaged head and big doe eyes sprang into Daire's head.

Bollocks.

"No, Hollingsworth. I haven't."

"Are you sure?"

"Yes," Daire said, trying not to sound impatient.

Hollingsworth patted him on the back. "Then I have one question for you."

Daire nodded. "Go ahead, ask it."

"My friend, are you lying to me or to yourself?"

Chapter Ten

BRENNA SPENT THE day being treated like a queen.

Goodness, one could easily get used to this pampering.

The inn's staff, at the duke's insistence, waited on her hand and foot. His suite, which was the finest in the inn, had now been turned over to her for the night. "Felicity, stop bouncing on the duke's bed," she called to her cousin from the sitting room. "One would think you lived in a hovel and had never seen a proper bedchamber before."

Felicity ignored her. "I have never seen a four-poster bed this size. It is massive. Why won't you come in here and stretch out on it? The *chaise longue* will not be nearly as comfortable. You should sleep in here and not out there in that narrow thing. What if you roll off it and bump your head again? But you won't fall out of this bed. It is the size of a frigate."

Brenna laughed. "Ow, don't make jokes. It only hurts my scalp where the doctor sewed the stitches."

She had taken a nap in the duke's bed earlier this afternoon because there had been too many comings and goings in his sitting room. But now, his divine musk scent was on her skin, and she could not breathe in without catching the scent of him.

She had been tingling since waking up from her nap because of it.

What was worse, it had put wild thoughts in her head,

thoughts of his sharing the bed with her. Kissing her and wrapping his muscled arms around her. Even now, thoughts of those rain droplets sliding down his rock-hard chest and taut stomach sent the butterflies in her stomach into a frenzy.

That bump on her head had definitely addled her senses.

It was much safer to simply spend the night sleeping in the sitting room, curled up on the *chaise* or the settee, or even on the carpeted floor.

Felicity walked into the sitting room. "Oh dear. Brenna, you look flushed. Are you running a fever?"

"No, I'm fine."

Just thinking of the duke standing naked before me. Nothing to be alarmed about. Ignore the fact that I have lost my mind.

One obviously lost vital brain matter when taking a tumble over a tea cart and striking one's head.

"Where is the duke, anyway?" Felicity asked. "I haven't seen him in hours."

"I don't know. Perhaps he is still trying to get rid of his friends."

"No, I think they departed hours ago. While you were napping. I think the two lords, Hollingsworth and Danson, were eager to leave, but the ladies were not. Can't say as I blame them, since they are not likely to find a better man than the Duke of Claymore, no matter where they search."

Brenna said nothing, merely tucked a light blanket around her legs and smiled at the maid, a sweet girl by the name of Mary, as she brought in a supper tray for them and set it on the small *demi-lune* table beside Brenna.

"Compliments of His Grace," Mary said, bobbing a curtsy before bustling out.

Felicity drew up a chair beside Brenna. "Good heavens, he certainly spares no expense for you."

"No, he doesn't," Thaddius said, walking in just then and drawing up another chair beside Brenna. "We need to talk before Claymore returns. Felicity, you can stay. I want you to hear this as well."

Brenna regarded him seriously. "What's wrong?"

Thaddius glanced around. "This. You have to be careful, Brenna. Now, I am not saying the Duke of Claymore is a bad man. In fact, I like him. But he has his faults."

"I am well aware," Brenna assured him with a roll of her eyes. "He knows how to get his way…and he always seems to get his way, doesn't he?"

"But he has also been very generous with you, Brenna," Felicity remarked. "Is this so terrible? He did not have to give up his suite for you or have meals brought to us."

"That's right," Thaddius said with a frown. "Nor did he have to insist on paying for Brenna's stitches or lease her house at a cost that is double what any other landlord in the area is charging. And he is now renovating your entire house at his expense. Does this not give you cause for concern?"

Brenna nodded. "Yes, of course. Have I not been vocal about it? But he did not push me into it. Albert's sabotage of my position at the school did that. The duke offered a practical and very generous solution. Not only will I make money off the lease, but I get a completely refurbished home in the process, and I will also be permitted to live there as his nephew's governess. He is paying me good wages for this, too."

Thaddius was not smiling. "Cousin Spencer at the bank says the duke deposited a hefty sum into your account to cover the renovations. Well, he is no miser, I will give him that. But what is he doing, Brenna?"

She pursed her lips. "What do you mean? He wants to settle his mother and nephew here."

"What is he doing to *you*?" Thaddius said. "He is a womanizing hound. Barely a fortnight ago, he was taking women into his bed as a regular habit. Mostly those two promiscuous ladies in his party, Lady Gemma and Lady Sarah. But they were not the only ones. He had only to glance at a woman and she would follow him wherever he led. He treated them all quite casually. Oh, always politely, but he did not give a fig about any of them once he had satisfied himself. To him, they were just disposable commodities."

Felicity cleared her throat. "Honestly, Thaddius. That is a little too much information for us. Brenna and I are still innocent when it comes to *that* sort of thing."

"I know, but it is all the more reason why Brenna in particular needs to heed my warning. He is circling you like a lion about to leap on its prey. Just be careful. Why is he here in Moonstone Landing, of all places? Why not anywhere else in England?"

"To find himself, I think," Brenna said. "He has obviously noticed how happy the Duke of Malvern and the Marquess of Burness are here. Not to mention Viscount Brennan, who won Lady Chloe's heart. He is trying to make a home for his mother and nephew. But most of all, I think he is trying to make a home for himself, an idyllic and safe place that he never had as a child. Do you not see how empty he feels inside?"

Thaddius tossed his head back and laughed. "Empty? This man has everything anyone could ever want, including exquisite women who will jump into his bed at the snap of his fingers. And now he has discarded these very ladies who have warmed his bed for years."

"Is that not a good thing?" Brenna asked.

"Perhaps. But what if he wakes up one day and suddenly decides to do the same to you?"

Brenna inhaled sharply. "Thaddius! I am not one of those women!"

"No, but it will be much worse for you because you are at risk of falling in love with him. You do not have that toughness these other women have, Brenna. In fact, I am sure he is drawn to you because you are soft and innocent."

She pursed her lips and frowned. "I am not a delicate ninny."

"I know. You are intelligent, thoughtful, and can stand on your own, which is more reason why the duke is attracted to you. I just don't want to see him break your heart. I won't let him do this to my little cousin."

"He won't," she said, although this was her fear as well. In truth, she was very afraid it was already happening. The Duke of Claymore overpowered her in every way. She had never thought of men in physical terms before, but she could not stop thinking of how wonderful his skin had felt against her cheek when he carried her into his suite after she fell. Nor could she forget the magnificent body on this man.

Yes, she had noticed handsome men before. But she had never felt an ache to kiss them or run her hands along their sleek muscles.

Even Felicity had been bouncing on the mattress, breathing in his scent on the pillows, and urging her to hop onto that massive bed.

Brenna closed her eyes a moment and emitted a soft groan. "He may speak to us politely, but we are not equals to him. I am painfully aware that dukes do not marry schoolteachers. Yes, Cara and her Duke of Strathmore are the exception, but I know this is something quite rare and not likely ever to be repeated. I understand this. He is more likely to marry Lady Gemma or Lady Sarah than ever—"

"Those promiscuous cats," Felicity interjected.

"Yes, them, before he would ever consider me. Which is the point I am trying to make. He will *never* consider me suitable to be his wife. So, I will be very careful not to allow anything between us beyond a polite friendship."

"And what of your professor?" Thaddius asked.

Brenna put a hand to her head as it began to throb. "He is out of the question, too. I will never marry a man who thinks to win my hand by undermining the thing I love most."

"You mentioned it might all have been a terrible misunderstanding," Thaddius reminded her. "Give me the letters you wrote to him and your headmistress, and I shall post them in time for tomorrow's mail coach. You said you wanted to send them off as soon as possible."

"I haven't written them yet," Brenna admitted.

Thaddius slapped his hands on his thighs and rose to leave. "Well, if you are not too tired, then you must write them tonight. You need to do this, Brenna. Don't put it off."

He left her and Felicity to return to his innkeeper duties.

She and Felicity ate their supper, then Felicity helped set her up at the duke's writing desk so that she could write those important letters. The writing desk was in the duke's bedchamber and not in the sitting room.

Brenna felt like a trespasser, for being in the same room where he slept felt so intimate, even though the duke was not around. "Why don't you look through more of those fabric samples while I finish my correspondence, Felicity?"

Her cousin laughed. "Not on your life. We've gone through enough of them for today, and my head is spinning. Besides, I think we're done with our selections. The duke will be quite pleased by all we've accomplished, since he seems to be pleased with everything you do."

"Oh, stop. He wasn't too happy I took a spill trying to *discreetly* run out of his room and managed to wake the entire inn." Brenna laughingly groaned. "I cannot believe he did not sever all relations with me on the spot. Done with the lease. Done with the governess offer. Done with me."

"If anything, your injury seems to have brought you closer."

"Don't say that. There is nothing between him and me." But Brenna wondered whether the duke would stop in to see her before retiring. She heard he had taken over Lord Hollingsworth's room for this evening. Of course, most of his clothes remained here, and now Felicity was with her in his bedchamber, and…was her cousin foraging through the armoire? "Felicity! Get out of there. What you are doing is unforgivably rude!"

"He has wonderful taste in clothes."

"I know." He had wonderful taste in everything, in addition to being witty, charming, intelligent, wealthy, and so handsome he made her ache just looking at him. He even had an exquisite horse. This man had everything, and yet he was so unhappy.

Felicity began to dig through his drawers.

"For pity's sake! Have you no sense of propriety? I am going to kick you out if you do not stop going through his unmentionables."

"Brenna, you are no fun. Where's the harm? He'll never know."

"He will because he seems to have an instinctive sense about everything. Stop. You are distracting me, and I am almost done with my letters. You heard Thaddius. I need to hand them over to him tonight."

"All right," Felicity said with a huff, and put Daire's clothes back in order just as someone knocked lightly at the suite's door. "Oh dear. Do you think it is him?"

"I don't know."

Felicity tossed Brenna a wicked grin. "Has he come to kiss you goodnight?"

"Honestly, Felicity." Brenna rolled her eyes and gave her cousin a warning glance before she rose and crossed into the sitting room.

"Do come in, Your Grace," she said, her heart beating a little faster as she opened the door and took him in. He was a big man and filled the doorway.

Dear heaven, she was doomed. He looked glorious.

"How do you feel, Brenna?" He studied her with genuine concern. She knew he was worried about her, but there was such a gentleness in the way he regarded her.

"Much better, Your Grace. Thank you for sending up our supper. You did not have to do it."

"I know, but it is my pleasure." He placed his hand lightly atop her brow. "Good, no fever."

"Please have a seat," she said, motioning toward the settee. "This is your suite, after all. I'm sorry I have taken it over for the night."

He waited for her to sit and then settled beside her. "Don't be. You haven't demanded anything of me, which is something quite unusual. It feels good to be in the company of someone I know is not scheming to take from me."

Brenna blushed. "Good grief, why should I scheme when you have given me all of this without my needing to ask for a thing? You know I would not have insisted on any of it. In fact, I really ought to contribute something toward—"

"No," he said with a chuckle. "Have you gotten any rest?"

She nodded. "Yes, plus a bit of work done. Felicity and I finished going through all the fabric samples. I took the liberty of setting out our choices and adding their descriptions and designs in a new journal I started just for these decorations. Would you care to see what we've done?"

He nodded. "Yes."

"I'll fetch the samples and your book," Felicity said, joining in their conversation. She brought the samples and Brenna's journal over and handed them to the duke.

He quickly reviewed the items and then grinned at Brenna. "I should have known. You are remarkably organized and efficient. I suppose this is the schoolmistress training in you. Since you have detailed the work so well, even taken down all the measurements and made drawings for each room, I could ride to Plymouth tomorrow myself and have these ordered. There's no reason to bring you and Felicity along, is there?"

Brenna did her best to hide her disappointment. "No, I suppose not."

"The worst of the storm has passed and the rain has stopped. The air is drying out, as well. I should have easy travels if I leave tomorrow." He turned to her cousin, who had taken a chair beside them. "Felicity, is there a reason you cannot start on the garden work immediately?"

"No reason, my lord. I'll gather the supplies I need and start first thing in the morning."

"Good. Brenna, do you feel well enough to oversee your Uncle Simon's work? You know exactly what needs to be done, and I would not expect you to do anything other than make certain he is doing the right job, and be available to him if he has any questions."

"Yes, that is a sensible idea." She would have liked to visit Plymouth, but this was a trip she could always take at her leisure later. With a proper chaperone, of course.

Also, she sensed the duke was feeling on edge and eager to be away from Moonstone Landing. Riding to Plymouth to put in his orders with the fabric company was as good a reason as any. Plus, it was productive and would keep them on their fast schedule to have much of the house ready for his mother and nephew by the time they arrived.

No doubt he was feeling a bit out of sorts now that his friends were gone. Even though he had been the one to push them away, he was possibly regretting his decision. A man like him would be too proud to admit he might have acted hastily.

Would he seek out female company while in Plymouth?

Was this really the reason he was eager to leave? Not that it was any of her business if he stayed overnight and did whatever sordid things wealthy bachelors did during evenings on their own.

None of her business at all.

"Well, now that we've sorted this out..." He rose to take his leave, tucking her journal under his arm. "Do you mind if I take it and the samples with me tomorrow? I'll leave at first light, so I had better hold on to them now. I'll pack a few items for overnight, as well. Do you mind if I take a moment to gather my belongings?"

She rose with him. "Not at all. Do you need any help?"

He grinned. "I think I can manage to toss whatever I need into a travel pouch all on my own."

"I did not mean to imply you were incompetent." She cast him a wry smile. "My father, however, was quite a child when it came to such things. He was helpless and needed me to tend to the task for him. But I think you take it as a point of pride that you can fend for yourself and never rely on others."

He shrugged. "One learns in order to survive."

The remark twisted around her heart, for it seemed everything he did, every task he undertook, no matter how small, everything he mastered or strove to conquer, arose from this haunting need to rely only on himself and never depend on others.

He did not even have a valet with him. What duke ever traveled without a valet? Was he that closed off he could not even trust a personal servant?

He excused himself to stride into his bedchamber and fetch the few items he needed. The man did not waste time, and he meant to ride to Plymouth at first light tomorrow. As he was gathering a few belongings, he must have noticed Brenna had been at his desk, for he called out to her. "Did you finish your letters, Brenna?"

"Yes, just now." She joined him in the bedchamber while he continued to dig into his armoire. Felicity remained in the sitting room, but could easily see them from her position. Although her cousin was meant to serve as chaperone, Brenna doubted she would ever rush in and stop the duke if he attempted to kiss her.

Quite the opposite—she feared Felicity would be goading him on.

In any event, the duke was not likely to grab her and kiss her when she was nursing a lump on her head and had on that unsightly bandage. Her hair probably looked a fright, tumbling over one shoulder in an unruly cascade of curls.

"The ink ought to be dry by now, and I can seal them up," she said, finding it almost impossible to breathe as the duke stared at her with his smoldering gaze.

"Good—do it and I'll take them to Thaddius for tomorrow's mail coach. Did you ask the important questions, or are you still avoiding the obvious?"

"Feel free to read them if you must. In fact, I would appreciate it if you would. I'm not very good at this sort of thing."

She did not want to come across as too soft and ready to forgive, and knew the duke would tell her if the letters, especially the one to Albert, were inadequate.

She watched him as he quickly read each. "What do you think?"

"They are good letters, Brenna."

"You aren't just saying this to appease me, are you?"

He grinned. "No, the thought never crossed my mind. You know my feelings about your beau. He is a horse's arse."

Felicity was listening in and laughed. "Well said, Your Grace."

"Felicity! Do not encourage him." Brenna frowned at him, then took the letters and properly sealed them. "Not every man can be as insufferably perfect as you, Your Grace."

"Insufferable, am I?" He took the letters from her hand, tucked them in the inside pocket of his jacket, and then gave her chin a light tweak. "I suppose I am. Sorry, little dove. You are not the only one who has strong opinions."

"Which I voice tactfully."

"This is why you are the perfect choice to be Matthew's governess. I have already proved I am an utter failure when it comes to him." He placed her journal in his travel pouch, along with the shirt, cravat, and other items one needed for an overnight stay. "Do not berate me for being blunt about your beau. I told you I would never lie to you."

He kissed her lightly on the brow, a gesture neither of them expected, for he appeared as surprised as she was. "Couldn't resist, little dove. You are looking up at me with those big doe eyes, and it just felt right. By the way, I will not be back until the day after tomorrow at the earliest, so sleep here tomorrow night as well. I do not think you should be alone in your cousin Cara's cottage yet, not after you put in a full day tomorrow at Stoningham Manor."

"All I will be doing is watching the work. It isn't as if I will be doing any heavy lifting."

"Good gracious, I do not want you lifting so much as a spoon.

I mean it, Brenna. Those stitches are still too fresh and might rip if you exert yourself. All the more reason to have you sleep here another night. I'll make certain Thaddius is aware. The inn's maids can look in on you throughout the evening, if necessary."

He poked his head into the sitting room. "Felicity, that goes for you, too. Keep Brenna company here tomorrow night. The inn's staff will attend to both of you."

Felicity chuckled. "You don't have to ask me twice. Sure, I'll stay. Do we get dinner, as well?"

Brenna gasped. "Felicity!"

He laughed heartily. "Yes, and pay no attention to Brenna's griping. Anyway, Thaddius knows to ignore her if she dares take out her coin purse."

Felicity sauntered to the doorway. "You don't happen to have a brother interested in a wife of humble birth who enjoys toiling in gardens, do you?"

Brenna noticed a shadow darken his eyes for just a moment, but he recovered quickly, setting his mask firmly back in place as he turned to Felicity and responded with a casual smile. "Sorry, no."

He then turned back to Brenna, running his thumb along the line of her jaw. "Take care of yourself," he said in a hoarse whisper.

She found it hard to draw her gaze away. "You too, Your Grace. Safe journey."

Felicity sighed and flopped back on the massive bed the moment the duke left the suite. "Why can there not be more men like him in Moonstone Landing? He must like you, Brenna. He treats you like a princess."

"Have you already forgotten Thaddius's warning? And look at how he treated his friends, bringing them along everywhere until abruptly dismissing them and packing them off to Bath?"

"Well, they had been moaning about going there ever since they first arrived. Can you blame him for finally getting fed up and sending them off? They aren't exactly suffering, since they are traveling there in his fine carriage, and he's letting them stay at his townhouse in one of the finest crescents. This duke does not scrimp. Everything he does is the height of elegance."

Brenna said nothing as her cousin rambled on about Daire's qualities.

Yes, he had many fine qualities.

But he was also a womanizer.

Her head began to throb, but it had little to do with the stitches, since the doctor had given her a little laudanum to ease that pain. She could handle a little physical pain.

The pain in her heart was the problem.

Would the duke take any of the Plymouth ladies to his bed?

He had promised not to lie to her.

Would he tell her the truth if she asked him?

Did she dare ask him?

Chapter Eleven

DAIRE RODE OFF for Plymouth at dawn the following morning, feeling as restless as Scipio, who needed his daily run or else would be kicking down his stall. They were going to make good time, Daire knew, for his big warhorse was a sturdy beast and used to riding long distances under the worst of conditions.

But the weather was no impediment today, for the air still held the cooling breeze of night, and there was no sign of rain. Indeed, the storm had deposited every last drop of rain onto the village yesterday, leaving quite a bit of mud but also a crisp, dry day ahead of him. The breeze carried the familiar saltiness of the sea and the sweet scent of honeysuckle that grew along the hedgerows.

Daire spurred Scipio past the field of poppies along Brenna's hillside. He resisted looking toward Stoningham Manor or back at the little village of Moonstone Landing, for he already felt a palpable tug, as though a rope connecting him to the manor and the village had wrapped itself around his heart and was pulling him back.

But it wasn't *things* that held him in this heavenly patch of Cornwall—it was Brenna.

For this reason, he had grabbed the samples and her journal and hurried off to Plymouth in the hope of putting distance between him and the girl. He needed to slow things down between them. He needed to contain the fire that tore through him whenever he laid eyes on her. Hollingsworth had put his finger on something yesterday, asking if there was anyone whose happiness meant more to Daire than his own.

The answer was Brenna.

Was it not obvious?

He took pleasure in spoiling her. Indeed, he wanted to do so much more for her.

But to admit it, even to himself, was to give Brenna too much control over him. He was not ready to cede power to anyone yet, and certainly not to this little dove with big green eyes and a gentle heart he could so easily crush.

He tore along the countryside, eager to put that necessary distance between him and the girl. Why else would he bother dealing with something as trivial as draperies and bed canopies? Well, the days were passing, and he wanted to have as much put in order as possible when his mother and Matthew arrived.

He reached Plymouth by early evening and immediately sought the business establishment whose samples he carried. The Dumbley & Hayworth owners were just closing up as he arrived. Daire, with his usual rampaging bull approach to all business dealings, insisted they reopen for him, and soon had them hopping to his demands. It was amazing what offering to pay double the fee accomplished in very little time.

Not only did the owners stay on to review all his samples and requirements, but they left instructions for their workers to immediately halt all other commissions and start work on his orders first thing in the morning.

Brenna would purse her cherry lips and frown at him, but where was the harm in paying top price to jump ahead of the queue and get the work done? It was not possible to have everything completed within ten days, but the drapery, cushions, and bedding for his mother's bedchamber and private parlor would be done first. Afterward, wagons hauling the other finished items would begin to arrive on a weekly basis until all was completed.

Content with his accomplishments and bone weary, Daire next rode to one of the Plymouth gaming hells owned by a friend of his, Ajax Monteith, the newly installed Earl of Bradford. This newfound respectability did not sit well with his friend, for he had been merely a distant relative of the earl's, cast off from his family, and never expected to succeed to the title. But Daire always thought of Jax as far worthier than any of his useless relatives, even though the man's line of work was not at all wholesome.

"Jax," he said, relieved to find his friend at the elegant gaming establishment he owned that managed to quietly prosper among the gentry in this more dignified part of town. Yes, gaming and probably a bit of bootlegging on the side was not exactly honorable, but Jax had never cheated anyone and could always be relied upon to follow through on his word.

"Daire, what brings you here?" Jax greeted him warmly and ordered one of his footmen to take Scipio to his stable. "Tell Grimm this horse is to be treated like a king."

"I had business not far from here, and hoped I might impose on your hospitality for a day or two."

"Of course. You know you are always welcome here. Stay as long as you like." Jax ushered him inside and offered him food and drink. "I was just sitting down to supper. Care to join me? We'll dine and catch up with each other while I have a room prepared for you."

"Sounds good."

"Ah…would you care for some entertainment after we dine?" He motioned in the direction of several finely gowned ladies seated at the gaming tables.

Daire shook his head. "No. I've sworn off those amusements for now."

Jax arched an eyebrow. "Sworn off the ladies? Dare I ask what happened?"

"Nothing happened. I just got bored. Same greedy look in their eyes. Same meaningless romps. It began to feel dull and distasteful, my using them and their using me."

Jax led him into his private dining room and crossed to the tall cupboard. He took out a bottle of brandy and two crystal glasses, then poured the amber liquid into each glass. "I know what you mean. I have been feeling quite restless lately, too. Perhaps this is the reason why. There's not an ounce of genuineness to any of it. Returning to London is even worse. The ladies here in Plymouth are easily satisfied with coins or pretty trinkets. But in London, especially the Upper Crust ladies who frequent my copper hells, they can eat your soul. I thought I was hardhearted, but I am a lamb compared to some of them."

Daire laughed. "I doubt anyone would ever describe you as a lamb. You are almost as ruthless as I am."

His friend held up his glass in toast. "And almost as wealthy as you because of it."

After dining, they spent the rest of the night catching up over drinks. "So we are to be neighbors now?" Jax asked. "You in Moonstone Landing and me here in Plymouth?"

Daire nodded. "I would hardly call us neighbors, but certainly we are much closer than between here and London. I am determined to set up my mother and Matthew in Moonstone Landing. I'll make more permanent arrangements if they take well to the quieter life the village offers. Perhaps I will settle there too. I haven't decided yet."

"I beg to differ. It seems you have firmly made up your mind to set roots there. I've never heard you speak of anything with as much enthusiasm before. What makes you reluctant to admit it to yourself?"

Daire sighed. "I don't know. Perhaps because it is such a big change for me."

"One for the better, it seems. I will have to stop by and visit you in Moonstone Landing. You have accomplished quite a bit in the few weeks since you arrived there. Secured a house, now having it refurbished inside and out, and you seem quite confident in this governess you have hired. Teaching girls at the Rainard Academy is not at all the same as trying to manage your nephew. He's a damaged lad…scared, angry, trusting of no one."

He may as well have been describing Daire at that age. "If anyone can do it, it is Brenna."

Jax arched an eyebrow. "Brenna, is it? I did not realize the two of you are on a first-name basis."

Daire settled in one of the cozy tufted leather chairs beside the hearth. "Do not make anything of it. The villagers are all welcoming, and there is a refreshing innocence about them… Most of them, anyway. Sometimes I feel as though I have stepped through the mists of time and come upon a strange new world where people are helpful and friendly."

Jax settled in the chair beside his and chuckled. "Now I definitely must pay you a visit. In fact, let me ride back with you once you've finished your business in Plymouth. I have nothing pressing at the moment and could do with a few days away from here."

Daire shrugged. "Suit yourself. You will find it quite dull, just as Hollingsworth and Danson did."

Jax shook his head. "I think I will enjoy the change of pace. I really need to get away from the sophisticated women and discontented men who come here looking for a nightly thrill. People only come to my gaming hells because they are dissatisfied with their lives. Some are more desperate than others, but by and large they are unhappy people."

"And you, Jax?"

"Oh, I am quite happy making a profit off them. But this is not what I want for myself. Unfortunately, one does not meet the right sort of woman here, and until I recently became Earl of Bradford, who would ever allow their sweet daughters near me? No, it is time for me to look seriously for someone worthy to marry. I'm ready for it," he said, his manner quite earnest. "The ache grows inside me with each passing day. Do you think I will find what I am looking for in Moonstone Landing?"

"I have no idea." Daire had not meant to bring along a companion, but Jax was a good friend. Probably as close a friend as Daire ever had, although he never allowed anyone to get truly close to him. But he was determined to try harder, because Jax had always been generous, never asking him for anything in return, not even in those hard days when Jax was obviously struggling to set up his gaming hells.

THE NEXT MORNING, Daire strode out of the gaming club on his way to Dumbley & Hayworth and heard Jax call after him. "Wait for me. I'm coming with you."

Daire tried not to appear impatient. "Why? All I am doing is selecting curtains, for pity's sake."

His friend grinned. "Precisely. I need to see this for myself. The fierce Daire Claymore ordering decorative fabrics. I promise not to laugh, at least not while we are in their shop. However, I reserve the right to tease you mercilessly afterward."

Daire groaned. "All right, come along. But I shall kick your arse to London and back if you give me a hard time about it."

"I'll be quiet as a mouse in the shop, I promise."

"Ha!" Daire shook his head. "Come on, then."

They walked in to find the place already bustling. Mr. Dumbley fussed over Daire to the point of irritation, but he could not complain, since everything was moving more swiftly than he ever expected. The seamstresses were following Brenna's designs to the letter. The fabrics were all in stock. The delivery dates were all going to be met.

Daire was waiting for the hammer to drop, because things never went this smoothly. But Brenna and Felicity had been quite thorough and precise, so Mr. Dumbley had no trouble finding all the right patterns, while Mr. Hayworth supervised his staff of seamstresses to make certain they kept to the precise measurements. "The styles drawn by your decorator are quite elegant and will always remain popular," Mr. Dumbley assured him.

Daire and Jax walked out by late morning, all arrangements in place, including delivery of the first completed items to commence next week. Since everything was moving along with military precision, Daire thought about packing up and leaving Plymouth immediately. It was early enough that he could be back in Moonstone Landing by nightfall, which fell late at this time of the year.

Jax must have sensed what he was thinking. "Stay the night and I'll ride back with you tomorrow morning."

Daire agreed, for no reason other than he considered it wise to keep that distance between him and Brenna. There wasn't much for him to do in Plymouth, but he joined Jax in a ride around the countryside in order to exercise Scipio and Jax's stallion. Whenever they were not riding along the seacoast, they rode beside streams and rivers that led into the sea. Afterward, they stopped at a quaint pub, where they had their fill of crab stew, roasted rabbit, pasties, and ale.

The distraction did not prove much of a distraction at all, because Daire could not get his mind off Brenna and how disappointed she had looked when he announced he was coming here on his own. Well, perhaps he would take her to Plymouth along with his family later in the summer. She would enjoy the excursion.

He grinned at the thought of her frowning at him because he had no intention of allowing her to pay for anything along the way, not even any purchases she made while browsing the Plymouth shops.

Perhaps he would buy her something now, something pretty to match her eyes.

Bollocks.

Was he that besotted with the girl?

Daire looked in at Dumbley & Hayworth later that afternoon, saw all was still in perfect order, then spent a quiet evening at the card tables in Jax's gaming hell. He later shared a bottle of gin with his friend. "Be ready at first light," he told Jax.

"I'll be ready," his friend assured him.

IN ALL, DAIRE had been away three days, but when he and Jax walked into the Kestrel Inn, one would think he had been gone for years. The young attendant on duty at the registration desk uttered a cry of surprise and hurried off to wake Thaddius.

Jax arched an eyebrow. "Trouble?"

Daire shrugged. "I cannot imagine what it might be. He could not have given my room away, since I paid for it and left all my belongings there." Not to mention he had left Brenna sleeping there for at least one more night.

Thaddius, his ginger hair sticking out from his nightcap and obviously having thrown on his clothes in haste, rushed forward. "Your Grace, thank goodness you have returned."

Daire frowned. "Why? Has something happened to Brenna?"

Thaddius shook his head. "No, my cousin is fine. In fact, she has been tutoring your nephew for the past two days."

Daire shook his head, certain there had to be a mistake. "What?"

Thaddius, realizing he was still wearing his cap, tugged it off and tossed it on the registration table. "Your mother and nephew arrived with their entourage the same day you left. They drew up in front of the inn around suppertime. I sent word to Brenna, who was still up at the house supervising repairs, and told her to come here straight away because I was not certain what to do."

"Where are my mother and nephew now?"

"They are settled at Stoningham Manor."

Daire's jaw dropped open. "In the house? But it isn't ready for them yet. In fact, that house is completely upside down."

"That's what Brenna, Felicity, and I tried to tell them, but your mother would not hear of staying anywhere but there. Her rooms and your nephew's rooms are in fairly good shape because Brenna had the foresight to insist they be completed first. All they are lacking are elegant beddings and new curtains, but your mother did not seem to care about those. Her kitchen staff put the kitchen in order and have already started preparing meals there. The quarters for your butler, footmen, maids, and cook are livable, although Brenna insisted they were not quite ready yet."

Daire nodded. "They only needed to be swept clean and have a fresh coat of paint applied to the walls."

"Brenna had Uncle Simon's crew attend to that yesterday. The kitchen is up and running, and your staff is slowly unpacking all your mother's belongings."

Daire raked a hand through his hair. "They weren't supposed to be here for another ten days."

"Brenna has it all in hand, Your Grace. She got Duchess Henley to invite your mother and nephew to St. Austell Grange for cream tea yesterday, so they were out of the way during the dustiest parts of the work. This morning," Thaddius said, glancing at the clock and noting it was after midnight, "she intends to take Matthew on a nature walk around Stoningham Manor. Then Lady Phoebe and the marquess have invited them to Westgate Hall for the afternoon. His nieces, Ella and Imogen, are visiting again. She thought your nephew might enjoy their company. They are a bit older than him, but I don't think they'll mind building sandcastles on the beach together. Does anyone ever grow out of that fun?"

Daire wouldn't know, since his father had never allowed him any idle pleasures. But he liked that Brenna was already on task with Matthew. "And what has she arranged for the following day?" he asked with a grin, knowing she was quite efficient.

"Brenna got the fort's commander, Major Brennan," Thaddius said, "to give your mother and nephew a tour of Fort Arundel, after which Lady Chloe will take them for tea and cakes at Mrs.

Halsey's tea shop. You needn't worry for their comfort. Everyone is helping out so that Brenna can keep the work going at Stoningham Manor."

"She appears to be handling this most efficiently," Jax remarked.

Thaddius nodded. "She's good that way. Quite organized. Always has been."

"Seems I have nothing to worry about," Daire muttered, amazed but also quite pleased by Brenna's handling of things. Of course, he knew she was wonderful in every way. Was this not precisely the reason he'd felt the need to put distance between them? "Well, it is late, and I am sure Lord Bradford would like to get to his room and retire to bed."

"He'll have the guest chamber across the hall from your suite, Your Grace. Do either of you need anything more? Refreshments? A bath brought in?"

Daire shook his head. "Yes to refreshments. Send a bath to each of us tomorrow morning. The ewer and basin will do for tonight." He turned to his friend. "Jax, do you wish to sleep in or ride up to Stoningham Manor with me in the morning?"

His friend cast him a lazy smile. "I'll ride over with you to pay my respects to Duchess Juliana, but mostly I need to see this paragon of efficiency, Brenna."

Thaddius immediately frowned.

So did Daire. "You are not to interfere with her work, or treat her as anything less than a lady. Have I made myself clear?"

Jax held up his hands. "Don't bite my head off. Of course I will be a gentleman. I was merely curious about her, since I've never seen you so concerned about a lady before. She must be something special."

"She is," Daire and Thaddius said at the same time.

Jax shook his head and laughed. "Dear heaven, I cannot wait until tomorrow."

Daire walked down the hall with his friend, and they parted ways as they each got to their door and entered. Daire lit a taper and glanced around the sitting room. None of Duchess Henley's fabric books were here. No doubt Brenna had made certain to return them as soon as possible. Nor was there any sign that Brenna had been here except for the lightest hint of lavender in the air. She had sat in here while working on the drapery designs. She had slept in his bed when napping after taking that lump to her head. She had been at his writing desk to write her letters to her beau and the headmistress.

Gad, he missed her.

Well, he would see her soon enough tomorrow.

He left instructions for Thaddius to wake him and his friend up at nine o'clock in the morning, which was much later than he was used to rising, but there was no point in getting out of bed sooner. By the time they would each have washed up, dressed, and met for breakfast in the dining room, it would be close to ten o'clock. He knew his mother would not be ready to see them before eleven at the earliest, so he was not in any rush to ride up to Stoningham Manor.

He wanted to see Brenna, of course. But he also wanted to give her time to get the day's work underway before he interrupted her.

Despite the long ride from Plymouth to Moonstone Landing, Daire found it hard to fall asleep. He drank a glass of port before undressing and washing up. He then fell naked onto his bed and closed his eyes. It took him a while to stop thinking of Brenna and lose himself in dreams. Those dreams were not helpful either, since they were of Brenna.

He cast a wry smile into the dark.

So much for putting a little distance between them. He had not been back five minutes before thoughts of her filled his head.

In truth, they had never left his head even while he was off in Plymouth.

Come morning, he shaved, had his bath, dressed casually on the chance there would be work required of him, and took a seat at one of the dining room tables. He was having his morning coffee when Jax strode in.

He had also cleaned up and put on casual riding attire. "Sorry I'm late," he said, taking the seat beside Daire's.

"You're on time. I got here a little early. I'd like to head over to Stoningham Manor as soon as possible. Duchess Juliana will not be down to meet us yet, but I'm eager to see Matthew and the work that's been done to the house so far."

Jax nodded. "Give me a minute to have my coffee and we'll be on our way."

The sky was a deep, bright blue and filled with tufts of white clouds, the sort that held no rain and provided occasional shade from the sun as the wind blew them across the sky. Daire's heartbeat quickened as they rode along the field of poppies, their red petals looking particularly bright against the green of the meadow grass.

Jax drew up his mount to stare back toward the village and the glimmering sea. "Daire, this is spectacular. No wonder you wanted to move them here." He shook his head and laughed. "Even I want to move here."

Daire arched an eyebrow. "I don't think the villagers will welcome a gaming hell."

"Dear heaven, I wouldn't bring that business here. No, I'd find something respectable. Perhaps I'll buy the Kestrel Inn. That young innkeeper has done a good job with it. Do you think he would be willing to sell?"

"I don't know. He just bought it from the old proprietor, Mr. Egdon."

Jax pursed his lips in thought. "Probably carrying a hefty debt on it. Even if he did not wish to sell, he might be open to taking on a partner to relieve the debt load that must be crushingly large right now. I would agree to keeping him on at full wages to run the place, since I cannot see myself bowing and scraping or indulging the whims of anyone. I'd destroy that business within a week because I'm such an arse. But I cannot abide demanding people. I routinely toss out anyone I deem insufferable in my gaming hell, no matter how heavily they are losing to the house or how powerful and important they might be. But it doesn't work quite the same way in a hotel. People actually expect to be served."

Daire chuckled. "Come on. Aren't you getting a little ahead of yourself? You haven't been here more than a few hours and are already planning to buy up half the village."

Jax grinned. "Can you blame me? Did you not feel this way upon first coming here? It is spectacular, Daire. One feels as though magic happens here."

Daire fully understood his friend's sense of awe.

"It is a bit like stumbling into heaven, isn't it? A man can heal in a place like this," he said quietly. This was as close as Daire had come to admitting what Moonstone Landing and its occupants meant to him… What Brenna meant to him.

Was she even aware how important she was to him? That he actually considered marrying her? He and Jax were alike in that neither cared much about status or bloodlines. His father had tried to beat this sense of privilege and superiority into him, but all he'd made Daire do was detest everything Society had to offer.

Lady Gemma and Lady Sarah would soon be among the richest ladies in England, with lofty titles to boot. But Brenna was worth immeasurably more than them.

What price could a man put on happiness?

What price on love?

Brenna was nowhere in sight as they rode up to the manor house. Daire swallowed his disappointment as Simon Angel hurried out to greet him.

Daire introduced Jax to Brenna's uncle and asked him to give them a tour of the work done so far. "My pleasure, Your Grace. Rain's hampered us a bit, but hasn't slowed us down at all indoors. Good thing, since we had Her Grace's rooms mostly done by the time she arrived."

To Daire's surprise, quite a lot had been accomplished, albeit mostly the interior work, as Simon had indicated.

"We're doing our best not to disturb Her Grace," Simon remarked. "But we'll be doing quite a bit of banging and hammering in the coming days. We'll complete the noisy work as fast as possible, but it will take us a few days. I'm glad you have returned, Your Grace. Do we have your permission to keep to our schedule, or should we wait on the noisier work until Her Grace is awake? It will slow us down a little, but nothing that cannot be handled with a little extra planning."

"Keep to your schedule, Mr. Angel. My mother is a late riser, but she can endure a few days of discomfort to have this place in order as soon as possible."

"Very good, Your Grace. I'll let my men know to continue as usual."

"I expect my mother has not come out of her bedchamber yet, but where is my nephew?"

"Aw, what a sweet boy he is."

Daire arched an eyebrow in surprise. "Sweet?"

"Oh, yes. Quite curious and helpful, too. Felicity and Brenna took him on a nature walk, and then plan a quick stop to take a dip in the pool by the glade."

Daire's eyebrow shot up again, for there had to be some mistake. Helpful? The child was a devil's spawn, if his prior governesses were to be believed. Nor did Brenna's taking Matthew for a swim sound right. "Brenna plans to swim?"

Simon shook his head. "Oh, dear me. No. That's why Felicity went with her. Brenna's afraid of the water. Any water. No matter how tranquil it appears."

"Timid, is she?" Jax asked.

Daire and Simon glared at him.

"She isn't timid," Daire said. "I'll explain later. You'll under-stand."

"Lead on. I'm intrigued to meet her."

Daire was leaping out of his skin to see Brenna again. One would think he had not seen her in years, but they had only been apart for three days.

It was not long before they neared the glade. Daire could hear the sound of rushing water. The stream running beside the glade must have filled to capacity after the storm earlier in the week. He also heard the lilting sounds of laughter. He immediately recognized Brenna's melodic voice and the slightly throatier trills of Felicity. His nephew was with them, for he also heard a child's gleeful giggles along with water splashing.

He stopped and simply stared at the glade.

Matthew laughing? Chattering, too.

Where was the sullen, withdrawn lad he had expected?

Matthew emitted another gleeful shout, soon followed by a loud splash. Then more laughter from the three of them. Was this not exactly what Daire had hoped for with Matthew? This was the first time he had ever heard the boy respond to anything with joyful abandon.

"Something wrong, Daire?" his friend asked. "You have the oddest expression on your face."

"No. Finally things seem to be just right."

They walked closer, their steps quiet as curiosity got the better of both of them. Perhaps it was not right to spy on the ladies and Matthew, but Daire did not want to interfere with their happy moment. He knew Matthew would close himself up the moment he noticed his uncle.

Jax inhaled sharply and then elbowed Daire in the ribs. "Praise heaven," he whispered. "Am I seeing right? Who are these beautiful wood nymphs?"

"Quiet," Daire warned, suppressing a groan. The ladies had taken off their gowns and wore only their shifts. The fabric was so sheer that he could see the dusky outline of the tips of Brenna's breasts beneath the fabric. Felicity had her back to them, thank goodness. He would not look at her, for he was no lewd peeper. But Brenna? He wanted to devour the girl whole. "Take your eyes off Brenna, Jax. I vow, I'll blind you if you look at her."

"Which one is Brenna?"

"The one on the rock."

"Suits me fine. I can't take my eyes off the nymph in the water. I suppose that's her cousin, Felicity? Gad, I'm going to spill myself if she turns toward me." Which she did a moment later, but Daire's gaze was still on Brenna.

Jax sucked in a breath. "Lord, I'm done for. I am going to marry that girl."

Daire stared at his friend, who had obviously turned into a babbling nitwit.

"You heard me, Daire. Don't give me that look. I've never seen anyone so beautiful in all my days, and I've seen plenty of beautiful women. Most of them unclad."

"Don't go thinking lewd thoughts. Brenna and Felicity are innocent about that sort of thing."

"Don't you think I can tell? I've seen enough used women to know the difference. Felicity is a vision from heaven. I am going to expire if she gets out of the water and takes off her shift... Oh, Lord!" he said, suddenly clutching his heart. "She's stepping out of the water. That shift is peeled to her arse. And look at her long, dark hair. No, don't look. I vow I will blind *you*, if you dare look at her. Felicity is mine and I am not letting her go."

"Shut up, Jax. Stop thinking with your privates."

"Actually, I am thinking with my heart for once. That blasted organ has been numb for so long, I was sure it had died out long ago."

Daire snorted.

"Why the dismissive snort? Aren't you the thick one? What are you doing all this for if it isn't to woo Brenna? How long have you been in love with her? Is this why you have been coming back here all these years?"

"I met her less than a week ago. Jax, come back to your senses. You cannot propose to Felicity when you haven't even spoken to her."

The ladies had taken off their gowns to keep them from getting wet. Matthew, that lucky six-year-old, had taken off all his clothes and was nakedly cavorting in the water with Felicity, while Brenna, obviously scared of the water, was perched on a flat rock overhanging the pool and calling out for her companions to be careful even as she tried to appear relaxed and cheerful.

Daire could see the magnificent swell of her breasts spilling out and dangerously close to revealing all their creamy splendor. Adding to the wild glory was the erotic tumble of her dark hair cascading down her back and over her shoulders.

He was going to pass out if he did not suck in a breath.

Neither the ladies nor Matthew had noticed them yet.

"Jax, we have to go. They cannot know we saw them."

"Not yet. Let me die a happy man on this very spot."

"Felicity and Brenna have seven uncles who are very protective of these girls. We both will die on this very spot if we are found out."

"Oh, all right. Let's step back twenty paces, and then you ought to call out to them as though we have just arrived and are trying to find them."

"What are we, idiot schoolboys?" But Daire grabbed him and dragged him away from the glade. Only then did he recover his breath and manage a quiet laugh. "Bloody hell, Jax. This is not the introduction I had planned."

Jax grinned. "I cannot tell you how pleased I am to be here. Just punch me if I start to leer at Felicity. Isn't she spectacular? No wonder your nephew is having the time of his life. Who wouldn't be in raptures while in the company of those two wood nymphs? My eyeballs are still throbbing in their sockets. Dare I mention what my male parts are doing?"

Daire rubbed a hand across the back of his neck and took several deep breaths to calm himself, for his male parts were also misbehaving at the moment.

He and his friend were standing back, both of them laughing quietly, when Matthew suddenly tore out of the glade with breeches half buttoned and his shirt hanging open. The boy was barefoot and laughing, but his laughter died the moment he spotted Daire.

On instinct, Daire bent on his haunches and held out his arms to the boy. "Matthew, I missed you. This is my friend, Jax. We came up here looking for you."

To Daire's disappointment, Matthew's expression turned to one of fear and he raced back into the glade.

Jax frowned. "He seems terrified of you."

"Not of me, but I closely resemble my bastard of a brother, who must have beaten that boy mercilessly…just as our bastard of a father did to us. He is so afraid whenever he sees me. I've tried to remain in the background and let my mother take charge of him. He doesn't cower as much around her, but nor does he trust her yet. He fears to say or do anything around us, for one wrong step and he thinks we'll show our true colors and beat him. The poor lad must have been receiving thrashings from his mother, as well. So he's learned never to trust family."

"Dear heaven," Jax muttered. "My heart goes out to him. My life was hard, but nothing like the ordeal he must have gone through."

Daire nodded. "We hired governesses from the best agencies to look after him once I found him and took him in, but I think our choices only compounded the problem. These governesses were trained to rule with a firm hand, completely the wrong approach to take with that boy."

"Well, you've finally done something right in hiring Brenna. His joy was genuine."

"I know."

Brenna and Felicity emerged from the glade, now clad in their gowns. But they were holding their wet shifts in their hands. Daire tried to keep his imagination from running wild, for they must have been naked and drying themselves off mere minutes ago.

Brenna naked?

He struggled to tamp down the fireworks exploding in his body.

Unaware, Brenna cast him the sweetest smile. "Welcome

home, Your Grace. We did not realize you were back."

"I arrived late last night." Was that his voice, so thick and raspy?

"We were swimming, as you can plainly see. Well," she said with a light blush, "Felicity was teaching your nephew how to swim. Master Matthew is doing beautifully, and he also knows how to count to one hundred. Would you like him to show you?"

Matthew began to sniffle.

Daire felt a jolt to his heart. What he would not give to have the boy trust him enough to give him a heartfelt embrace. "Matthew, that is remarkable. Well done, lad. Perhaps we shall count together later. How about counting the poppies in the nearby field? Or we can count the birds we see. Or the clouds. Would you like that?"

Brenna spoke up for the boy, who was now hiding behind her and tugging on her gown. "We shall like that very much." She turned to the lad. "I shall be by your side, too. No one is going to hurt you here, Matthew. No one wants to do you any harm."

Matthew just stared at Daire, his eyes shadowed.

"Your Grace," Brenna said with obvious heartache, "your nephew is an utter delight. Clever. Helpful. Funny. We have been having quite a lot of fun learning our numbers, and next week we shall start on our letters."

Daire smiled at the boy. "That's very good, Matthew. I'm glad you are enjoying your studies with Miss Angel. She is quite charming, isn't she?"

Matthew just cast him another shadowed stare.

"I like her, too. I think she is an excellent governess. I wish mine were as nice when I was your age. But they were all quite horrid. What do you think of our Miss Angel?" When he still received no response, Daire decided to leave the boy as he was for the moment and introduce Jax to the ladies.

He was about to do so when Matthew spoke to him from behind Brenna. "I can dress myself."

Daire let out a breath. "I see, although you seem to have

dressed in a hurry. But that's all right. I'm glad you were having fun. Was the water pleasant?"

He nodded. "Miss Standish said I was a wicked boy and always misbehaved. She said I was stupid and would never learn."

Daire spared a glance at Brenna. "Seems to me that Miss Standish was the wicked one. She should never have spoken to you so cruelly. You will never hear a cruel word from Miss Angel's lips, Matthew. In fact, I think she will box the ears of anyone who dares be mean to you."

Jax emitted a low growl. "A pox on all these charlatans who call themselves governesses and tutors. They hold themselves out as experts, but all they are is bullies who single out children because they are too weak to fight back."

Daire thought back to his own childhood, to a time before his stepmother came into his life and that of his older brother. Their tutors and governesses were a cold-hearted lot, but their father had been the cruelest of all. He'd noticed a bruise on Matthew's chest when he had run out of the glade toward him earlier.

He would ask Brenna about it later. Not that he suspected her of ever laying a brutish hand on Matthew.

No, that deep bruise must have been put there by Miss Standish or any one of the governesses who came before her. He recognized those marks, for he still had a few that had been so brutally beaten into his back that they had never disappeared.

Matthew screwed up a little courage and spoke directly to Daire. "Shall I show you how well I can count to one hundred?"

Daire would pull out his hair if he had to listen to the boy count the entire way to one hundred, but he was not going to deprive the lad of the pleasure of showing off. As he was about to nod, Brenna spoke up. "I think your uncle has many questions for us, Master Matthew. How about we shorten it for today and you just count by tens?"

The lad nodded and immediately started. "Ten, twenty, thirty..."

Daire smiled, for that was a much better idea. When the boy

finished, he patted him on the head and congratulated him. "Well done, lad. An admirable job. Give me a moment to properly greet the Misses Angel and catch up on all that has happened since I've been away. Then you and I shall take a long walk and you can tell me all about what you've done since arriving here. How does that sound to you?"

Fear shot into the boy's eyes again, and he stared at his toes.

Brenna tweaked Matthew's nose. "Yes, we would love to take a walk with you, Your Grace. I hope you don't mind my being with you at every step."

"Not at all, Miss Angel. I look forward to having you with us."

Matthew's tension appeared to ease.

Daire now got around to the business of introducing them to Jax. "Miss Angel, I would like to present a good friend of mine, Ajax Monteith, Earl of Bradford. He resides in Plymouth, and I stayed with him while attending to the Dumbley & Hayworth draperies. By the way, that business went very smoothly because of your excellent preparatory work," he told both Brenna and Felicity.

Then he introduced Felicity to Jax.

Felicity curtsied demurely.

Jax took her hand and bowed over it. "May I say it is an exquisite pleasure to meet you."

She shot a questioning glance at Daire, especially since Jax retained hold of her hand. "The pleasure is all mine, Lord Bradford." But her tone was curt, and she appeared decidedly uncomfortable, since Jax was not only holding her hand but grinning at her like a besotted dolt.

"Jax," Daire said quietly, knowing his friend was taking uncalled-for liberties.

Jax cleared his throat and released Felicity. "I hope you will allow me to get to know you better, Miss Angel."

Felicity shot Daire another disquieted glance. "Why, my lord? I am merely the hired gardener."

Jax arched an eyebrow. "Is that so? Well, I expect it is as respectable a profession as any for a future countess."

Felicity's eyes turned stormy. "A future what?"

Daire groaned.

"I'm serious," Jax said, his gaze on the girl remaining as sharp as a hawk's while he eyed her as though she was his prey.

Since when did Jax spill every stupid thought that popped into his head? And then compound it by spilling more stupid thoughts? Not that admiring Felicity was stupid. In fact, Daire could not think of any women finer than Brenna or Felicity.

But to spout off about marrying Felicity upon a minute's acquaintance? Had Jax taken total leave of his senses?

Chapter Twelve

Daire wanted to throttle Jax but dared not say or do anything in front of Matthew for fear of frightening the lad. Brenna and Felicity were also tossing daggers at his friend with their dark emerald eyes.

Felicity, obviously aware of Matthew's sensitivity, tried to keep her tone unaffected as she responded to Jax's statement. "And what makes you think an earl is worthy to be the husband of a gardener?"

Jax smiled. "Perhaps this earl is not quite the prize yet, but I assure you he will be trying very hard to prove himself in the coming days."

"Just how long do you plan to stay here?" Brenna asked, trying not to curl her hands into fists as she rose to the defense of her cousin.

Jax glanced at Daire. "As long as it takes me to finish a bit of business in Moonstone Landing."

Felicity eyed him warily. "What sort of business could a man like you have here?"

"Do you mean because I am an earl? Or are you referring to what I was until a few months ago before I came into the title? I assure you, Miss Angel, you were far worthier than I ever was back then. Indeed, you are far worthier than I even now. Do not be put off by a title I acquired merely by the fortuitous deaths of two uncles and several worthless cousins. Nor do I want you to look askance because of the speed with which I have made my decision about you. I hope you do not consider me rude."

Felicity snorted. "How else am I to take your words?"

"As honest. When you've seen and done the things I have, you will be quick to recognize a good thing when it comes along and not hesitate to reach for it."

Felicity merely shook her head and walked away.

Jax excused himself and followed her.

Brenna watched them with concern. "He won't do anything untoward, will he?"

Daire shook his head. "No. He may come across as a dolt, but he is one of the smartest, finest men I know. He is serious, by the way. Don't worry about your cousin. He will do right by her."

"He had better," she said with quiet determination.

Daire raked a hand through his hair. "I'll make certain he does."

"Will you? Or are you both cut from the same cloth?"

He frowned. "What does that mean?"

"Do you really need explanation?"

"Yes, in fact, I do. How have I stepped out of line?" He cleared his throat, recalling the kiss he'd taken on the first day they had met. But hadn't he been on his behavior ever since? Well, if he had kept his stupid mouth shut, she wouldn't be walking around with stitches in her head either. But considering his formerly debauched ways, he truly was on his best behavior around Brenna. Which was no small accomplishment, considering how thoroughly the sight of this girl ravaged his senses.

"You've come here and overwhelmed us all. You toss your coin about and everyone jumps to do your bidding...even me."

"Brenna, you are the best thing in Moonstone Landing. How is it wrong of me to recognize it and rely on you? You are worth ten times what I have offered you. What price am I to put on all you have accomplished in a matter of days?" He spared a glance at Matthew, who was holding tightly to her gown and hardly dared to breathe. "And you know I am not merely referring to the manor renovations."

"Forgive me, Your Grace. Obviously, I spoke out of turn."

He shook his head. "No, I always want you to speak your mind to me. My friend's behavior has rattled me, too. But he is serious, and I fully expect Felicity will be a countess before the month is out."

What he left unsaid was Brenna's status. This was the true disquiet Brenna was talking about. She wanted to know Daire's intentions toward her.

He was not Jax. He needed time to open his heart even to someone as worthy as her.

"Well, it is not quite eleven o'clock yet, so I doubt my mother will be receiving visitors for at least another quarter of an hour. How about we take a walk, the three of us? Matthew, do you have your shoes? Shall I help you put them on?"

Brenna held out his shoes. "I have them right here, Your Grace. Sit down, Matthew. Show your uncle how well you put them on all by yourself."

The lad seemed to take instruction from Brenna like a duckling to its mother. He sat on the grass and took his time struggling with one and then the other shoe. Daire was twitching with impatience, but Brenna lightly touched his hand, a sign for him not to rush the boy. "Well done," she said once Matthew had laced them up.

She then knelt down beside him and properly tightened the laces so he would not trip as they loosened. "It takes a little bit more strength than Matthew has just yet, being as he is only six years old. Isn't that right, Matthew? But it all works out in the end, since he helps me with anything I am not quite able to do on my own."

She chattered away in a deliciously soothing voice.

Matthew nodded all the while. "I'm going to help Felicity in her garden. We're to grow strawberries along the hedgerows borders because they are my favorite."

Daire smiled at the lad. "That is an excellent idea. May I watch you? I have never planted strawberries and am curious to learn. Do you think Felicity would mind if I joined you? I can do some of the heavier digging, if that is required."

"Miss Standish said that only nobodies like me—"

"You are not a nobody," Daire said harshly.

Matthew yelped and hid behind Brenna.

Daire sighed. "Matthew, I was not angry with you. It is Miss Standish who got my blood boiling. You are a fine young man. Never believe anyone who tells you otherwise. And never think anyone is better than you merely because they carry a title. It means they might have more power than you, but they are not necessarily any worthier than you are."

The lad did not respond, merely buried himself tighter against Brenna.

Daire sighed again. "Sorry, I bungled that, didn't I?"

"No, Your Grace. In time Matthew will learn that you won't ever hurt him. I know this, but give him time to come around because he has had a very difficult upbringing. Haven't you, Matthew?"

The boy nodded.

He did not speak to Daire again for the entire walk, not even as they ambled through the field of poppies and began to count them. "Matthew," Daire said, feeling as though he were talking to himself, "I think I shall purchase us some kites so we can fly them up here. Does that sound like fun to you?"

The boy looked to Brenna.

She smiled and nodded. "That is a hearty yes."

The lad then glanced at Daire and gave a curt nod.

Well, small steps. He was glad Matthew felt a kinship to Brenna and Felicity, even if the lad held a loathing for him.

APPARENTLY, THE BOY'S kinship extended to Brenna's uncle and his work crew. Not an hour later, Daire noticed the boy smiling as he watched Simon Angel paint the dining room walls. They had returned to the house a short while earlier. Daire had found his mother in her private parlor having breakfast. While he greeted her, Brenna had taken the boy to watch the workers.

Daire did not need long to greet Duchess Juliana. "What do you think of Miss Angel?" he asked, taking quick assessment of this woman he considered his mother, and finding her hair a little grayer than he last recalled, and her complexion a little paler. He hoped her fatigue was attributable to her long journey from London and nothing more.

Duchess Juliana arched an eyebrow. "Seems the question to ask is what do *you* think of her, my dear boy?"

Daire avoided the question. "She seems to have worked a miracle with Matthew."

"Yes, and impressed me immediately. Felicity, too. They are very clever young ladies, and very kind. Matthew sensed it, too. He's already quite attached to them."

Daire sighed. "I never thought of myself as an ogre. But he is still in fear of me."

"Because you look so much like Morgan. There is nothing you can do about this for now. One can only hope the boy will grow out of it in time. He is still wary around me, as well. It is family he distrusts because it is family who has hurt him."

Daire settled in the chair beside her. "What brought you out here ten days early, Juliana? And why did you not simply settle into rooms at the Kestrel Inn? Thaddius would have known to give you the best."

"London became intolerable," she said, her smile faltering. "The heat, the odors, and the house simply became too much for me to manage on my own, especially with Matthew acting out constantly. That last governess, Miss Standish, was horrid. I caught her hitting him with a ruler. Then she had the gall to declare the boy was at fault for failing to learn his numbers."

"He knows them very well. In fact, he counted for me just a few minutes ago and did it perfectly."

"Oh, dear heaven. And still that horrid Standish beat the soul out of him? I sensed something was terribly wrong. Daire, it all became too much for me. I felt as though I had trapped the poor boy in a prison. So I dismissed Miss Standish, packed up the household, and came straight here. I know it was earlier than planned."

"But why stay at the house when the rooms have not been put right yet?"

"I've lived under far worse conditions, and so has Matthew, that poor child," she replied. "I chose to move us in because there is room for the boy to run around here. He could not have done so at the inn, although it looks to be a lovely place to stay. We weren't here more than fifteen minutes before Miss Angel had us settled and Matthew was following her like a puppy everywhere she went. She told us that she was the governess you had hired, but she is obviously so much more."

Daire nodded. "She is. I've never seen anyone operate as efficiently as she does."

"When we told her we had not had our supper, she commandeered her uncle's wagon, rode off to town, and returned with meals for us all. And I mean all of us, the entire staff. Not only did she bring back meals, but she also had a picnic hamper filled with strawberry tarts, lemon cake, ginger cake, and tall bottles of lemonade."

He chuckled. "Sounds like something Brenna would do."

"Brenna, is it? I thought there might be something between the two of you."

"It is only a professional friendship."

"I see. By the way, she told me to tell you that she put all the meals on your account."

Daire threw back his head and laughed. "Did she now?"

"Yes. She also said you would find it amusing. But I think it is Brenna that puts the smile on your face." She cast him a knowing look, but did not press him with more questions. "While the staff and I settled in, she took Matthew into the poppy field for a picnic supper. It was only to get him out of the way while everyone bustled in and out to unload our trunks. But the boy did not realize this. They were on an adventure. It was as though the world opened up to him in that moment. He thinks she is a fairy princess."

Daire could not help but grin. "Sometimes I think so, too. I've never met anyone quite like her, Juliana. Clever, earnest, organized...innocent. Kind. Brave. Honest."

"Daire, are you opening your heart to the girl?"

He shifted uncomfortably in his chair. "My heart? What heart?"

"The one you keep securely hidden in darkness. But it seems that girl is pure sunlight, and you cannot hide from her."

His grin faded. "I don't know. Maybe. Much too soon to tell."

He wasn't like Jax, able to decide in a moment that a girl he'd seen—and not even spoken to yet—was the one he would marry. Yes, he'd felt an immediate attraction to Brenna. But that was a far thing from being ready to make a lifetime commitment, especially to someone like her. She believed in a love match.

He, on the other hand, wanted anything but a love match. How could he pledge to be faithful and loving when he had survived all these years by keeping his heart locked away?

Yet he had contemplated marriage to Brenna from the first.

More than contemplated it, since she was constantly in his thoughts. Even now, he was eager to return to her side.

"Brenna is taking us to Westgate Hall this afternoon," Juliana said, breaking into his momentary thoughts. "Would you care to come along? After all, you are the boy's guardian, and it would be appropriate for you to join us now that you have unexpectedly returned from Plymouth."

"I'm here with Jax. It would be too much of an imposition for both of us to simply show up unannounced at the marquess's door. Enjoy your afternoon with Burness and his wife. Matthew will have fun with his little nieces, Ella and Imogen. His twin boys are probably a little too young to play with him, but it is good to have other children around no matter their age."

"Oh, I agree."

"Burness's wife, Phoebe, is one of the Killigrew sisters," he continued. "Henley, the eldest, is married to the Duke of Malvern, and Chloe, the youngest, is married to Viscount Brennan, who is commander of the local fort. I understand Brenna has arranged a tour of the fort for you and Matthew tomorrow."

She nodded. "Your Brenna seems to know everyone and fit in everywhere. We met the Duke and Duchess of Malvern yesterday, and the duchess seemed particularly friendly with Brenna."

Daire nodded. "Everyone adores her."

"Even you."

He frowned. "Stop prying. Yes, I like her. What's not to like? Are you now going to warn me not to get involved with the hired help?"

"Ah, am I supposed to tell you that you ought to know better than to entangle yourself with someone beneath your station? Well, you will not hear this caution from me. If you must know, I was going to suggest you stop getting in your own way and court her. Daire, you are ruthless in going after what you want. So why are you holding back now? Grab her for your own before someone wiser comes along and claims her first."

Daire squirmed in his seat once again. These blasted chairs were made for delicate females and not men the size of him. "Someone has already come along. Brenna met an Oxford professor while she was teaching at the exclusive Rainard Academy. He asked her to marry him."

His mother frowned. "Oh dear. I did not realize she was already betrothed."

"She isn't."

"Has she refused this professor? Then what are you waiting

for, Daire? I am serious. If you care for her, then you cannot let her get away."

"She has not refused him, but I know she will never accept him."

"You say this with such certainty. Why?"

"When the school term finished, she returned to Moonstone Landing to contemplate his offer and tend to other affairs," he replied. "Seems to me, if she needed to think this hard about his offer, then she ought to have declined immediately. But Brenna is soft hearted. I think she was trying to find a gentle way to tell him they were not suited. While she delayed, the oaf contacted her school's headmistress and told her that Brenna would not be returning next term because she was to be his wife."

Juliana gasped. "Oh dear. What an abominably presumptuous and arrogant thing to do."

"The headmistress, believing the churl, went ahead and replaced Brenna. I suppose this worked in my favor. She will never accept her professor now. I immediately offered her the position as governess to Matthew. Wisest decision I ever made."

"No, the wisest decision you make will be revealing your feelings to the girl. No one is stopping you but yourself."

He laughed. "Leap into a lifetime commitment upon one week's acquaintance? What has gotten into you? This rushing things is not like you at all, and it worries me."

Juliana reached for his hand. "My only thought is for your happiness. Do you have any idea how your eyes shine when you speak of her? Your father turned Morgan into a monster, and I could not save him. But I got to you in time. I know I did, Daire. You are not like them. You have a good heart, so do not be afraid to share it with Brenna. She will never hurt you."

"How do you know? How long have you known her? A day or two? I haven't known her that much longer. But she is soft and sweet, incapable of hurting anyone. The important question to ask is, will I hurt her? And I mean this in every sense. Will I break her heart? Will I physically beat her? Will I be faithless and shatter her spirit?"

"This I will answer with an emphatic no, to all of it. I know you, Daire. Perhaps better than you know yourself. I don't believe you capable of hurting her. Now, you must learn to believe in yourself." Juliana eased back in her chair and took a sip of her tea. "I've said whatever needed to be said. I won't press you further because you will turn stubborn and do the opposite thing."

He rose with a sigh. "I'm glad you have arrived, albeit early. I think you will settle in nicely here. Let me find Jax. He'll want to greet you before you leave for Westgate Hall. You'll like Lord Burness and his wife."

"If she is anything like her sister, Duchess Henley, I am sure I will."

He grinned. "Henley is gentle. Burness calls his Phoebe a little lioness, but you will like her very much. You'll meet their youngest sister tomorrow."

"Ah, Chloe. Yes, I've heard about her, too. You considered marrying her."

"A halfhearted consideration at best. I acted because I felt remorse for almost running her down with my phaeton. We were never in danger of falling in love with each other. She's a good soul, as are her sisters. News travels fast here, doesn't it?" He cast her a wry smile. "Is there anything you need? I can attend to it while you are paying your visit."

"No, not a thing. Brenna and Felicity have helped us organize the household. We've settled in quite well. Even Cook is liking it here. The fish is fresh, and so are the vegetables available at market. She and her scullery maids look forward to walking down to the harbor every morning. Mrs. Halsey's husband comes by in the early afternoon with the most delicious cakes and pies from the tea shop. I think we are quite well supplied."

He nodded. "Sounds like I am not needed at all."

"You are head of the household, Daire. Of course you are needed. Quite desperately by Matthew, only the boy doesn't know it yet. But go find Jax for me and tell him to come in and greet me properly. He always was one of your nicer friends. The others are just leeches. I thought your fast-set friends would be here with you."

"I sent them away. Grew tired of them."

"It is about time, Daire. I am happy to hear it."

He strode out and found Jax in the garden with Brenna, Felicity, and Matthew. "Jax," he said, curious as to what they were doing. "Mother is asking for you."

His friend nodded and immediately excused himself. "I'll be back shortly."

Daire knelt beside Brenna as they watched Felicity and Matthew till the soil. The boy had a small spade in hand and was mimicking Felicity's actions as she prepared the flowerbeds for their plants. "Strawberries are Matthew's favorite," Brenna said in a whisper, "so Felicity has set aside this little patch for Matthew to grow them himself."

"He seems to be enjoying the work."

"Because he does not view it as a chore. We thought it would be a good way to bolster his morale and learn he can create something out of nothing. He is going to help Felicity plant flowers, too. This boy needs to build happy memories in order to push out the bad ones that have dominated his early life."

Daire nodded.

As they watched Matthew at work, Daire's thoughts drifted back to Juliana's words about him standing in his own way. It was true. So why could he not move forward? Logically, it was too soon to ask Brenna to marry him. But would his opinion change in a month from now? Or a year?

He did not bother to answer his own questions. Nor could he toss caution to the wind, as Jax seemed able to do.

Yet he was falling in love with Brenna. Why lie to himself? Every time he saw her, she worked her way deeper into his soul. He could not look at her without his blood heating. His heart soared every time she smiled at him.

But to be sure this was love? Or that he could handle it if it proved to be love? That would take time and a willingness to give up control over his life, over his surroundings, dismantle the barricades that had sheltered him all these years—for Brenna would never be satisfied with anything less than a complete commitment from him.

He'd seen the damage his family had done to his brother. He still bore the scars of the damage to himself.

Right now, looking at Brenna and Matthew, he could not imagine ever hurting them. But what if he was wrong? What if there was a monster lurking inside him and determined to come out?

He had spent so much of his life behind a carefully crafted façade that he no longer knew who the real Daire Claymore was.

Brenna, unaware of his thoughts, smiled at him.

He could have sworn the sun came out from behind a cloud at just that moment, shining its rays on her so that she truly looked like an angel. Meanwhile, Felicity and Matthew were still happily digging away in the garden.

Was he being a fool? Making up reasons not to grab at the happiness that had so long eluded him?

AROUND NOONTIME, BRENNA and Matthew left the garden in order to prepare themselves for their visit to the home of Lord and Lady Burness. Daire strolled indoors to see how Simon Angel and his workmen were progressing.

"Moving along quite nicely, Your Grace," Simon responded with cheer, because these Angels were the most contented family Daire had ever met. "Let me know if you spot anything amiss."

"It is all very well done, as far as I can tell," Daire replied.

Since Juliana had also retreated to her quarters to ready herself for the Burness visit, Daire strolled back outside. He saw Jax beside Felicity, his coat off and sleeves rolled up as he assisted her with the heavier work that would have been done by Simon's men if not for Jax offering to do it himself.

Gad, was his friend truly serious about Felicity?

Jax stayed on at Stoningham Manor to assist Felicity as she worked on her garden designs. Daire simply shook his head and rode back to Moonstone Landing, stopping first at Bedwell's Mercantile in order to look for kites.

"Yes, Your Grace. You'll find them in the back corner. Let me show you," Mr. Bedwell said, leaving his other customers to wait while he led Daire through his shop.

Daire chose three kites, each of a different color. A red, a blue, and a yellow.

He was now eager to fly them with Matthew and Brenna, but this would have to wait until tomorrow afternoon, since she had already arranged a late-morning tour of the fort for the lad and then a treat afterward at Mrs. Halsey's tea shop.

Matthew would adore the day.

Perhaps Daire would hold off on the kite flying until after tomorrow. He was feeling greedy and wanted to spend an entire, uninterrupted day with Brenna and Matthew. Kites, a picnic, and anything else they cared to do.

He had no preference. He just wanted to be with them.

The afternoon invitation to the Burnesses' turned into a dinner invitation, since Matthew was having so much fun with Ella and Imogen. Thaddius knocked at the door of Daire's suite to deliver the invitation the marquess had sent for him and Jax. "This just arrived for you, Your Grace. The messenger is here and awaiting a response."

Daire read the invitation. "Let him know I have accepted on behalf of both of us. My friend is still up at the manor house. I had better go fetch him."

"Very good, Your Grace."

Daire had been working on the latest documents arrived from London pertaining to Claymore matters, but he set them aside to see what Jax was up to. He should not have left him alone at the manor with Felicity, but hopefully the presence of Simon and his crew were enough to keep Jax in line.

Then again, despite owning some of the most lucrative gaming hells in all of England, Jax was one of the most decent men Daire had ever met. He was all business and never dallied with the help. He was always discreet, and Daire had never known him to seduce innocents.

To his relief, Jax was still toiling away in the garden when he rode up. "Felicity, do you mind if I take your assistant away now? We have been invited to dine with Lord and Lady Burness."

"Not at all," she said, emitting a gentle laugh. "He's been a marvel. I could not have asked for a better worker."

Jax beamed with pride.

Felicity cast him a soft smile in return. "I'm well ahead of my schedule because of you. Thank you, my lord. It has been a pleasure."

He bowed but made no move to take hold of her hand, since his were covered in dirt. "The pleasure is all mine, Miss Angel. Same time tomorrow?"

She turned to glance in surprise at Daire, obviously uncertain what to say.

While Daire did not know what to make of his friend's behavior, he did not doubt his honor. "I certainly have no objections," he said, "if this is what my friend wishes."

Felicity cast Jax another smile. "Well, then. Yes, my lord. Same time tomorrow."

Daire was not one to meddle in another's business. But he had hired Felicity and Brenna, and now felt a duty to deliver another warning to his friend as they rode back to the inn. "Jax, what in bloody blazes are you doing?"

"Getting to know Felicity. Is this not what you insisted I do?"

"Just don't behave like a nitwit and hurt the girl."

"Hurt her?" Jax laughed. "Daire, do you not see I am already in love with her? I want to ride off this moment and secure the marriage license. The only reason I hesitate is because none of you, not even Felicity, will ever believe me if I were to propose. I'm sure she will club me over the head with her shovel. So, I will wait until she feels more comfortable around me. However, it does not diminish my feelings for her. That girl is a gem. Frankly, I do not understand how she is still unmarried. For that matter, Brenna too. There is something quite special about them."

Daire listened quietly as Jax continued spouting their virtues. He agreed with everything his friend said.

Thoughts of Brenna swamped him as they rode past the field of poppies toward the village.

Those poppies.

Why did they stir his heart every time he looked at them?

Jax drew his mount closer to Scipio as they rode, feeling the warm wind swirling around them. "Let me turn the tables on you, my friend. What in bloody blazes are you doing with Brenna? If anyone is likely to do any hurting, it is you, Daire. You do not get to have it both ways with a nice girl like her. I can see you care for her. You cannot contain your smile whenever you see her. So what's holding you back?"

First Juliana and now Jax getting on him? Was this what Daire was doomed to endure throughout the summer?

He knew he was the problem. But time was also a problem. A duke did not propose to a girl he'd met merely a week ago. Why were Jax and Juliana being so thick about it?

"Bah," Jax grumbled. "Go on, be stubborn. But I'm sure you fell in love with her within a minute of meeting her. You and I are alike in this way. We immediately know what we want. It is only a matter of figuring out how much we are willing to pay to acquire it."

"It? Doesn't Brenna deserve better than to be treated as an object? And doesn't she deserve to be kept safe? You know what my brother was. What if I turn out to be just like him?"

"First of all, you never were anything like him, or your father and grandfather before him. Nor will you ever be. You are no green boy just out of knee pants, either. Certainly your character is well formed by now. When have you ever raised a hand to a woman? Or to a child? When have you ever lost control of your temper?"

Daire said nothing, although he knew his friend was likely right.

"But it is all about control with you, isn't it? You cannot bring yourself to allow anyone else to hold power over you. Well, my friend, it is too late. Brenna already has that power, specifically over your heart."

Daire snorted.

"She does, so just admit it and seek your happiness with her. I am not suggesting you behave like me. I know I am an impulsive arse. But I trust my instincts. They have never failed me. Having met Felicity, I know I will never be happy without her. Simple as that. Is this how you feel about Brenna?"

"You've been toiling in the sun too long." Daire cut short their discussion, for he was irritated by everyone's meddling in his business.

Wasn't he already lecturing himself? And resisting the obvious conclusion—he had to marry Brenna or get out of her life completely.

But life without this lovely girl would be a barren existence for him.

Daire and Jax rode over to Westgate Hall in the early evening. Brenna, Juliana, and Matthew were there, all of them having a wonderful time. Matthew's cheeks were pink from the sun, and his shirt was pulled out of his breeches as he played spillikins in a quiet corner of the parlor with the girls.

Daire decided to leave the boy to his friends. In truth, he was worried Matthew would withdraw inside himself the moment he noticed his uncle had arrived. But the lad was lost in the game with Ella and Imogen, who were fussing over him like a pair of mother hens.

Was this not exactly what the boy needed?

Daire greeted Burness and his wife warmly and introduced them to Jax.

To Daire's relief, the children were to be taken upstairs to the nursery quarters and fed there, along with Burness's twin boys, who the marquess claimed were little terrors and could not be set loose in decent company.

Phoebe laughed. "It is not so. They are wonderful boys. They helped Matthew, Ella, and Imogen build sandcastles on the beach until it was time for their nap. They all had a wonderful afternoon."

"We will happily return the invitation as soon as Stoningham Manor is put in order," Daire said. "Bringing Matthew to Moonstone Landing is the best thing I could have done."

Brenna agreed and then excused herself to follow the children out, but Daire stopped her. "Are you not dining with us?"

Lady Phoebe nodded. "Yes, Brenna. Do not be ridiculous."

"But I am the boy's governess. Is it not right that I should attend to him?" The blush on Brenna's cheeks said it all. She was the only one present without a title, and obviously felt the class difference acutely.

Daire growled. "He will be fine with Burness's nieces and his little boys."

Burness nodded. "We have two governesses up there already. Not to mention Ella and Imogen are going to fuss over him, too. He will not even notice your absence."

Daire smiled. "So you see, it is all in order. Join us, Miss Angel."

He knew it was brazen of him to demand it, especially after all the protestations he'd made when pressed on the matter of his feelings for Brenna by Jax and Juliana. He would not have said anything were it not obvious Burness and his wife felt the same and wanted her at their table.

Lady Phoebe took her by the arm and led her into the dining room. "As you can see, we included you in our count. I am not having the place setting taken away. Besides, you will completely throw off our numbers if you take your meal in the nursery. With you, we are a balanced table. Three men. Three ladies."

Brenna blushed, her discomfort still obvious. "All right."

Juliana cast Daire a disapproving look. It wasn't that she disapproved of Brenna. She disapproved of his stalling to do what was right.

Bollocks.

Was no one ever going to let up on him? No matter what anyone said, he was not about to bare his heart to a girl he'd known less than a week. It did not matter that he felt as though he had known her forever. Time was important. Actual days, weeks, months.

Why was Juliana rushing him? Was there something going on with her that he ought to know about? She had looked a little wan. Perhaps it was more than travel fatigue.

He would pursue the matter later.

Since they were only six in the party, the Burnesses had chosen to use what they called their winter dining room, which was small and cozy. Brenna was seated across from him and beside Jax. The marquess and his wife sat at opposite ends of the table, while Juliana was seated beside Daire.

By the time the soup course was served, everyone was on a first-name basis.

"Daire," Cormac, the marquess, said, "give the boy time to heal. He will come around to it, especially with Brenna's guidance."

Phoebe nodded. "It took Cormac three years after he lost his arm, and he was a grown man. Although I think children heal much faster. I noticed that horrid welt on his chest. He told Brenna that his former governess had hit him."

"Those on his back were done by his father and mother," Juliana added, pain etched in her features. "The boy was so badly bruised when Daire found him and brought him home. I do not understand how people can be so cruel."

"Nor do I," Jax said. "But we three men faced barbarity almost daily on the battlefield. Perhaps life is meant to be cruel and we must grab our happiness wherever we can find it."

Daire shot him a look.

He wasn't going to mention Felicity, was he?

Jax said nothing more.

Conversation turned to Juliana's plans for the next few days. She smiled toward Brenna. "Phoebe, tomorrow we shall be with your sister and her husband, as I am sure the entire village already knows."

Phoebe laughed. "Oh, yes. Our gossip lines operate with military precision. Chloe and Fionn are very much looking forward to it."

"The day after tomorrow will be a day of leisure, I expect. The house won't be ready yet for visitors, but perhaps by next week."

"I've purchased a kite for Matthew," Daire said. "I hope to spend some time over the next few days showing him how to fly it."

Brenna smiled in approval. "He will enjoy it much more than he will his school lessons."

Daire smiled back at her. "You'll come along, of course."

She nodded. "Of course. I take my job as his governess quite seriously. Does it not warm your heart every time you hear him laughing?"

"You have no idea," he said, trying to keep the anger out of his voice. "I am still shaking my head over the miracle you have accomplished in this short a time. I did not think it possible for the lad ever to feel any joy."

Brenna set down her fork, having hardly touched her fish course. "The joy is always there within children. It takes so little to bring it out. A kind word. A compliment. A squeeze of their hand. A moment to listen to what they have to say. And yet it is not something that ever happens for many of them."

"Well," Cormac said, "speaking as an adult who managed to botch countless years of his own life behaving like an arrogant, temperamental child, it is a good thing there are wise women like you and my wife in the world, or else there would be no hope for any of us."

Jax raised his cup of wine. "Hear, hear."

They all raised their glasses in cheer.

BRENNA WENT UPSTAIRS with Phoebe to fetch Matthew once the evening had come to an end. Daire and Jax escorted them and Juliana to Stoningham Manor before they headed back to the inn.

Once back at the inn, the two of them shared a bottle of port in Daire's suite and reminisced about old times before each retired to their quarters for the night.

By morning, Jax had awakened early and was already up at the manor house by the time Daire finished going through his morning pile of documents. Once done responding to the most important ones, he strode to the dining room. "Thaddius, when did my friend ride up to the manor?" he asked, encountering Brenna's cousin in the hall.

"Oh, quite early. No later than seven o'clock this morning, I would say. But Felicity rides up there with Uncle Simon, and he likes to start early. Lord Bradford mentioned something about helping Felicity move rocks."

"Rocks?" Daire shook his head. "What rocks? Never mind. I'll see for myself."

He was also eager to see Brenna. Mere hours had passed since he had last been in her company, and yet he was already missing her.

To his surprise, he noticed her walking across the poppy field when he rode up. She waved to him and smiled. "Good morning, Your Grace."

"Daire," he said, dismounting and leaving Scipio to nibble on the sweet grass at the edge of the road. "I thought we had resolved last night to call each other by our given names."

"Well, that was last night. I did not really belong at the table."

"That is utter nonsense. Do not forget Matthew called you a fairy princess. So, you see? A princess ranks above everyone, even a duke."

"I shall remember this next time I put on my fairy wings," she said with a soft laugh.

He joined her in walking across the field, having no idea where she was going and not particularly caring so long as he was beside her. "Where is the boy now?"

"Assisting Felicity and Jax." She frowned lightly. "I know I have asked this before, but is he truly besotted with my cousin? Can he be trusted?"

"Yes, Brenna. He's quite serious about her. If anything, I am the one holding him back. He's chosen well, mind you. I like Felicity. But how can one know anything about a person in less than a day?"

She nodded. "I agree. One must be sensible about these things. Especially men in your position, titled and wealthy, who have only to tip their head and women will come running."

Daire paused amid the sea of red petals. "There haven't been women for either of us, Brenna. Jax is serious, and so am I."

"What are you serious about, Your Grace?"

"Daire." He took her gently by the shoulders. "Not *what*, but *who*. You, of course. Have I not been clear about it?"

"Actually, you have not. In truth, you constantly leave me in confusion." She surprised him by drawing out of his grasp. "Is this some game you two are now playing? Lord Bradford intent on seducing Felicity and your having set your trap for me? Do you think we are easy marks because we are approaching spinsterhood? Let me assure you, Felicity and I are not sad, desperately unhappy women. We are quite content with our lot."

"The thought never crossed my mind. You are both too beautiful and clever, and have likely been fending off beaus for years. As for me and Jax, if you consider marriage a trap, then yes, we have set our traps for you and Felicity."

She regarded him warily. "Marriage? You are suggesting this is not a game for either of you?"

"I did not think I had been particularly secretive about my intentions. I'm sure the entire village is waiting for me to say something to you."

Her expression softened. "Are you saying it now?"

Daire swallowed hard. "I hadn't intended to."

Her smile faltered. "I see."

"No, I don't think you do. Blast it, Brenna. I did not intend to have this conversation with you at this time."

"I understand. A man in your position… A girl in mine. How can it ever be right?"

"That's just it—it can be. Everything already feels easy and natural with you. Give me time, will you? I'm fairly certain I already know where my heart will lead me. But as you've acknowledged, I am a duke, and a wealthy one at that. No, it is coming out all wrong. You never cared about my wealth or title. You sought to know me. But I am a mess inside."

"Yes, I know," she said, her smile returning as they walked on through the field. "I care about you, as you have probably guessed. Very much. As you said, it is not because of your title or the careless way you toss your coins about. Actually, I find this spendthrift habit of yours quite irritating."

He laughed. "It gets me what I want, and I can easily afford it. I am not a spendthrift. How can I be when I know exactly where every farthing is spent? I am fully aware and completely in control of why and where each coin goes."

"Daire," she said softly. "Is this not exactly the problem? In truth, I am worried about you."

He arched an eyebrow in surprise. "Why are you worried?"

"Seeing Matthew has helped me to understand you better."

"Is that so?" His heart began to beat faster. He was not certain he was ready to have her probe so deeply into his soul. But was this not Brenna? Inquisitive, determined, and compassionate to a fault? She wanted to love him and to save him.

Did he not need saving?

She nodded. "Yes, quite so. He is a little boy and therefore has not learned to hide his fears. They are open to be seen by all. But you, as a man, have learned to hide yours very well. You are completely Matthew on the inside."

He growled. "I do not have fears."

"Everyone does, and you are no exception. You are afraid to ever let anyone into your heart because those who should have loved you and protected you were the very ones who always hurt you. Were you raised as cruelly? Never mind, I know the answer."

"What has Juliana told you?"

She cast him a wry smile. "Probably too much, to your way of thinking. She agonizes over you and still regrets being unable to save your brother. It haunts her to this day."

"There was nothing she could do about Morgan then, and there is nothing she can do about him now. My brother is dead. He could have saved himself at one time, but he did not. He could have treated Matthew decently, but he did not. Do not waste a tear over my brother. He was never worth it."

She gave him a worried look. "You think you are like him, don't you?"

"We are of the same blood. We received the same beatings from the same father. We look so much alike that Matthew cannot look at me without thinking I am his father come to beat him again. How are we different?"

"Your strength and spirit were never the same. You were always stronger, Daire. You were always kinder."

How could she know? How could she trust him not to become the monster his father and brother had been?

He raked a hand through his hair. "Brenna, I am not having this conversation with you."

She looked up at him with gentle eyes. "Perhaps at a later time, then."

He grunted. "No."

Having made clear there was to be no more discussion about him, he changed the topic. "Where are you walking?"

"Nowhere in particular. I just like to wander through this field of poppies."

"There's something about them. I'm drawn to them too. I don't know why."

"I think I do."

He groaned. "Gad, are you always going to have an opinion on everything?"

But he spoke with gentle teasing, for he was more curious than annoyed. He was also quite a bit amused that she, a complete innocent, had answers for everything.

She cast him a heartfelt smile. "No, not on everything. However, I do tend to think a lot, and I am determined to figure you out. Do you mind?"

"Do I have a choice?" he asked.

"I suppose not, for you cannot stop me from thinking about you. For many, a field of red poppies represents death. Blood. But it also represents peace. Perhaps a peace found in death. But also simply peace. I think this is what you see whenever you look across this field. Peace. Release. Freedom from your agony. It is a field of hope for you. A field where you can escape into your dreams. Good dreams, not the nightmares that probably haunted your childhood and perhaps plague your adult life, too."

She pointed toward the sea. "Just look at this view... The water, blue and glistening. The sky, an even deeper blue and dotted with white clouds. The sweet grass, a deep, vibrant green. And those poppies. Bright red and swaying in the breeze. One feels transported to an idyllic place."

"Go on."

"You are in another world here, a world where you can forget your pain and open your heart to new possibilities, allow yourself the happiness you seem determined to deny yourself. This is the essence of the problem, isn't it? You don't know what happiness feels like, nor are you certain you deserve it.”

“Ah, Brenna. I had no idea you were such a philosopher.”

She frowned. “Please, do not mock me. I could not bear it from you. This is what Albert and his professor friends did to me. What makes any of you wiser? Why can I not think about things and wonder what might be? Who says men are the only ones capable of higher reasoning?”

“Forgive me, little dove. I was not mocking you or condescending to you.” He took her gently by the shoulders and turned her to face him. “Everything you have said is true. But so what? I do not live in a world of dreams. I go by hard facts. Knowing what I am will not necessarily change me. Knowing it and being able to do something about it are quite separate things.”

“But that’s just it. I don’t think you know yourself. You have convinced yourself that you are a horrible monster like your brother. It isn’t true.”

“Are you sure? Because I am not sure of this at all. Enjoying a field of poppies will not fix the darkness in me. Yes, it will soothe me for a while. But what if I become angry? What if I ever raised a hand to you?” He shook his head and tried to ignore the pain in his heart. “Looking at flowers is not going to cure me. Do not be naïve.”

“And you ought to stop being a stubborn dolt.” She gave him a tender frown, if there was such a thing. But this was Brenna, irritated with him and also wanting to hug him and love him. “You would die before ever hurting me.”

“Brenna,” he whispered, drawing her into his arms. “Matthew was treated like a little beast. Those marks on Matthew… I have the same across my back. Put there by my father. You did not see them when I had my shirt off because I was always careful to face you. They are not only etched in my skin but in my soul.”

“I’m so sorry you had to endure this, Daire.” She placed a hand to his cheek and gently stroked it.

“I adapted to survive. I adapted by remaining numb as I was beaten. I have continued to survive by remaining numb to everything I face as an adult."

"So you approach everything with logic and detachment?"

"Yes, it helped particularly to get me through the war. This is how I now deal with those in Society. With business affairs regarding the Claymore estate. This is how I deal with cheats and liars, coldly cutting them off at the knees."

"And you think you can deal with a loved one in this way?"

He drew her closer and rested his forehead against hers. "I don't know how to deal with a loved one, little dove. I don't know how to deal with you. You turn my feelings upside down. I cannot think straight around you. I cannot breathe when I am around you."

"I suffocate you?"

He chuckled. "No, you simply take my breath away. Brenna, I crave you. I crave you and I fear to hurt you. Meeting you has been the best thing for me, and also the worst. What will I do to you if ever we disagree?"

"Haven't we disagreed on things already?"

"No, little dove. We haven't yet, but it is inevitable we will fight about something at some point. Do I let you win? Will I seethe with resentment afterward? Will I beat you?"

"Oh, Daire. You are looking at it all wrong." She wrapped her arms around his neck. Her body was so soft and warm pressed to his.

"How am I looking at this wrong?"

"If you loved me, you would not care who won or lost. You would not look at our differences of opinion as combat postures. We would listen to each other and come up with a compromise together."

"And if we could not?"

"Then one of us would give in. Even if we both stubbornly held to our ground, you would never hurt me. You are not capable of this. Your heart is too good. Just ask Juliana—she knows." She looked up at him, and he wanted to kiss her into eternity.

She sighed as his lips hovered over hers. "Daire, this is the way love works. We willingly sacrifice to make the other happy. Yes, one of us is likely to sacrifice more. It is rarely an even balance."

"Are you going to keep talking, Brenna?"

She smiled up at him. "Do you wish me to keep talking?"

He laughed. "No, you lovely, opinionated, bossy bit of goods. I want to kiss you until we are both in flames. I want to lose myself in you."

"Lose yourself in me?"

Gad, she was so innocent. She did not know what this meant.

To be inside her.

To make her howl with pleasure.

Scream his name.

"I'll explain it to you another time. Just know that I will not take you outside of marriage, although my body has not stopped aching to know yours since the day I met you."

"Outside of marriage?"

"Do you think there can ever be anyone else for me?" He did not wait for an answer, but lowered his head to hers and kissed her with all the passion she had stirred in him. Molten heat poured over him like lava. He covered her mouth with his, aching to possess her, conquer her, gain her surrender. Earn her love.

She was so sweet. Her lips tasted like honey. He dipped his tongue inside her mouth, probing the velvet warmth, tasting tea and strawberries.

"Brenna, my little dove," he whispered, lifting her up against him and shuddering as her beautiful, softly rounded breasts pressed against his hard chest.

He wanted to be inside of her and delve into her soul.

She responded with innocent ardor, her mouth soft and welcoming, her tongue hesitantly matching his thrusts.

"Brenna, what am I to do with you?" he asked, tearing his lips from hers. "My smart-mouthed governess. My fairy princess."

She still had her arms wrapped around his neck and was trying to draw him closer still. She met the heat of his mouth again
and again. After a moment, she let out a soft cry. "Oh, Daire. Let
me go. What have we done? What are we doing to each other?"

Chapter Thirteen

HOW HAD IT suddenly come to this? Had they fallen in love with each other? To what end?

This was so much worse than dealing with Albert's marriage proposal.

Brenna and Albert had known each other a full year before he proposed. She'd known Daire a mere week and was already lost to him.

But his fear of ever loving because of his cruel upbringing was a barrier that stood between them, and no amount of kisses would convince him otherwise.

His rank was also an enormous barrier, although he did not appear to find it as important as she did.

Was it possible he and his friend Jax, with respect to Felicity, were willing to ignore the demands placed on them by their titles and marry commoners? They might have gotten away with it if she and Felicity were heiresses.

But they weren't.

Of greatest concern were her lingering doubts. Was she ready to believe that Daire cared for her? He had every reason to seduce her, pretend to court her. He wanted Stoningham Manor. Was this his way of tricking her out of it? And had he brought his friend in on the ruse? Pretending to court two spinsters. Lulling everyone into complacency.

Well, he had not attempted to lure her into his bed, although he claimed to crave her body. Perhaps her doubts about Daire's feelings for her would resolve in time.

But this fear of his, this worry he had a monster lurking within him, was quite real. She saw the worry in his eyes and the genuine fear in Matthew.

How was she to convince Daire that he did not have a cruel heart?

He needed time, just as he had said. He needed people not to push him and dismiss his fears as groundless.

She ran back to the house, leaving him alone in the field of poppies.

In any event, she had to ready Matthew for their excursion into town. He would enjoy the tour of Fort Arundel and the new hospital built to take in the overflow of wounded soldiers from Plymouth.

Once she and Matthew were ready, she knocked at Duchess Juliana's door. The duchess's lady's maid opened the door.

The room was dark, and it took Brenna a moment for her eyes to adjust to the lack of light. "Oh, my dear," Juliana said, her voice sounding weak as she lay burrowed under her covers. "Please convey my apologies to Viscount Brennan. But do go on ahead with Matthew. He is so looking forward to the tour."

"Very well, Your Grace. Is there anything I can do for you?"

"No, dear. I shall be fine. A little too much sun yesterday, I fear. It has brought on a megrim. I have these often."

Brenna did not know whether to summon Daire, but decided to leave it alone for now. She would send word if Juliana took a turn for the worse. "Very well."

As expected, Matthew was quite fascinated by the fort and soldiers, his smile broad and eyes gleaming as the fort commander, Fionn Brennan, showed them around.

Afterward, he escorted them to Mrs. Halsey's tea shop, where they met his wife, Chloe, and the four of them had tea and cakes together.

Matthew chatted with Viscount Brennan, excitedly asking question after question about the ancient fort and the life of a soldier. "This is what I want to be," the boy declared. "Or I might be a gardener. I'm growing strawberries."

The viscount was duly impressed. "We have a small garden beside the hospital. Did you notice it, Matthew? Would you like to plant strawberries there? I'm not sure the soil is rich enough or if there is enough sunlight. I am not good with matters of gardening. But I would be grateful if you tried."

Matthew was overjoyed. "Yes! Miss Brenna, is that all right?"

He had taken to calling her by that name and Felicity as Miss Felicity to distinguish them, since they both had the family name of Angel. Brenna heartily approved of the idea. "That will be a fun project. Give us a couple of days to get our plants and proper soil and supplies gathered."

By the time they parted ways with the viscount and his wife, Matthew was floating like a bird in the air. Brenna took a moment to thank the viscount profusely. "Just look at him. Have you ever seen a happier child?"

"I know what his life must have been like, having lived through similar. It is worth everything to see his smile."

Chloe was equally gracious. "We will have you all over to Moonstone Cottage soon," she promised. "Please let us know if there is anything we can do for Duchess Juliana."

"I will." Brenna thanked them again and walked off with Matthew.

Daire happened to be coming out of the inn as they strolled by. The boy immediately stopped smiling and ducked behind Brenna. "Matthew, he is not your father. Your Uncle Daire loves you. Has he not been nice to you?"

The lad nodded, but still was not convinced to trust him.

She saw the pain etched on Daire's face the moment he noticed them and saw his nephew already hiding behind her gown.

How awful the men in his family must have been to damage him and Matthew as they had. Despite her disappointing conversation with him, she knew Daire was struggling to overcome the hurt he had endured.

Was it truly because he wanted to marry her?

She dared not hope or think about it. Just because her cousin Cara had found love, that did not mean she had a chance at the same happiness. This remained an improbable outcome for her. Perhaps less improbable for Felicity, because the Earl of Bradford, unless he was a consummate actor and had taken them all in, seemed not to care a whit for Society's rules. Nor did he have Daire's concerns about a monster hidden within his soul.

But Daire? He had spent so many years in a very, very dark place and grown quite adept at hiding his misery.

Instead of fretting about what might or might not be between them, Brenna put her thoughts toward establishing a relationship between Daire and Matthew. How was she to fix these broken Claymore men?

"Good afternoon, Your Grace," she said, putting on a bright smile.

"You seem to have enjoyed your time with Viscount Brennan and his wife." Daire knelt to address Matthew. "Did you have fun touring the fort?"

The lad nodded, but would not look him in the eyes.

"What was the most fun thing you saw, Matthew?" Daire asked.

The boy was too scared to answer.

Daire rose with a sigh.

"I'm sorry," Brenna said softly.

He shook his head. "Early days, yet. I'll keep trying. You haven't forgotten our kite-flying outing tomorrow, have you?"

Brenna gave Matthew's chin a little tweak. "Kite flying, Matthew. We are going to have so much fun. I'll pack us a picnic basket and we'll make an afternoon of it."

Daire began to walk along with them as they started toward Stoningham Manor. "How is my mother, by the way? I see she did not join you."

"She had a megrim and sent her regrets. I suggested calling for the doctor, but she dismissed the idea rather forcefully and insisted I take Matthew on his outing. Is she all right, do you think? I mean, other than these occasional headaches?"

He shook his head. "I don't know. She isn't all that much older than me—about a fifteen-year gap in our ages. But she seems frail, doesn't she?"

Brenna nodded. "I'll check on her when we return and send for Dr. Hewitt if she is not feeling any better."

Daire lightly touched her forehead. "What about you? When is he taking out your stitches?"

"Oh, a few more days yet. He said they must stay in a full week. But it shouldn't hurt or take very long to take them out. I think the cut is healing quite nicely. It does not bother me at all. I haven't required laudanum since that very first day."

"Will removing your stitches take place in his infirmary? What time? I'll meet you there and hold your hand while he takes them out."

She arched an eyebrow. "Daire, that is hardly necessary."

"I know. I want to be there for you." He gave a pained laugh. "And yet I've been such an arse holding you off. Honestly, Brenna. I don't know what I am waiting for."

"I do," she said softly, motioning toward Matthew, who still had his head buried against her gown. "He shows it outwardly, but is this not you on the inside? He'll come out of it in time, and so will you."

Daire shrugged.

"I have an idea that I would like to put past you. I'll tell you more about it when we meet tomorrow to fly our kites."

"Why not tell me now? I'm intrigued," he said as they slowly walked up the high street toward the edge of town.

She shook her head. "Not yet. I have to think it through."

"All right, little dove." He escorted them up the hill to Stoningham Manor.

Brenna never tired of the magnificent view no matter the hour of the day. She knew Daire felt the same.

Matthew was exhausted from his excursion and the walk back home. Brenna helped him wash up and then tucked him in bed for a nap while Daire went to see how his mother was faring.

They met in the parlor thirty minutes later. "How is Duchess Juliana?" Brenna asked, noting his furrowed brow.

"She insists that she is fine. Simply a megrim. But I'm not sure. I am beginning to think she hurried out here ten days early for a reason."

Brenna began to fret her lip. "Shall I have one of the footmen summon Dr. Hewitt now?"

"Let's leave it for tomorrow. She insists she will be fully recovered by morning. Honestly, I cannot see anything wrong with her other than she looks a little pale. But that could also be a trick of the light. What do I know?"

"I'll keep an eye on her," Brenna assured him. "I expect to have an easy night. Matthew will spend the evening playing with his tin soldiers, I'm sure. He'll fall asleep with very little difficulty tonight even if he manages a solid nap."

"Summon me at the inn if you need anything. I'll be around, just finishing off the last of my work. I received a full pouch this morning, and it has taken me much of the day to get through the most pressing matters. If I can tear Jax away from your cousin," he said with a wry smile, "I'll share a late supper with him and a glass of port before retiring."

"Sounds awfully dull, Your Grace," she teased.

"Well, I could scrap all plans with Jax and simply do what I've wanted to do since the first moment I met you, but you will slap me if I go into elaborate detail. Can't have you tearing out and tumbling over tea carts, can we?"

She lightly patted the spot of her stitches. "Oh, don't remind me."

But Brenna smiled at him because she was not really overset that he found her attractive. Not that she would make too much of it, because she dared not believe he could have eyes only for her when there were several more beautiful women in town who would appeal to him, not to mention the *ton* beauties he encountered in London.

Just as he had his doubts, she had a few of her own.

He was ruthless, by his own admission. He knew how to kiss a woman to gain what he wanted. He certainly wanted something from her.

Hadn't Thaddius warned her that Daire was circling her like a lion? But did he just want her home? Or did he want her?

In her heart, she knew he was not using her. Daire genuinely liked her. He treated her well and respected her opinions. He did not spout trite flattery.

In fact, he was deathly afraid of ever admitting he might be in love with her.

Why did love have to be so complicated? Why did it have to be so confusing?

"I have learned my lesson," she said with a soft laugh. "I will not run off like a goose and tumble over tea carts just because you toss a saucy remark. I shall take it in stride and simply thank you for thinking I am pretty enough for you to take notice."

He groaned. "Pretty enough? There is no one more beautiful than you, Brenna. All I want to do is kiss you."

"Again?"

He chuckled. "Again and always."

She noted the heat in his eyes, but had no time to respond because Matthew suddenly came hopping in and interrupted their conversation. "I'm hungry, Miss Brenna."

"Matthew, how is it possible? We just finished an entire lemon cake at Mrs. Halsey's tea shop." But she smiled at the boy and took his hand. "Oh, very well. Since it seems you are not going to take a nap, let's see what Cook has prepared for us. Your Grace, will you be staying for supper?"

"I'm not sure yet. I'll reserve my answer until I see Juliana again. I'll give it another hour before I look in on her."

Daire remained with Brenna while she attended to his very hungry nephew. They sat with the boy on the terrace, since her uncle's men were working indoors and stirring up quite a bit of dust throughout the main floor. Felicity and Jax had finished their gardening for the day, and joined them for lemonade and more cakes while Matthew continued to dig into his plate of hearty stew.

"How was your outing, Matthew?" Jax asked.

The boy smiled. "I saw soldiers and an old fort and ships in the harbor. Tomorrow, Uncle Daire and Miss Brenna are going to take me to fly a kite. We're going to have a picnic, too."

Brenna looked on in surprise. The boy had been listening, after all. He had even mentioned his uncle by name. Was he getting over his fear of Daire?

"We are going to weed the flowerbeds tomorrow," Felicity said with cheer.

Jax laughed. "What fun. I cannot wait."

Since Jax seemed to be occupying Matthew, Daire took the opportunity to slip away to look in on Juliana. Brenna knew he was concerned about his mother. She felt the same. Perhaps they were both overreacting, but Brenna sensed this lovely woman was not suffering merely from a megrim.

Daire returned a few minutes later, settling in the chair beside Brenna's but ever careful not to get too close to Matthew and upset the boy.

"How is she?" Brenna asked.

"Same. Claims she is feeling much better. I don't think she is."

Brenna nibbled her lip. "Then is it time to summon Dr. Hewitt?"

"I left instruction for her lady's maid to report to you immediately if she takes a turn for the worse. If she passes a peaceful night, I'll look in on her tomorrow morning and decide what to do then. The doctor will be summoned if she shows no improvement." He looked around. "Your uncle and his crew are packing up for the day."

Jax reached out and took Felicity's hand. "If you wish to stay longer, Daire and I can escort you home later."

She shook her head and rose. "No, I'll see you all tomorrow. I enjoy the work immensely, but it is physically strenuous and tires me out."

Jax rose along with her. "I'll ride up early tomorrow to help you."

"All right." Felicity cast him a soft smile.

Daire stared at his friend, but said nothing.

Brenna wondered what Daire was thinking. What were *both* these men thinking?

Matthew had now finished his stew, so Brenna bade both men a good evening and went upstairs with the boy to ready him for bed. It was early yet, but he needed to wash up and play with his soldiers, and then Brenna was going to read to him.

She peered from the nursery window an hour later and saw the two men striding down the lane toward Moonstone Landing. The house suddenly fell quiet, even though there was a full staff.

Later that night, shortly before retiring to bed herself, Brenna sought out Duchess Juliana's lady's maid. "Oh, Miss Brenna. I don't know. She has slept all day and not eaten a thing. She could barely hold down her tea. I added honey to it to thicken it a little. She ate none of Cook's stew."

The stew had been delicious, which added to Brenna's concern. Perhaps Daire ought to have called for the doctor.

When she mentioned it to Juliana's maid, the girl shook her head. "No, Miss Brenna. Give it until tomorrow. She's had these episodes before. A little more frequently lately, but I'm hoping the fresh country air will clear out her lungs and have her feeling better in no time."

To Brenna's relief, Daire's mother did appear much better the following day. She came down in time to join her and Matthew for breakfast on the terrace, and seemed quite comfortable as she watched Brenna and Matthew toss around a ball on the grass afterward.

Daire arrived by late morning and went straight over to Juliana. "How are you doing, darling?" He gave her a light kiss on the forehead.

"I am in the pink, my boy. Do take Matthew and Brenna on your outing. He will never tell you, but he is excited to learn how to fly a kite. Cook prepared a picnic basket for you. Daire, why are you still frowning at me?"

"I am concerned for you."

"Well, don't be. You must stop frowning. I'll have Betty bring out my embroidery, and Jax and Felicity will keep me company should it become necessary while you are off on your adventure."

"All right. But you must tell Jax at once if you do not feel well. Will you promise me?"

Juliana nodded. "I will."

Brenna had been listening in on the exchange and now took Matthew's hand to walk over to Daire.

He cast her a soft smile. "Ready to fly kites?"

She nodded.

Matthew surprised them by addressing Daire directly. "I'm ready, too."

Daire let out a soft breath. "I'm glad, Matthew. We will have fun."

They walked into the kitchen to retrieve the picnic basket, which Daire hauled over his massive shoulder. She and Matthew carried the kites and a blanket for them to sit on while they ate. The head butler had asked if he ought to set up chairs and a table for them in the field beneath a shade tree, but Brenna did not want the formality. "Blanket will do, Mr. Greggson." She wanted Daire and Matthew to stretch out and look up at the sky, comment on the shapes of clouds, set aside their anguish.

The picnic basket and blanket were placed under a nearby shade tree while Daire prepared their kites and showed her and Matthew how to get them in the air. It was not long before she and Matthew were laughing and running through the poppy field, while their kites caught the wind to soar above them.

Matthew had chosen the yellow one, while Brenna had taken the red. This left the blue one for Daire. After helping them get their kites in the air, Daire joined in, his expression lighter than she had ever seen before.

It was not long afterward that Brenna's kite got tangled in the trees and ripped. "Oh, no. Daire, I think I've broken it."

He strode over and gave her his while he climbed the tree to retrieve hers. "Yes, it's torn," he called down to her from a high branch. "I'll see if Mr. Bedwell can have it mended. Use mine in the meanwhile, Brenna."

Matthew looked on in surprise. "He didn't yell at you."

"Nor would he yell at you had it been yours that got ripped, Matthew. Accidents happen."

Daire hopped down from the tree. "Shall I help you get the kites flying again?"

Matthew shook his head. "I can do it, Uncle Daire. Look." He then ran off through the field, cheering as his kite caught the breeze and soared.

"Blessed saints," Daire said in wonder. "Did you hear what he just said?"

"Yes. Isn't it marvelous?" Brenna watched the boy, his little head bobbing as he ran. "I think I ought to sit this one out. Why don't you take your kite and join your nephew?"

"I'd rather have my arms around you as I pretend to care about helping you make that kite soar." Daire sighed when she tossed him a stubborn look. "All right, I'll go play with Matthew."

"He called you Uncle Daire and wanted to show you his

accomplishment. Is that not amazing?"

"Yes, did I not just say this very thing? Brenna, I am sincerely cheering this breakthrough. However, I still want to hold you in my arms. Even more so because you are the one responsible for making this day happen."

"Remember when I told you I had a plan?"

He nodded. "You mentioned something yesterday. What did you have in mind?"

She kept her eyes on Matthew as he tore back and forth across the field, his heart as light as the butterflies flitting along the flowers. "We each have a fear. Mine is water. Matthew's is fear of getting beaten. Yours is fear that you will turn into a monster and beat him…or beat me. You never will, Daire. That cruelty isn't in you. But we are not going to think about it today. We shall start tomorrow, weather permitting."

He arched an eyebrow. "Start what?"

"Overcoming our fears."

He groaned. "You are not my governess. I have no intention of becoming one of your students."

She folded her arms across her chest. "Fine, then we'll start with me. I'll be your student. You are going to teach me to swim."

"Brenna," he said with a soft ache to his voice. "Truly?"

She nodded. "I don't want to be afraid of the water. It is long past time I conquered my fear, especially since Matthew also wants to learn how to swim. Felicity cannot be with us all the time. She went through the same ordeal as I did, and yet she is not afraid. So why am I still so cowardly? I have to stop holding myself back. It is time. Don't you agree? Will you teach me?"

"You do realize it is highly inappropriate for us to swim together? One might say it would compromise you if ever we were caught."

Her heart sank. "Oh… You're right. I did not think of it that way. I should have, of course."

He caressed her cheek. "I'll teach you, little dove. I will also step up and do the honorable thing if ever we are found out. Never doubt it."

"I don't doubt it, Daire. I know you are honorable. But I'll ask Felicity to help me once she finishes the landscaping job. It was never my intention to trap you."

"I know." He gave her cheek another light caress. "Nor could you trap me, unless I wished to be caught. Do not bring Felicity into this. I am going to teach you."

"No matter the consequences? That sounds awful."

He emitted a heavy sigh. "No, it sounds wonderful. Surely you cannot doubt…there is no one else for me. I know I have not made my feelings clear enough. Well, I never had doubt about my feelings for you. But can a monster ever truly be in love?"

She wanted to scream that he wasn't a monster, and yes, he could be in love. Who else could ever make her happy? But he would not listen to anyone telling him what to think or feel. He had to come to the realization himself.

He slapped his hands on his thighs. "I had better see to Matthew."

Brenna's head was still a whirl of confusion as she set out their picnic fare while Matthew and Daire flew their kites. She watched them run back and forth for several minutes more until calling them over. The pair hurried back and sank onto the blanket quite exhilarated and hungry. Brenna thought Cook had overstocked their basket, but the chicken, ham, apples, cheese, and bread were all devoured within minutes. Since tearing across fields was thirsty work, the lemonade and ale were also polished off with due efficiency.

Brenna laughed. "I don't think there is so much as a crumb to be found on our plates."

The two Claymore men then stretched out on the blanket to study the clouds. "I see a bear," Daire said, pointing to a cluster of tufted clouds.

"I see a hawk," Matthew said, scrambling closer to his uncle and pointing to a wispy string of clouds toward the horizon.

Brenna's heart filled with happiness.

She held her breath and simply watched nephew and uncle as they played their game. Daire was so gentle and patient with the boy.

"No rain tomorrow," she whispered, praying for another beautiful day such as this one. She was serious about getting over her fear of water. It was important that both Claymores saw her do it, because they needed her to set the example and prove it was possible to get over one's fears, although she did not want Matthew there for her first attempt, which could very well go awry because she was a coward.

She smiled again, watching those two.

Matthew appeared to be well on his way toward healing. He was laughing at Daire's jests and talking to him without hesitation.

After finishing their cloud game, Daire and the boy flew their kites again.

Daire helped Matthew untangle his kite string when it got caught in a row of gorse bushes. Brenna sighed, knowing she was falling even more deeply in love with Daire as he knelt beside Matthew and the two of them worked on unraveling the knotted string together.

The lad ran across the poppy field cheering like a Pictish warrior once his kite was liberated.

Yes, liberation.

There was something quite freeing about this place, something that helped these Claymore men open their hearts and feel joy.

Daire walked over to her, grinning from ear to ear. "Don't say it, Brenna. I know this afternoon has been a triumph. Matthew chattered the whole time. He called me Uncle Daire and forgot to be afraid of me. We still have a way to go, but it is an incredibly good start."

"How does it feel?"

"Miraculous."

As the clouds began to thicken, Daire suggested they head back to the house. Matthew skipped by his side, and then, without hesitation, took Daire's hand when he held it out to the boy.

Daire cast Brenna a look of surprise, but he was happy and his expression filled with love. It was a feeling he was not used to having.

Brenna kept quiet as she watched them, standing back and trying not to show her elation.

Daire thought he was helping the boy open his little heart, but did Daire realize he was doing the same, opening his heart to let the boy in?

Would Daire let her in next?

Chapter Fourteen

DAIRE WENT UP to Stoningham Manor the following day, arriving drenched to the bone because the rain had fallen in torrents. Scipio was not too pleased with him, his mount having gone soft during their daily rides across the countryside in what had been idyllic weather until now. "Where is everyone, Greggson?"

He had not expected Simon and his workers to be here, since the work that remained was mostly outside work and could not be done in a storm. Nor could Felicity work outdoors on such a day. He had no idea where Jax had gone, but he would not be surprised if he were paying a call on Felicity and her family. His friend had not left Felicity's side since the moment they met, and everyone in the village had noticed…including Lady Dowling.

He only hoped Jax knew better than to fall into that widow's trap.

Should he have said something? Given warning? He would make a point of mentioning it the next time he saw Jax.

Not that his friend was ever likely to rise to her bait. He had eyes only for Felicity.

"Duchess Juliana, Miss Brenna, and Master Matthew are in the music room," the stately Greggson said, helping him off with his coat and waistcoat, then watching as Daire removed his cravat. "Your Grace, you are still soaked."

"There's no help for it. I cannot remove all my clothes, can I?"

"No, I suppose not. Shall I search for something for you to wear? Staff livery? It isn't perfect, but you have none of your own clothes here."

"My fault. I should have thought to bring some up before this." Daire heard a lively country air being played on the pianoforte and a young lady delicately singing. He recognized Brenna's sweet voice. "Just bring me a cup of tea. I'll join the others. Thank you, Greggson."

He raked his fingers through his hair to put himself in some kind of order. But his shirt and riding breeches were still damp and plastered to his body. "No help for it," he muttered, striding in and unwittingly disrupting Brenna's song.

Juliana was sitting on a settee, embroidering while listening to Brenna's playing. Matthew had his tin soldiers and was lining them up in battle formations in a corner of the room. He scrambled to his feet, but did not approach. "Good morning, Uncle Daire," he said with an aching hopefulness to his voice.

This was a huge advancement, and one Daire had no intention of letting go to waste. "Good morning, Matthew," he said with equal cheer. "You seem to be enjoying your soldiers."

"I am. I'm setting up the armies."

"Would you like to learn about battle tactics?"

The boy's eyes lit up. "Would you teach me?"

Daire nodded. "Yes, but give me a few minutes to dry off and have my tea."

Brenna was a vision of loveliness seated at the pianoforte, her gown a pale blue muslin that seemed to enhance the pink of her cheeks and ruby sweetness of her lips. But she shot to her feet now. "Oh dear. Your Grace, you are completely…wet. Let me fetch you a towel."

He grinned. "I'll be fine. Don't let me interrupt your dulcet tones."

She blushed, no doubt remembering the last time she had

seen him wet. "My singing voice is adequate, at best," she said, making one of those little, breathy sounds that shot heat through him. "I'll ring for tea."

"Already done, Brenna. Go on with what you were doing." He turned to Juliana. "How are you today, darling?"

She smiled up at him. "Quite well. But you will catch a chill if you stay in those wet clothes."

"Must you all comment?" Daire laughed. "I can hardly take them off, can I?"

Brenna's face was once more suffused with color, and she made another of those breathy sounds that put his heart in spasms because he wanted her so badly.

He was in no danger of catching a chill. No danger at all.

"I'll have Greggson light a fire," Brenna said, obviously wanting to fuss over him.

He smiled, quite liking the tender attention she was paying him. "Not necessary. It's already too hot in here."

Her pretty eyes widened, for she understood his meaning, obviously feeling a little warmth herself, which had everything to do with his nearness and nothing to do with the inclement weather.

She licked her lips.

He wanted to kiss her.

Instead, he grabbed a wooden chair and sank his large frame into it. "Do keep playing. Ah, Greggson, just in time."

The butler handed him his cup. "Will you require anything else, Your Grace?"

"No, Greggson. This is perfect," Daire said with a nod of dismissal.

Brenna plunked her delicate derriere back down on the piano stool.

Daire listened to her play another lively air and sing while he drank his tea. His insides were warmed by her sweet voice as much as by the hot liquid. This was another moment he wished to hold on to—Juliana at her embroidery, Matthew humming along while playing with his soldiers, and Brenna, his little dove, seated at the pianoforte.

This was what his heart needed. This was what his heart ached for most.

He thought back to the lazy hours in his own sitting room at the Kestrel Inn when Hollingsworth, his sisters, and Danson were with him, all of them doing absolutely nothing worthwhile. Just griping, yawning, passing snide comments about others in the *ton*. How dull and empty their conversation had been.

How full and rich this scene in the music room was in comparison.

When he finished his tea, he walked over to Matthew. "Shall I join you and your soldiers?"

The boy did not need to glance at Brenna before he nodded. "Yes, Uncle Daire."

Indeed, a breakthrough.

Daire stretched out on the carpet as he taught Matthew how to set up his battalions. "There is an order to these army formations, because one must protect one's flanks from attack as well as maintain strength along the middle. Where will you position your cannons?"

Brenna was watching them out of the corner of her eye, just tinkling a soft tune so as not to disturb their conversation. Juliana was watching them as well.

Daire engaged in play for another half-hour before the luncheon bell sounded. "Are you hungry, lad?"

The boy nodded.

"Leave the soldiers where they are. We'll return to the game later." Daire rose and held out his hand. The boy looked up at him, then smiled and took it.

Daire turned to Brenna.

She cast him a delicious grin. "Well done," she mouthed.

Indeed, he could not have felt prouder.

Matthew held his hand while they walked down the hall to the dining room. Daire noticed only two places had been set, and quickly motioned to Greggson to have two more added. "We dine as a family from now on."

Daire had done nothing but play tin soldiers with Matthew, but he knew it was one of the most productive days he'd ever had.

THE SUN WAS out the following day as Daire rode up to the manor house in the morning. Simon and his workers were fixing the roof. Jax was already in the garden helping Felicity.

Daire seemed to have gained an unpaid worker in Jax, who had no interest in ever leaving Felicity's side. He was not sure whether to step in and draw Jax back a bit. Since no one in Felicity's family was expressing concern, he decided not to interfere.

He kept telling himself that Jax, despite having a reputation as a womanizer and the capability of being ruthless in his dealings whenever needed, was extremely honorable at his core. But what if, despite his good intentions, Jax decided Felicity was not right for him?

"Jax," Daire said, coming upon his friend and motioning him over.

Jax left Felicity's side and strode to him. "I know what you are going to say. Drop it, Daire. I haven't changed my mind, nor will I ever."

"All right, but you must understand I feel responsible for Brenna and Felicity."

"I know, and rest assured, Felicity will soon be my responsibility. I only meant to wait the week before officially asking her. But I will be proposing as soon as the week is up. I hope you will ride over to the parish church with me to obtain the license."

Daire nodded. "Just let me know when you are ready."

He supposed this ought to have calmed him. And in truth, it

did. Having made the decision to marry Felicity, rash as it was, Jax was going to honor and protect her to the day he died.

He had also laughed off Daire's warning about Lady Dowling last night as they sat in Daire's sitting room sharing a bottle of port. "Such women are rife in the *ton*," he'd said. "She already approached me, and believe me, I immediately felt her trying to spin her little web around me. But Felicity is solid in my heart. Every minute I am with her only confirms how right my instincts were. No, I'm ready to make that commitment. But I have to figure out what to do about my gaming hells. I don't think Felicity knows yet this is how I made my fortune."

Daire's advice was to be forthright and tell her. "Jax, you cannot build a marriage on lies."

He'd felt quite wise and proud of himself when giving that advice.

He was still watching Jax help out Felicity with the gardening work when Felicity whispered something. Jax nodded and then rose to approach him again. "Daire, would you mind if we took your nephew for the day? Felicity said something about the fort commander setting aside a patch of garden for Matthew's strawberries and other plants. Felicity thinks it is a good day for it."

Daire chuckled. "I don't mind at all. He'll be thrilled."

This would also give him time alone with Brenna. He had tucked a change of clothes for himself in his pouch because he was going to work on her fear of water today. Since he had not completely taken leave of his senses, he was not about to strip down naked. He'd brought along a pair of old breeches to cover his privates, and a fresh set of clothes to change into after the swimming lesson.

Jax's plan worked out well, because Daire did not want Matthew, who also could not swim, with him as he was teaching Brenna. Having to keep his eyes on both of them would prove difficult, especially if Matthew jumped into the water as Brenna was fearfully clinging to him at the same time.

Daire knew that sharing a swim with Brenna was also a major step for himself. He knew the consequences if they were discovered. She would be compromised. He would be honor bound to marry her.

In truth, he *wanted* to marry her.

She was probably right about his never being able to hurt her. All he wanted to do was love her and protect her.

Love her.

Yes, this was what he was—in love with her.

He chose a moment when Simon and his workers headed back to town to gather more supplies. Daire's staff had been with him for years, first when he was a viscount and now as a duke. Not one of them would talk if they happened upon him and Brenna in the water, although the glade was fairly remote and no one was likely to wander by there.

Nor would Juliana ever gossip about such a thing if she found out what they were doing.

Brenna hurried to the glade with her own pouch that doubtless contained a clean shift and gown. He had already stripped down to his old breeches and was waiting for her. "Shall I help you off with your gown?" he asked, trying hard not to cast her a wicked grin, because she was shy and probably doubting the wisdom of her decision.

She blushed. "I can manage it."

"All right, Brenna. I'll be here whenever you are ready." She was as skittish as a filly let out to pasture for the first time.

He stepped into the water and waited for her to join him.

After several minutes, she poked her head out from behind the trees.

"Ready yet, Brenna?"

"I don't know. This might be a mistake. My shift…"

"Little dove, there is nothing you can show me that I have not already seen."

She gasped. "On me?"

"No, love. On other women." Well, he'd seen a bit of her,

too. But this was not the time to admit he and Jax had been spying on them in the glade. "Don't change your mind. You need to do this."

"All right. I know. Give me a moment." He heard her inhale softly, and then she stepped out from behind the trees.

Daire was glad he was in the water up to his waist, for his response to Brenna was one of immediate arousal. Did she realize just how sheer the fabric of her shift was? And how beautiful her body appeared beneath it?

She set his blood on fire.

There was something quite sensual about having only glimpses of her, a dark shadow between her legs, and softer shadows at her bosom.

He was glad the water was on the cool side, because he needed to calm the heated mess she was making of his body.

This was about Brenna conquering her fears, not his notching another conquest.

He held out his arms to her. "Come to me, love. Don't be afraid. The water will not be over your head."

"You have to hold on to me, Daire."

"I will, love." He nodded. "I won't ever let you go. All right? Today, we are just going to have you stand in the water. No swimming. No floating on your back."

Dear heaven.

He would expire if she ever went on her back with her breasts thrust out, the wet shift clinging to her body, and those stiff little buds straining against the fabric.

He began to sweat.

Had he thought this was a good idea when she suggested it?

Well, he wasn't complaining. He just did not think he could control his body's response to her. It might prove a little embarrassing, but she was going to be safe with him.

"Come into my arms, love."

Her hair was piled atop her head in a mass of dark curls. Her body was beautiful.

She put a toe in the water. "It's cold."

"A little cool, but you'll quickly get used to it."

She hiked her shift above her knees and carefully stepped in.

Gorgeous legs.

"That's it. Take another step toward me." His arms were still held out to her.

The stream rushed by behind him, its water clear as crystal. But this pool, also a crystal blue, had a gentle flow that should not have frightened Brenna. It was quiet and lapped gently within the secluded glade. He said not another word, merely waited patiently for her to take another step deeper.

"Daire," she said in a shaky whisper.

"You can do it, love."

The wind rustled through the leaves, although he could hardly hear them for the stream's current rushing past them in a steady *whoosh*. Brenna was now almost within reach of him. He leaned forward and took her hand, then wrapped an arm around her waist as he slowly drew her up against his chest. "There, love. You did it."

She was shaking and clinging tightly to him. "Daire, please don't let me go."

Their bodies were pressed together, her soft breasts against his chest. Her legs tangled with his because she seemed afraid to set them down, as though the sand beneath their feet was unsteady.

It wasn't. She simply did not trust that her feet would find firm ground. She thought they would slip out from under her, so she held on to him for dear life. She was a little thing, and so scared.

He wrapped both arms around her, holding her close and inhaling the warm scent of her skin. "You're doing great, Brenna."

She laughed. "You are too kind, Your Grace."

"No one has ever described me as kind," he said with a wry smile. "But you *are* doing great. Perhaps not quite the fearsome pirate yet, but it is your first time, love."

"Why do you call me that?" Her eyes were closed and her lips brushed his neck as she spoke.

"Love?"

She nodded.

He sighed deeply. "Because this is what you are to me. It's true, Brenna. I am in love with you. I've loved you from the moment I set eyes on you. I have also realized something very important while holding you."

She opened her eyes to look at him. "What have you realized?"

"That I don't need another week or month or year to be certain of my feelings for you. Nor do I need more time to know I will never hurt you. I love you now and will love you forever, little dove. I want to marry you."

She gasped. "You do? What changed your mind?"

"It wasn't a change of mind so much as gaining confidence in my decision. I always knew you were someone permanent. What I did not know was myself. Would I turn into my brutish forebears? I know the answer now. I could never lose control and beat you like my dog of a father did to me. I would sooner die than ever lift a hand to you."

"I know," she whispered. "I never doubted it, not for a moment."

"Then you had more faith in me than I had in myself. I'm beginning to understand how love works. It is just as you said, not about control but about making the other person happy. I think you could ask anything of me, ask me to catch the stars in the celestial sky for you, and I would do all in my power to accomplish it."

"I would never ask you for anything so impossible."

"When there is love, I think nothing is impossible. Is this not what you have been trying to tell me? Is this not what all the tales surrounding Moonstone Landing prove? A ghost who falls in love? Moonstones that shimmer in the night whenever true love is present? How do you feel about me, little dove? Would you have me for a husband?"

"Are you asking hypothetically, or are you truly proposing to me, Daire?"

"True proposal." He chuckled. "I would get down on one knee, but that would put us both underwater, and I do not think you are ready for that."

She laughed and held him tighter. "Oh, it is much too soon for certain. I am not nearly brave enough yet."

"Will you marry me, Brenna?"

"Are you sure, Daire? I am only your nephew's governess. No title. No connections. You will be cut from Society, perhaps even by your closest friends."

"If you are referring to Hollingsworth and his family, I assure you they are too enamored of my wealth to cut ties with me. As for Jax, I think it will be a race to see who gets to the altar first. Besides, you are not without your powerful supporters, your cousin Cara and her Duke of Strathmore. The Killigrew sisters and their titled husbands, duke, marquess, and viscount. You'll also have the support of Jax, the earl. That's quite an impressive start." He kissed her on the brow. "You'll always have me, little dove."

She nodded. "I love you so much, Daire. I cannot think of anything more wonderful than to be your wife. I love *you*. I love your strength and kindness. I love that you burst into my life with all your bullheaded determination. Does this mean we are betrothed?"

He smiled. "Are you accepting me?"

"I cannot imagine my life without you. It would be a sad one, indeed." She nodded. "Yes, I am accepting. I could never love anyone else. I couldn't. I trust you with my heart, with my hopes and dreams. Even with my greatest fears. Can we get out of the water now?"

Her sweet body was still trembling.

"You just got in, love. Can you give it another minute?" He

wasn't going to force her, but she really needed to stay in longer. He was holding tightly to her. She was safe in his arms. That fear she had built up over the years needed to come down. "Put your arms around my neck and just talk to me of anything that comes to mind. Do this for me, Brenna."

"Must I?"

"Yes." He knew she wanted to tear out of the water, but she might never go in again if he let her out now.

"You're right. I am being a coward."

"No, love. It isn't cowardly. Don't think of it that way. Pretend we are on land, for this is little different…just wetter."

She laughed softly.

"What's on your mind, love?"

"Daire, that day," she said, and he knew by the soft ache in her voice she was referring to the long-ago incident when she had been trapped on the sinking schooner as a child. "The waves were so high as they swept onto the deck. We all held on for dear life, grabbed on to whatever we could find. A mast. A stair rail. The wheel of the ship. But the waves were relentless as they crashed all around us."

He kissed her on the cheek. "Go on, love. You can tell me."

Tears started to roll down her cheeks. "Even though we were all very young, we understood the danger and knew we were about to die. Cara, Felicity, William, and me. We were all there, so little and helpless. We just stared at each other, too scared to talk or scream. This is what real fear does, simply paralyzes you. We held on and closed our eyes as the waves swamped us. After each wave, I would open my eyes with such fear, wondering whether one of us had been swept overboard. I shuddered with relief each time I saw them all still there. I know they must have been thinking the same. *We survived this wave. Will the next one take us?* Still, we held on and waited for the next wall of water to hit."

"Sweetheart," he whispered, glad she trusted him enough to let spill her feelings.

"Suddenly, Captain Arundel, this warrior angel, climbed aboard and loomed over us. He took William first because he was the littlest. Then he took Cara. He took all the children, one at a time, and told us we would be safe. He wasn't going to let anything bad happen to us."

He kissed her tears as they rolled down her cheeks. "And look at all you've accomplished since. I hope you know he would have been so proud of you. As I am, Brenna. I am yours, and I will always protect you. For any reason, if ever you are in danger, I will always come for you."

"I do know. I trust you with all my heart. I would brave anything for you and with you, Daire. Although I'm not really being brave right now, am I?" She took a deep, shuddering breath. "He died saving us. Why did he have to die? He was such a good man, so brave and fearless."

"I don't know, little dove. But he saved you, not only for all the important work you did at the Rainard Academy and will continue to do as my duchess. He saved you for me, as well. I now have my chance at happiness because you are here for me. Just as you are here for Matthew. He is conquering his fears because of you. I am conquering mine because I now have you."

"Daire, do you think the moonstones will shine for us?"

"Without a doubt, love. They'll shine brighter than the sun for us."

"I think so, too. I'm glad you kept coming back to Moonstone Landing year after year, even though you could not find a suitable house."

"I knew there was a reason I had to keep returning. You know it was never about a house. It was, and has always been, about you. I had to meet you. When I did, I knew you were the one. I felt it to depths of my damaged soul, Brenna."

He tucked a finger under her chin. "Look at me, love. Let me kiss you."

She nodded and raised her gaze to his.

He covered her mouth with his, pouring his heart into a

gentle kiss. The hot, passionate ones would come later, but not now. She was so fragile, he thought she might shatter like crystal. He deepened the kiss, but kept it soft, and then ended it slowly.

She smiled at him.

He could not resist kissing her on her pert, wet nose. "I think there will be a double wedding. You and me. Jax and Felicity. I'll take Jax with me tomorrow morning and we'll obtain the licenses."

"And marry here in Moonstone Landing? At St. Peter's Church? Vicar Trask will be delighted. I'm sure it will draw his biggest crowd yet. Do you think Jax is ready to marry Felicity?"

Daire laughed. "He is champing at the bit. He would have married her the day he met her, had I not held him back."

"Felicity and I survived the schooner together. As I mentioned, Captain Arundel took William first. Then he took Cara. The wave swells were getting bigger. Felicity and I were the last. We held hands, afraid to fall off the deck. Those waves were so big, time and again knocking us over. We thought we would die together. But we were happy that Cara and William were saved. It made us feel more at peace, knowing they would survive the squall even if we did not. Felicity said she loved me, and I told her that I loved her. We held on to each other and wrapped our arms around each other. Then Captain Arundel lifted us up."

"Dear heaven, Brenna." He kissed her closed eyes, her cheeks, and her lips. He then buried his lips against her soft neck.

"Nothing would make me happier than to marry on the same day as Felicity."

"I love you, Brenna. I love you so much, my Moonstone governess." He tipped her chin up so that she met his gaze. "Kiss me, little dove. Kiss me, my angel. A double wedding it shall be."

Chapter Fifteen

S EVERAL DAYS LATER, Daire and Jax returned to the Kestrel Inn, each one with a marriage license secured in his breast pocket. They marched in just as the mail coach rumbled to a halt beneath the inn's sheltered portico. Daire waited for the mail pouch to be handed over to Thaddius, since there was likely to be correspondence in it for him.

Several passengers descended, a young husband and wife, and a gentleman who carried himself with a superior air. Daire took an instant dislike to him, for he could tell by the cut of his clothes he was not *ton*.

Not that he was enamored of most members of the *ton*, who were as aimless and insufferable as the friends he had recently dispatched to Bath.

This man was pretentious.

However, Daire, in a frame of mind to be generous, moved aside to allow these new arrivals to register.

The husband and wife went first, obviously not used to an inn as fancy as this one. They were a sweet couple, and Daire realized they were probably newlyweds splurging on a wedding night and had never been to any place this grand. That they rode here in the mail coach was a strong indication they were not a couple with means and had to scrimp on their fare. Their clothes were modest as well.

But they looked happy.

As they chattered with Thaddius, Daire heard them mention being childhood sweethearts. "I knew I had to marry her the moment I met her," the man said, obviously still madly in love with his wife. "But it took me a while to gain her family's approval. I never gave up, and here we are finally."

The insolent man behind them grumbled impatiently.

"Thaddius," Daire said, calling him aside a moment. "Give those newlyweds a nice room and put it on my charge. Their meals, as well."

His eyes widened and he tossed Daire a lopsided grin. "That is most generous of you, Your Grace."

Daire shrugged. "Every once in a while I lose my mind and decide to do something nice. Do not go blabbing about what I've done. Keep it to yourself. Tell them they are lucky winners of some contest the inn is running."

Thaddius rolled his eyes and hurried back to his desk. "Well, look at that! You are our thousandth guest this year. Congratulations, Mr. and Mrs. Davenport."

They turned to each other, looking pleasantly muddled, and then turned back to Thaddius. "My word, you are a popular establishment. Congratulations to you, Mr. Angel. We heard the Kestrel Inn was a wonderful establishment."

"Well, put your coin purse away, Mr. Davenport. Just sign our registry. That's all we'll require of you, because your room and meals are on us tonight." Thaddius, obviously unable to keep a secret, turned his smiling countenance toward Daire and winked.

"My word," the husband said, shaking his head in awe.

His wife had tears in her eyes. "That is most generous of you."

"Not at all—it is our pleasure." Thaddius winked at Daire again.

The man behind the young couple grew more impatient. "Do you mind moving along? Others are waiting in queue to register."

Thaddius summoned one of his attendants to take the Davenports and their bags up to their room, and then turned to the priggish bag of wind. "My apologies for the delay, sir. We'll have you comfortably settled in the blink of an eye. Just sign the register, please."

As the man signed, Thaddius hastily opened the mail pouch and sorted through it. "Your Grace, these came for you." He handed Daire three letters. "I think that's everything. I'll deliver anything else I might have missed. Oh, and here's one for my cousin. May I put it in your custody, since I expect you will be seeing her shortly?"

"Yes, of course." Daire took it, noting it was from the headmistress of the Rainard Academy. Brenna had been eagerly awaiting her response. "Thank you, Thaddius."

The man cast Daire an insolent look.

Were he not in such pleasant humor, Daire would have punched the fellow. No one shot him a look of disdain and got away with it. Although Daire itched to give this man a comeuppance, he turned away and was about to shrug it off when the man began to snipe at Thaddius. "This delay is intolerable. I demand to speak to the manager."

"You are looking at him," Thaddius said, still smiling, but Daire caught the undercurrent of annoyance in his tone. "We are a busy establishment, sir. We strive to accommodate all of our guests. If you are displeased with our service, then may I recommend the Three Lions Tavern?"

"A tavern? For a man of my stature? Do not be ridiculous. Show me to my room."

"At once Mr., er...Swan..."

"Swanson. That's Professor Swanson to you. Professor Albert Swanson."

What the blazes?

How did this oaf dare set foot in Moonstone Landing after the way he had treated Brenna?

"Brenna's Albert?" Thaddius asked, his eyes wide in alarm as he glanced at Daire, who studied the man.

No wonder he had taken an instant dislike to him.

Priggish arse.

Daire shook his head slightly, motioning for Thaddius to keep quiet about his betrothal to Brenna. She and Felicity would be along soon. He knew Brenna would want to speak to Albert Swanson and gently break the news of their impending marriage to him.

Not that her Albert deserved to be handled politely. Daire intended to be present for that conversation, his purpose to scare off this windbag on the chance he thought to insult Brenna.

Thaddius gave a quick nod in understanding.

But he had no sooner registered the man than Brenna bounded into the inn. "Your Grace," she said, addressing Daire formally, since they were in public, "I think you are going to love what I have chosen for—" She came to an abrupt halt. "Albert? What are you doing here?"

"I've decided to give you another chance. I'm here to take you back to Oxford, at great expense and inconvenience to myself, I might add."

Jax, who had been standing next to Daire, muttered, "What an arse. This ought to be interesting."

Brenna's smile faded. "Thaddius, hold up the mail coach. They are to ship this man back to Oxford, or to blazes, for all I care. Albert, how dare you show your face here after what you did to me!"

"Me? Why, you ungrateful girl! I asked you to marry me."

Daire blocked the man when he started toward Brenna, not at all liking the angry look on his face. "Keep your distance," he said with a warning growl.

Brenna tipped her chin in the air. "Thank you, Your Grace. But this is my fight, and I would like to finish it. You needn't involve yourself."

He glanced at Jax, who was struggling to contain his laughter.

Daire did not think the situation was particularly humorous, other than this officious prig was about to get his arse set afire by Brenna. He wished to interfere, to protect her, but she would only take it as though he had no faith in her.

She curled her hands into fists and took in a lung full of air. "Albert, did you or did you not attempt to destroy my career?"

"Are you referring to that girls' school?" the prig said with disdain. "Surely you are not serious."

"Yes, the very one. It happens to be an elite preparatory school where I taught mathematics and literature. You sabotaged my teaching position in an underhanded attempt to force me into accepting you. Do you dare deny it?" She placed her hands on her hips and pursed her rosebud lips in that kissable way Daire adored. "I am merely awaiting the proof of your reprehensible behavior from independent sources."

"The proof? I do not owe you an explanation for my actions. Did you think I would allow my wife to demean my standing by having her work after our marriage?"

"You find the work I do demeaning?" Brenna approached him. "Well, go find yourself another woman's dreams to stifle and crush, for you shall never get your hands on mine. I will never marry you."

"Ungrateful girl! You ought to be kissing my hand that I even deigned to ask you. What are you other than a spinster with no prospects? Who better do you think to find in this miserable rabbit hole?"

Daire growled.

Brenna shot him a warning glance.

How could he keep out of it? The man was insulting his betrothed and Moonstone Landing. He was going to flatten the oaf.

He took a step forward and once again met Brenna's glower. "Your Grace, I asked you to keep out of this," she said.

He did not want to argue with Brenna, but he was not about to put up with this man insulting her. Then he remembered he had the letter just arrived from the headmistress of the Rainard Academy. "Brenna, take a moment to read this."

Her eyes widened as she took it from Daire's hand, gasping upon recognizing the sender's name. She opened the letter and quickly read it. Her chin shot to the moon again. "Aha! You wretch! I knew it. The headmistress has confirmed your heinous act by letter to me. I have my proof. You are a bounder and an ignorant oaf. I demand you leave Moonstone Landing at once! Thaddius, what are you waiting for? Stop that coach!"

Thaddius ran out with arms waving in order to hail the driver before he started on his return route. "Horace! Wait! The professor is returning to Oxford."

But Albert did not appear quite finished with her yet. "Fine, I shall return where I am appreciated. Go find a slovenly tavern keeper to marry you, Miss Angel. But do not think to come crawling back to me when you realize no one will have you. How are you going to manage now that you have no work? And no proposal of marriage from a gentleman? You are alone in the world, and I was willing to take you on as my wife. I deserved your gratitude, not your attack. But I was much mistaken in believing you were a demure young lady of good breeding. You are no better than an alewife."

"An alewife?" Her eyes became dark, fiery emeralds. "Here's my gratitude, you condescending oaf!" She grabbed a cane out of a nearby stand and went at him like a harpy.

Daire gave a hearty laugh as he caught her about the waist before she smashed the cane down on the poor man's head. "Love, I think he's got the message."

Albert stared at him in surprise. "Dear heaven, is she your mistress?"

"Mistress!" Brenna raised the cane again. "I am His Grace's betrothed, which is the only reason I do not hit him over the head with this cane right now for preventing me from hitting *you*."

Jax was laughing.

So was Thaddius.

Daire struggled to hold back his own laughter as he held on to her. "At least wait until we are married to do me in."

She leaned back against his chest and groaned. "You know I would never really hurt you."

"I know, love."

Daire might have felt some pity for Albert if he looked at all wounded or contrite. But he merely looked down his nose at all of them, climbed back in the coach, and kept his gaze forward as the team galloped off.

The moment Albert was gone, Brenna burst into tears.

This surprised all of them.

Daire wrapped his arms around her. "Love, why are you crying? You were marvelous in chasing him off."

"He called me an alewife."

He caressed her cheek. "Well, you did go at him like Attila the Hun with that thick cane in hand. He certainly deserved it."

"You would have handled it with far more tact. I flew at him like a demented witch. Are you terribly disappointed in me?"

He kissed her on the nose. "I am in danger of being more in love with you than ever. Brenna, you came so close to having your spirit crushed by that boor. Deep down you knew he wasn't right for you. This is why you had to come back to Moonstone Landing. You were searching for the same thing I was—the one person who could make those moonstones shine for you."

"Daire, what if the moonstones don't shine for us?"

He sighed. "They will. I'll bet my dukedom on it. I promise you, Brenna. They are going to glow brighter than the sun for us."

Chapter Sixteen

D ESPITE DAIRE AND Jax having obtained licenses, Brenna and Felicity's family insisted on having the banns read in St. Peter's Church each Sunday. Daire was not a patient man and meant to set down the law with these Angels, but Jax was the voice of wisdom this time. "They are insisting upon it for the sake of the girls, Daire. They are nothing as far as the *ton* is concerned and already bound to be looked down upon, although heaven knows they are a thousand times worthier than we are."

"And your point?"

"Having the banns read allows them to come into the marriage with pride. Everyone now knows it is not some rushed, patched-up affair. You need to give Brenna this respect."

So Daire did, although the wait to have her in his arms and in his bed was utter agony. It was worth it when he saw the happiness in her eyes as they stood before the altar and exchanged vows.

She was a shimmering ball of sunshine.

Vicar Trask, quite euphoric because of the size of the crowd amassed for his wedding sermon, put on quite a show for his flock. He added fire and brimstone to what should have been a simple wedding ceremony. Much of his fiery speech was aimed at Daire and Jax for their debauched pasts, his stentorian voice resounding with calls to repent and forsake their wicked ways—

which was completely unnecessary, since they had quite reformed and did not need to be lectured about it.

Finally, the vicar ended his theatrical performance and got down to the business at hand. "Do you, Brenna Angel…"

"I do," she said, her smile taking up her entire beautiful face.

"I do," Daire said at this turn. "With all my heart."

Jax and Felicity then exchanged their vows.

The crowd erupted in cheers, Matthew and Juliana loudest of all. Daire was glad these wedding plans had seemed to revive Juliana, who had not been looking very well upon first arriving in Moonstone Landing. But she seemed to be thriving now, the megrims fewer and farther between, and a healthy color added to her cheeks.

Matthew threw himself into his uncle's arms.

Daire lifted him and carried him as he and Brenna made their way out of the church to the Kestrel Inn, where the wedding breakfast was to take place. Although most of the Stoningham Manor renovations had been completed, the stately house was not quite ready for the entire village to descend on it.

However, he and Brenna were going to spend their wedding night there. He had planned it all out, giving Juliana and Matthew his suite at the inn, while he and Brenna were to sleep in the duke's quarters that had been expanded and decorated just for him and his wife.

The wedding breakfast continued through the day, and he and Brenna did not leave the inn until well into the evening. They rode to Stoningham Manor at twilight, but as they passed the poppy field with its sweeping view to the sea, Daire ordered their driver to stop the carriage. He climbed out and helped Brenna down. She looked like a fairy princess in her gown of ivory silk and lace. "Drive on, Mr. Poe. Duchess Brenna and I will walk the rest of the way."

"Very good, Your Grace."

Brenna arched an eyebrow. "Why are we here, Daire?"

He turned her to face the water as it now caught the hues of the fading sun, the lilacs and pinks, and the distant burst of orange, all now shimmering on the water. "We're going to wait until nightfall," he explained, moving behind her and wrapping her in his arms as they both watched the sunset over the cove.

"Oh, you're looking for the moonstones already, aren't you?"

"Yes, love."

"But Daire, it is high tide. I don't think we'll see them for hours yet, not until the tide rolls out. We ought to come back here in about six hours."

"No, I intend to have you naked in my bed by then. We are not going to haul our arses out of bed, get dressed again, and stumble our way down here in the dark."

"We could take lanterns," she said with a light chuckle, "something we should have thought to bring with us now."

"Not necessary. And I do not appreciate your logical suggestions," he teased. "This is about magic. The magic of our love. Those moonstones are going to shine for us whether low or high tide."

"Oh, have you ordered it so?" She nestled against his chest as they waited for the last rays of the sun to disappear on the horizon. "Tossing all your buckets of money at the moonstones will not help in this matter. Moonstones do not care how wealthy you are, or how bullheaded and demanding you are. You cannot bribe nature, Daire."

"I am not bribing anyone or anything. Nor am I tossing my wealth around. I am tossing my heart at them. A heart, I may add, that is completely yours from this day forward into forever." He gave her a kiss on the neck. "You should be doing the same instead of lecturing me, little dove."

"Your heart? Oh, Daire. That is the most romantic thing I have ever heard you say. You know I am yours and will love you eternally whether or not those moonstones shine for us."

"Now who is the cynic?"

"I am being sensible." She turned to glance up at him with a kissable purse of her lips. "It is a matter of the tides. It is high tide,

Daire."

He kissed the curve of her neck again. "Stop reminding me. You are not to be sensible about it. Those moonstones are going to glow for us with a brilliance never seen before."

"You love me that much?" She gave a lilting laugh.

"Yes, I do," he said with an ache and a joy he felt to the limitless depths of time. "How can I not? You are beautiful beyond description. That body of yours is going to fit perfectly to mine. But this is not merely about my finding a desirable wife. You have given me something I never imagined possible. Peace, happiness. A true family. Matthew, despite throwing the occasional childish tantrum, is no longer that scared, battered, angry boy."

Brenna nodded. "He is happy."

"Yes, but most important is that he has learned to trust and to laugh. To smile. Most of all, never to fear me. I want him to know that if I ever raise my hand, it will never be to hit him."

"He will, Daire. He does."

"I hope so." It was no small thing, for Daire was determined that no Claymore going forward would ever suffer the rages or beatings he and Matthew had suffered. "Look, little dove. The moon is now rising."

She sighed and rested against him as the night breeze swirled around them. "It is a full moon, so big and silver. We'll need its light to make our way back to the manor."

"Greggson will have torches lit for us. We'll only need to walk toward them to find our way home. Here we go, darkness falling."

They stood together in silence.

Brenna burrowed against his chest while his arms remained circled around her. He breathed in her light lavender scent along with the salt of the sea carried on the cooling breeze. The grass was also cooling beneath his feet, and the poppy petals were furled.

"Oh, Daire. It is high tide."

"Have faith, love. Be patient."

"All right. I cannot believe you are the one reminding me to be patient," she said in jest.

But the minutes passed, and Daire began to think he had approached this matter with his typical bullheadedness and demanded the impossible.

Yes, it was high tide. And he had not taken Brenna to bed yet.

Was this something he should have done first? Made her his own?

What did it matter? She was already so deeply etched in his heart.

And then they saw it. No more than the slightest glimmer of light, at first. Then a sparkle.

And more sparkles.

Each little burst of light shone as a different color beneath the dark water. "Little dove, look."

"I see it, Daire. Oh my. It's beautiful."

The sparkles of colored light now dazzled as they danced beneath the water.

Brenna began to hop excitedly. "Oh, Daire! You were right."

"See, you ought never doubt your stubborn husband. I knew it would happen for us. It had to happen, for no one but you could ever claim my heart."

"This is momentous," she said in awe.

He cast her a wicked grin. "Indeed, it is. I am about to have the best sex of my life."

Chapter Seventeen

BRENNA HAD NOT needed to see the moonstones sparkling to know she and Daire were to have a good marriage, but she found it nevertheless heartening to have the confirmation. After all, it was not every day that a former schoolteacher turned governess married a duke, especially one as handsome and perfect as Daire.

He lit several tapers to give their bedchamber a candlelit glow. The light enhanced the gleam in his deep blue eyes, and she noted their warm shine. "Let me help you out of your gown, love."

She nodded, eager to finally have his hands on her, to feel the rough pads of his fingers slide along her skin with a magical gentleness. "Shall I help you out of your clothes, too?" she asked.

He laughed softly. "You may, if you like. Otherwise, I'll just tear mine off, because I am so impatient to have at your sweet body. But I see that my thrifty wife is appalled at the thought of my ruining perfectly good clothes. Yes, we shall go slow. I want you to savor your first time."

She smiled. "You have such a wicked grin on you."

"Because I know what is in store for you." He removed his jacket, cravat, and waistcoat, then turned her slightly so that she had her back to him while he set to work on the buttons and tapes down her back. "This modiste of yours is quite nefarious.

She must have put a hundred buttons on this gown."

"Twenty at most, Daire."

"Well, seems like a hundred. There, done." He turned her around to face him and then kissed her softly on the lips, a deep, exquisitely perfect kiss that had her heart beating faster and her body heating. "Feeling warm, love?"

She laughed. "Yes, as I'm sure you fully expected. Oh, and my gown is off."

He had slipped it off her shoulders and over her hips sometime during their kiss. It now pooled at her feet, so she stepped out of it and bent to retrieve it. Daire took it from her hands and set it aside over one of the large, cushioned chairs beside the hearth in their large bedchamber. He had tossed his own clothes over the matching chair beside it.

He nudged her over to the bed and sat her on it, then knelt to remove her shoes and stockings. She shivered as his hands ran up her legs and he slowly removed her garters. "You have the prettiest legs," he said, his voice husky as he slid the stockings off her, his fingers exciting her as they skimmed along her thighs.

Then he leaned forward and feathered kisses along her thighs.

She shivered again as heat coursed through her body and turned her liquid. She wore only her chemise now, and he looked splendid in the stark white shirt that hugged his muscled contours. His dark trousers outlined his powerful, long legs.

There was not a hint of softness on his body except for the look in his eyes as he studied her. "Help me off with my cuffs, love."

She was glad to assist, but her hands shook because she had never felt excited like this. She got them off, and he quickly did the rest, removing his shirt in one flexing move that fascinated her as he casually displayed his sculpted torso.

Dear heaven.

No wonder women did not resist him.

He stood before her wearing only his trousers, his body so sleek and powerful, she could see him as a war god on a fiery chariot.

"Here we go, little dove. Hold on to the bedsheets, because I am going to make you soar." He nudged her onto her back and settled over her, and both of them sank into the soft mattress. Then he cupped her breast, though her chemise was frustratingly between his palm and her skin. But as he stroked, she found the sensation somehow heightened by that bit of added friction, so she closed her eyes and just let him do what he did best.

It did not take her long before she was indeed grabbing the bedsheets as he played her body with exquisite finesse, his hands all over her, cupping her breasts, stroking her thighs, clasping her hips. She emitted a sigh of relief when he finally removed her chemise, eliminating that last barrier between them so that she felt the heat of his skin against hers. "Brenna, my little dove, you are so beautiful."

He made her feel that way, the way he worshipped her body, teasing and suckling her breasts, kissing every inch of her, covering her mouth with his as he probed and delved, exciting her and teasing her with his tongue.

He moved down her body, suckling each sensitive spot. She seemed to be sensitive everywhere. Along her neck, her breasts, where she felt sensations so powerful that her entire body turned to flames, and between her legs.

She cried out softly.

"I have you, love," he whispered, keeping up his intimate onslaught.

She grasped his head, clung to his shoulders, felt boneless and breathless as his hot mouth closed over the bud of one breast and then moved to the other.

Her eyes shot open when his fingers slid up her thighs and he touched her *there.*

"Trust me, love," he said, now working with prowess and taking full possession of her body.

She closed her eyes once more and simply felt his touch, breathed in the musky, male heat of him.

There was a fire in her body that raged and intensified with each new sensation of pleasure. A feeling she could not name began to build within her. She called out Daire's name, not certain what she was asking for, only that she did not want this exquisite sensation to stop.

"You're almost there, love," he whispered.

Almost where?

Then she felt an exquisite build and release, a beautiful shattering like an explosion of shimmering stars. She soared above herself, her body lost to this pleasure Daire had evoked in her. "Daire."

"I love you, little dove." He kissed her and quickly undid his falls, tossing his trousers aside to free himself and enter her.

It was not long before he soared, and she joined him again, surprising herself because she thought she had spent every bit of herself. But there was magic in their coupling, in their bodies joining as one. She breathed in the heat of him, felt the delicious weight of his body atop hers. She kissed his damp skin as he thrust into her and cried out in pleasure as he spilled his essence into her.

When they were done, he rolled onto his back with a joyful chuckle. "I knew it would be spectacular. I knew you would taste like lavender and honey. So sweet, little dove."

He took her into his arms and kissed her lightly on the forehead. "I love you, Brenna."

"I love you too. Daire, I did not think I could ever be this happy."

He kissed her again, this time on the lips. "Nor did I ever dare give myself hope of finding the peace and contentment that had eluded me all of my life. But I have found it with you. I would not be surprised if our moonstones were lighting up the entire coast of Cornwall at this very moment."

She smiled. "They could be. Indeed, they must be after tonight."

They fell asleep wrapped in each other's arms.

COME MORNING, DAIRE sat up suddenly, and the abrupt motion wakened her. "Sorry, love. But I think Matthew is here."

She rolled toward him and said sleepily, "There must be some mistake. What time is it?"

"It's early yet. Not quite six in the morning." He slid out of bed, gloriously naked, and hastily donned the trousers and shirt he'd worn yesterday that were strewn atop the plump chair. "I thought I was imagining it, but listen. Do you hear him?"

"Yes." Brenna slipped out of bed too.

Daire paused to smile at her. "Good morning, beautiful."

She blushed, for she had not been wearing any clothes either. She looked around for something to cover herself. "I cannot put my wedding gown back on."

He strode to the armoire. "Here, take my robe. Your clothes are next door in the duchess's dressing room. I told the lady's maid we hired for you not to start until tomorrow. I had not planned on either of us getting out of bed at all today."

She blushed again.

"Ah, my sweet wife. We've only just started exploring each other. If I had my way, I would have you in my bed all week. But I suppose we shall not have even a day to ourselves."

He watched her slip into his robe that was much too big for her, and then helped her roll up the sleeves. "Gad, you look better in it than I do. Let's find out what is going on, then I am taking you straight back to bed."

He took her by the hand, and they followed the sound of Matthew's voice to the nursery. The boy was crying.

Brenna and Daire rushed to him.

Daire took the boy in his arms. "Matthew, what's wrong?"

"One of the maids at the inn said Brenna wasn't going to be my governess anymore." He reached out for Brenna, so Daire transferred the boy into her arms.

"Matthew, no one is going to take my place. I will always take care of you. But I am now something more permanent than a governess. Do you know what that means? The word permanent?"

He shook his head. "No."

"Well, it means that I am never going away. *Never*. I am not merely working for your uncle, but I am now his wife." And after last night, she certainly felt every bit claimed by Daire. "It also means I am your aunt. We are not only friends, but now related to each other. This means we belong to each other for all of our lives."

"Then you're not leaving me?"

"No, Matthew. We are a family. Your uncle and I shall always be with you. We love you." She feathered the boy's face with kisses until he was laughing.

That seemed to satisfy him.

Brenna was about to put him down because he was the size of a Claymore, which meant he was already almost as big as she was even though he was only six years old. But he was all lanky bones.

When she tried to put him down, Matthew reached out for Daire instead.

"All right, up you go." Daire wrapped him in his solid arms.

The boy threw his arms around Daire's neck. "I love you, Uncle Daire."

Brenna's heart burst with joy.

Daire looked at her, his heart no doubt fuller than it had ever been. "I love you too, Matthew. Never doubt it."

Matthew was still hugging Daire as he asked, "Am I in trouble?"

"You ought to be," Daire said, not sounding very severe, "but Brenna and I just spent a very good night, and we are feeling quite…pleased with ourselves at the moment."

She smothered a laugh. "Does anyone know you are gone?"

Matthew shook his head. "I dressed myself and was quiet as a mouse. Then I ran out of the inn and came up here."

She ran her fingers through the boy's hair to put some order into his windswept curls. "You could have gotten lost, Matthew. What you did was dangerous."

"No, I wasn't lost. I followed the lights."

Daire shrugged as he exchanged a look with her. "Greggson put out the lights last night."

Matthew shook his head. "Not those lights. The ones across the poppy field."

"Like dewdrops?" Brenna asked, wondering how the morning dew might form a glistening pathway up to the house.

"Yes, in all pretty colors from the water all the way up to the house. I just followed the pretty colors."

Daire grinned at her. "I had no idea my essence was so potent."

She laughed. "Oh, Daire. Put away that silly grin. Yes, you were wonderful and masterful. Satisfied?"

"Not nearly, but I hope to be after we get this young man back to the inn. Matthew, can you stay in here and play quietly with your tin soldiers while Brenna and I get dressed?"

The boy nodded.

Daire led her back to their bedchamber, closed the door, and then leaped onto the bed, falling onto his back on the mattress with a soft *whoop*. "He said he loves me."

Brenna came to his side. "Hearing it from his sweet lips... It was wonderful, wasn't it?"

He grabbed her by the waist and hauled her atop him. "Almost as wonderful as burying myself inside you."

"Daire!"

"All right, I am elated. It is nothing I ever thought to hear. Certainly never expected it so soon." He kissed her on the lips. "But I love you too. Everything good has come to me because of you." He untied the string of his robe and started to take it off her. "Do not turn prim. I am merely assisting you to undress and wash up. Then we'll have to find you a gown to wear."

"That boy is going to wander in here if you don't stop wasting time nuzzling my neck."

"Is this what fatherhood will be like?"

"Very likely. Do you mind terribly?"

"Sharing you with others? Especially miniature others who resemble me or you?" He laughed. "No, little dove. I will endure it with manly aplomb."

Despite Daire's attempts to distract her, Brenna managed to wash and then pull out one of her gowns from the duchess's dressing room. Daire was already dressed and then helped her, taking his naughty time about it. They finally returned to Matthew and walked him back to the inn.

Matthew was smiling from ear to ear now that he was walking between them, holding each of their hands. "Do I get an extra reward for this, Brenna?" Daire muttered.

Goodness, he was so gorgeous with that wicked smile of his. "Yes, my love. You have been a very good boy."

Matthew looked up at her. "Do I get a reward, too?"

Daire snorted. "You shall have an extra serving of pie at Mrs. Halsey's tea shop. I shall make certain Thaddius is aware and notifies your grandmother when she wakes up."

The boy cheered and took off at a run across the poppy field.

Daire wrapped his arm around Brenna's waist as they strolled into town. "What sort of reward do you have planned for me, love?"

"Oh, you are the expert. I shall let you choose. I only know what you taught me last night. I sense there is much to be learned from you. I'll have you know, I am an able student."

"Good, because I am a very thorough teacher."

Which he indeed proved to be later that night.

They fell asleep entwined in each other's arms after a wanton, slightly shocking, and utterly delicious coupling.

Daire nudged her awake in the middle of the night. He wrapped his robe around her and led her to the window. "Look, little dove. The moonstones are shining again."

"Oh, how lovely. They must be shining for someone else."

"No, love. For us. Can't you see? They are pointed toward us."

He seemed so proud, and she realized it had nothing to do with their activities in bed, during which they had been quite active.

He was proud because moonstones represented his ability to love. He had opened his heart to her, a heart he'd believed to be damaged beyond repair.

Brenna knew those moonstones had to be shining for someone else, but she was not going to tell him otherwise. This was his pride. This was his joy.

And perhaps he held so much love in his heart that those moonstones needed to shine for them two days in a row.

"I love you, Brenna."

"I love you," she whispered back, looking forward to everything wonderful that marriage to Daire was bound to bring.

Epilogue

St. Austell Grange
Moonstone Landing, Cornwall
July 1824

"T HE BLASTED MEETING of the Ladies' Hospital Auxiliary," Daire muttered, spurring Scipio to a gallop, his heart in his throat as he rode with all speed to St. Austell Grange, home of the Duke and Duchess of Malvern. *"I'm fine,* she says. *I'm weeks away,* she insists. *Trust me to know my own body, Daire.* Ha! Nobody knows Brenna's body better than I do. Scipio, why on earth did I listen to her?"

Jax was right behind him, probably muttering the same thing to his horse about Felicity, since their wives—both of them— seemed to have disrupted the auxiliary tea by going into labor at the same time.

But these cousins were as close as sisters. They had almost died together, got married together, and were now bringing new life into the world together. No doubt one of them had gone into labor and set the other one off.

As soon as he reached the elegant manor, Daire leaped off Scipio and tore past the Malvern butler, who barely had time to dive out of the way after opening the door. "Where is she?"

"Both ladies are comfortably settled upstairs, Your Grace.

The midwife and Dr. Hewitt have been sent for."

Cain met him and Jax at the foot of the staircase. "Your wives are fine. Hen and her sisters have everything under control. You need to calm down."

"Calm down?" Daire and Jax blurted at the same time.

Cain laughed. "Yes, although I understand how hard it is to do. I've been through this before. Follow me. I'll take you to your wives, but you cannot stay beyond a few minutes. They're going to be in pain, and you will not be able to bear it."

"Oh, Lord," Daire muttered. "We won't bear it? How about them?"

"They need to push and sweat and cry out. They won't do it while you are hovering beside them." Cain motioned for them to follow him up the grand staircase. "I will personally remove each of you if you are not back downstairs within five minutes."

"I'm not leaving her," Jax insisted.

"Yes, you are. We'll wait in my study. Just be prepared—this may take a while."

"How long?" Daire asked, his heart in his throat as Cain led them down the hall of bedchambers.

"I have no idea. Could be a few hours. Could be thirty hours."

Daire was sorry he'd asked.

Could Brenna hold out for thirty hours of pain? She was his little dove, so delicate and refined. She might be carrying a boy who was going to be as big as him.

He could tell by the fear in Jax's eyes that he was thinking the same thing of Felicity.

Cain knocked at one of the doors along the hall.

Hen popped her head out. "Oh, excellent. Daire, you're here. Come in, but you mustn't stay long."

Daire nodded and entered. "Cain gave me the warning."

Hen nodded and quietly left the room. "I'll be back in a few minutes."

Daire strode straight to Brenna, who was lying in bed and

looking remarkably beautiful despite her discomfort.

"Look, Daire. This is the peach room. Did you notice the wall color? And the draperies?"

He laughed despite the turmoil in his heart. "Did you ever tell Hen about sneaking up here the day of their annual village tea?"

"No, should I confess it now?"

"Dear heaven, no. It shall remain our little secret. How are you feeling, love?"

"I've had better days." She smiled up at him. "You are allowed to kiss me. I won't break."

He leaned over gingerly and kissed her softly on the lips. "I love you, little dove."

"I know. I love you too. I'll see you when our little boy cries out with his full set of lungs."

"A boy? Are you sure?"

She shook her head. "No, but the midwife lore is that if you carry up front as I have done, then you are carrying a boy. But if your weight is spread across your waistline, as Felicity's was, then you are carrying a girl."

He knelt beside her bed and took her hand in his. "Another piece of lore? Do we not have enough of them in Moonstone Landing?"

"We'll soon find out if this midwife tale is accurate. How are Matthew and Juliana?"

He ran his thumb in a slow circle over her hand. "They are fine. Phoebe is taking Matthew home with her so that he can play with her boys and the visiting nieces. He won't notice a thing. Juliana is on her way back to Stoningham Manor to prepare the nursery." He let out a ragged breath. "Brenna, how can I leave your side?"

"I know it is hard, Daire. But I don't want you to see me in pain. You will suffer worse than I will because there is nothing you can do to help me, and it will drive you mad. Go downstairs and have a stiff drink while I do what I need to do."

He heard the click of the door and saw Hen slip back inside.

"Brenna, I love you." He hugged her as gently as he could manage and left before she noticed his tears. When had he ever cried in his life? Not ever that he could remember, not even after his father's brutal beatings. Despite the open sores and welts, not a single tear had ever fallen.

Nor had he ever shed tears during the war, despite his heartache as soldiers, hardly more than boys, fell all around him.

But now?

He would never recover if he lost Brenna.

He did not go immediately to Cain's study but strode outside in order to calm himself down. He walked to the gazebo overlooking the cove. He'd chatted there with Brenna at last year's village tea, thinking she was the most beautiful girl he had ever seen and knowing he was going to marry her if ever he straightened himself out enough to be a proper husband.

Jax and Cain were in Cain's study by the time Daire composed himself enough to return. The three men shared a bottle of port. "I've had my staff prepare a bedchamber for each of you," Cain said. "You'll have time to ride home and collect a change of clothes, if you like. This could take the entire night."

Neither Daire nor Jax dared leave.

"I'm not going to sleep," Jax grumbled.

"Did you when Henley had your children?" Daire asked.

Cain cast him a wincing smile. "No. In fact, Hen threatened to have me tied down and tossed into our storage room if I did not stop pacing like a caged bear."

As MIDNIGHT APPROACHED and both ladies had been in labor for over eight hours, Henley suddenly burst into the study. "Jax, come upstairs and meet your daughter. Mother and daughter are doing well."

"Thank the Lord," Jax muttered, and tore upstairs.

"And Brenna?" Daire asked.

Henley forced a smile. "She's taking a little longer. She'll get there, Daire."

The night wore on.

Cain remained with him the entire time. Jax joined them once Felicity and his daughter had fallen asleep. They tried to cheer his spirits.

But how could they?

"I need air." He rose to walk back to the gazebo.

"It's four o'clock in the morning, Daire," Jax said. "It's pitch dark out there."

"I know the way. I won't be long. I'll suffocate if I don't get out."

He made his way in the blackness of the night, his ears attuned to the ebb and flow of the tide as it rolled into the cove, of the crash and whoosh of waves as they swamped the beach. "Keep Brenna safe. Please, help her." He had never prayed in his life, had never believed. But he prayed now for her safety. He bargained now with everything he possessed, even his own soul. "Take me instead."

He heard nothing but the sound of the waves.

Then he saw the glimmer of moonstones, and his heart lurched. "But it's high tide."

He thought of their wedding night and Brenna's sweet body against his, and her logical brain insisting the moonstones glowed only at low tide. But they didn't. For her, they glowed at all hours.

He hurried back inside and took the stairs two at a time.

He had to know. Whatever it was, he had to know.

He heard a baby's wail just as he stepped inside.

"Daire," Brenna said in a hoarse whisper, "we have a boy."

He came to her side. "So I hear. He has a lusty set of lungs. How are you, my little dove?"

"Sore, but I'll recover."

"I need to kiss you." When she did not object, he leaned over and kissed her lips with exquisite care. "I love you. I love you with every ounce of my being."

"I know, Daire. This must have been so hard for you."

He groaned. "Me? You're the one who did all the work... Suffered all the pain."

"I'm not suffering anymore. What brought you rushing up here just as our son popped out?"

"I saw the moonstones. They shone...even at high tide."

She closed her eyes and laughed. "Stay with me, Daire. Hold me while I sleep. Are you sure it is high tide?"

"Yes, love. Not a doubt."

"Well, isn't that something? Are they shining very brightly?

"Brighter than the sun, love."

She closed her eyes and sighed as she nestled against his chest. "Isn't it just wonderful?"

The End

The Miracle of Love
The Remembrance of Love (novella)
The Dream of Love (novella)
All I Want For Christmas (novella)

MOONSTONE LANDING
Moonstone Landing (novella)
Moonstone Angel (novella)
The Moonstone Duke
The Moonstone Marquess
The Moonstone Major
The Moonstone Governess

DARK GARDENS SERIES
Garden of Shadows
Garden of Light
Garden of Dragons
Garden of Destiny
Garden of Angels

LYON'S DEN
The Lyon's Surprise
Kiss of the Lyon
Lyon in the Rough

THE BRAYDENS
A Match Made In Duty
Earl of Westcliff
Fortune's Dragon
Earl of Kinross
Earl of Alnwick
Aislin
Gennalyn
Pearls of Fire
A Rescued Heart
Tempting Taffy

About the Author

Meara Platt is a *USA Today* bestselling author and an award winning, Amazon UK All-star. Her favorite place in all the world is England's Lake District, which may not come as a surprise, since many of her stories are set in that idyllic landscape, including her award-winning fantasy-romance Dark Gardens series. If you'd like to learn more about the ancient Fae prophecy that is about to unfold in the Dark Gardens series, as well as Meara's lighthearted, international bestselling Regency romances in the Farthingale series and Book of Love series, or her more emotional Braydens series, please visit her website at www.meara platt.com.